emerge

···

HEATHER SUNSERI

Sun Publishing
VERSAILLES, KENTUCKY

Heather Sunseri/Sun Publishing
PO Box 1264
Versailles, Kentucky 40383
www.heathersunseri.com

Publisher's Note: This is a work of fiction. Names, characters,
places, and incidents are a product of the author's imagination.
Locales and public names are sometimes used for atmospheric
purposes. Any resemblance to actual people, living or dead, or
to businesses, companies, events, institutions, or locales is
completely coincidental.

Book Layout ©2014 BookDesignTemplates.com
Cover design by Mike Sunseri
Edited by David Gatewood

Ordering Information:
Quantity sales. Special discounts are available on quantity pur-
chases by corporations, associations, and others. For details,
contact the "Special Sales Department" at the address above.

EMERGE/ Heather Sunseri. -- 1st ed.
ISBN 978-0-9887153-9-4

For Dad.

....

chapter one

Cricket

L ife first began to disintegrate, for me anyway, on the day the president of New Caelum suspended all travel in and out of the United States, thereby closing off the last bit of hope that my parents would ever return to me.

I developed a fever two days later.

Three weeks after that, I became the first and only person out of millions to survive the disease that decimated the population.

I ran from the president, all of her people, and the city that should have kept me safe.

Not to be heard from again.

I was twelve.

~~~~~

The sound of the incinerator jolted me from sleep. It took little more than a second for the low rumble of the machine to register in my brain, and it took less than a millisecond after that for me to register what the sound meant.

I nudged Dax. "There it is again. That's three nights in a row." I quickly threw dirt over the remaining ashes of the campfire.

"Shit, Cricket. They're just burning trash." Dax was tucked in the sleeping bag next to mine, his arm bent over his head trying to drown out any and everything that might disturb him from a few hours of sleep. "Get some sleep." He rolled over and burrowed his head further under the covers.

Nina rose on her elbows across the fire pit that had now been reduced to nothing more than a pile of charred logs and a thick ribbon of smoke. She shook her head. "It's going to get cold quickly." She lay back down and closed her eyes.

At least no one would track us by the smoke of a burning fire. I pushed back my covers and began pulling on my boots, not bothering with the laces. "I know. I'm sorry." Nina Snow deserved better than the paranoid, crazy person she got for a best friend.

She snuggled in closer to Dylan, who had zipped a couple of sleeping bags together for the two of them to share—the power of body heat and all. Dylan was Dax's identical twin brother, and the nicer of the two siblings.

It had gotten colder the last few days. Dylan, Dax, Nina, and I had been making plans to move south soon. To explore, maybe. Search for other settlements. Or, at the very least, discover that there *were* no other settlements in the southeast, forcing us once and for all to remain at Boone Blackston, the settlement I'd called home off and on for six years.

Grabbing my thin jacket—much too lightweight for the weather moving in—I stood to witness the smoke billowing from the twin towers in the distance. Puffs of white, like clouds, rose from the sleek steel smokestacks of the incinerator and glowed against the midnight blue sky. I stared at the disappearing shapes, remembering how my mom and I once lay on a blanket in the middle of the park, identifying animals in the cloud formations.

Giving my head a quick shake at the memory, I secured a sheath to my leg, allowing my cargo pants to cover the knife.

"Where are you going?" Dax grabbed my forearm. I hadn't even heard him rise.

I let my line of sight drift from the distant smoke, down my arm, to Dax's fingers as they slowly traced a direct path to my hand, linking with mine. "I'm just going to get a little closer. I'll be back before morning. You don't need to come."

"You think I'm just going to let you wander off toward that place? Alone?"

I rotated my shoulders back and took a step closer to him. "You don't have a choice. I don't want you to come. I'll check it out on my own, and I'll be back before you're even awake."

"When are you going to stop trying to save everyone?"

"As soon as everyone's saved, I guess." I met his stare. I knew my face remained expressionless, whereas Dax's chest rose and fell with rapid breaths, his nostrils flared, and his cheeks burned red. And that had nothing to do with the campfire I had just extinguished.

"Fine. Have it your way. But when you get yourself captured by the goons behind those walls," he pointed toward the city in the distance, "don't expect me to save your ass."

I bit my lower lip for a second, pretending to consider what Dax was saying, then answered, "I understand."

I turned and began making my way closer to the city of New Caelum. I didn't expect Dax, or anyone else, to "save my ass." If what I suspected was happening inside those incinerators was actually occurring? *I'd* be the one doing the saving.

7

....

chapter two

West

The virus was gone from our world. That's what the experts inside New Caelum thought. Everyone who'd contracted the illness all those years ago had died. Everyone but one.

A girl.

Only one person knew the identity of this girl. I didn't even know her name.

I knew she would have been protected though, just like I was, inside this city.

But she ran away.

~~~~~

The alarm sounded on a Thursday night. And not just any Thursday night—the eve of the election that would decide the fate of my family going forward. Would my mother remain president of the city, or would the council decide that the citizens of New Caelum needed a new leader?

If Mother lost, we'd have to move from the private wing at the top of the city to a lower level with other people in our social class.

I knew that the alarms that sounded now were not part of a drill. If this were a drill, then as a member of leadership, I'd have been notified on my PulsePoint. I lifted the device from my waist. No messages.

Medics dressed in red hazmat suits jogged past me like trained military. They were headed straight for the leadership residence wing—my home.

Ryder, my best friend since we were two years old, rounded the corner, followed closely by Key, his girlfriend. They stopped in front of me.

"Where are they going?" Ryder proudly wore charcoal gray and black—the colors of government—a societal promotion that meant he would serve the city's leaders and eventually be eligible to hold an elected position.

Key bent over at the waist, attempting to catch her breath. Her pale blue lab coat covered her royal blue pantsuit, both colors carrying significant meaning. The pale blue told everyone she was of age and chosen for the medical profession within New Caelum. She'd keep the pale blue forever, a respectable color in its own right, or she would graduate to white when she became a doctor.

What the royal blue signified was arguably of much greater importance.

I touched her arm, prompting her to look up at me. "You've been matched? You're wearing royal blue."

She smiled, then traded an uneasy glance with Ryder. "You didn't tell him? Come on, Ryder!" She lightly punched him in the shoulder, causing him to stumble. "Must I do everything?"

Ryder sidled up to Key and threw his arm around her. "Dude. If you'd check your messages? I've been trying to get a hold of you since late last night."

I pulled them both into a hug, rubbing Ryder's black curly hair and doing my level best to mess it up. "What am I going to do with you two? That's fantastic."

He pulled away. "Stop it, man. She hasn't married me yet. I might still need my good looks."

Key rolled her eyes.

My smile faded and turned more severe. "What do you know about the medics?" I asked Key. "Is it a drill? I didn't get word of any drill."

"I don't know," Key answered. "I don't think so. I was working in the lab when the call came in. The senior medics dropped everything and convened in the emergency lab next door. I heard them say 'Code 51.'"

I grabbed Key by her arms and forced her to face me. "Are you sure?"

She tried to wriggle from my hold. "Chill out, West. You're hurting me."

"Just tell me. Is that what they said? Code 51?"

Ryder stepped between us and shoved me backward. "Get off her, man. What is with you?"

Key's eyes remained fixed on mine. "Yes, I'm sure. Why? What does that mean?"

I stood tall and faced them both. "I want you both to listen to me very closely. Turn around and go back to your daily tasks. Key, go back to the lab. Pretend you never left the medical sector. Neither of you are to tell anyone you've seen me or been in the leadership wing today. Okay?"

"What is it?" Ryder asked.

"Code 51 means Bad Sam is back."

Key gasped. "And if they're running toward the leadership wing—"

"Someone in my family or on Mother's staff has the Samael Strain."

~~~~~

My sister Willow stared at me from the isolation room, her eyes red from crying.

The medics said her fever was holding steady at 101.4, and that the virus hadn't taken over her body yet. Which, I figured, was why she was still standing.

The Samael Strain, nicknamed Bad Sam, was named after the doctor in Africa who had first discovered the deadly virus. At least, according to the scientists inside New Caelum. The more popular claim was that the viral death sentence was named for Samael, the archangel of death in some religions. Given my memories and my own studies of the disease, I always thought the latter seemed more fitting.

On the other side of the glass, a nurse messed with Willow's bedding while another organized supplies in a cabinet against the wall. Both were dressed in pale blue personal protective suits—a less alarming color than the red hazmat suits of the medics who'd escorted my family to the isolation suite. This wasn't a standard medical enclosure; it had been specially set up within the government quarters in order to keep this outbreak confidential for as long as possible.

Willow, who now wore a hospital gown, slipped into the hospital bed with the help of a nurse. Her face was flushed. Her hands shook, causing the IV in her arm to vibrate.

Dr. Pooley, the doctor in charge of studying the Samael Strain for the past six years—and Willow's and my biology teacher—spoke to Mother in a room just behind me. He wore white, the color of a successful doctor within our city, but I knew that underneath his protective gear he had donned a combination of doctor-white *and* black, identifying him as a member of council. Mother stood at the same height as Dr. Pooley, her black business suit and sophisticated high heels screaming power, and the two of them discussed not only the fate of her daughter, but what Willow's illness meant for tomorrow's election.

"She'll have two nurses assigned to her at all times, Ms. President. She'll be kept comfortable." Dr. Pooley spoke through a small microphone in his protective mask.

The fact that neither Mother nor I wore a hazmat suit made it pretty clear that these would be our quarantine rooms until they could prove that we hadn't contracted the virus. Fortunately, my mother's room and mine were side by side and connected with a speaker that allowed us audio contact, so I could listen in on her conversation with the doctor.

"How close are we to a treatment? What can you do for her?" Mother crossed her arms and stuck a hip out while tapping her foot.

"As we reported to you last week, ma'am, a treatment is still being tested."

"Yes, but you also said that your recent efforts were primarily geared toward developing a vaccine."

"With your daughter sick, we've altered that plan. But you know what we'll need if we're to develop either a cure or a vaccine." Dr. Pooley leaned closer to Mother. "I know you know where she is, Ginger." His voice was gruff, demanding. "If you'd just tell the council, we'll—"

"No." My mother's eyes darted to me for a brief moment, the tone in her answer sending a chill along my spine, before she looked back at the doctor. "I want this medication administered to my daughter. I'll accept full responsibility if it fails."

"You know we can't do that, ma'am. If we give it to her too soon, she'll die. A team of doctors will study her labs as her illness develops, and we'll do our best to see her through this."

I moved closer to the window separating me from Mother and the doctor. "How many have the disease?" I asked. And who was the council looking for?

"I'm sorry?" Dr. Pooley acted like I'd spoken a different language. I think he was surprised that I could hear him through the glass partition.

"You can't stand there and tell me that my sixteen-year-old sister is the first to contract the virus in six years. And out of thin air? How many have it?"

Dr. Pooley turned his back on me and spoke to Mother. "Ms. President, we don't know yet that this is the Samael Strain. I will monitor your daughter's progress. I *am* sorry. You and West will have to remain inside this suite until we can be sure exactly what your daughter has and that neither you nor your son has it."

Mother's voice dropped to just above a whisper, and I had to strain my ears to hear. "What does this mean for the election?"

"The council has postponed their decision for one week to give you time to be near your daughter." The doctor placed a gentle hand on Mother's arm, and something about it made me want to jump between them. "But I wouldn't worry," he continued. "The people of New Caelum love you." Then he turned and exited the isolation suite.

I backed away from the glass, watching Dr. Pooley go. His words, though encouraging to Mother, bothered me. It didn't matter if the people of New Caelum loved Mother. The council didn't answer to the people. They could easily decide that it was time for a change, and therefore a new president.

A glass door slid open, allowing Dr. Pooley to enter one of two small compartments separating the isolation room from the rest of the city. Once inside the compartment, a sanitizing liquid spewed from multiple nozzles, killing any trace of the virus that may have been on his protective suit. Just seeing the sudsy substance made my nose tingle with the smell of bleach. Then he stepped into a second compartment, which first dried his outer layers before bombarding him with an ultraviolet light. It started at the top of the chamber and slowly moved down his entire body, shining from all sides.

When he was gone, Mom turned and faced the one window she had to the outside world. I stared past her toward the thick forest that lined the eastern side of our city.

New Caelum was designed as a fortress, a collection of buildings connected by airtight tunnels and surrounded on all sides by a tall fence designed to keep the uninvited out. Its main purpose, I'd come to learn, was to shelter and protect the elite people of this country—people who had the best chance of rebuilding our civilization after the great Samael Strain had shattered our lives and our country forever. The people who were allowed inside were the most brilliant scientists, doctors, teachers, architects, engineers, military leaders, and policemen—to name a few. The richest and most powerful people were also given the opportunity to purchase a spot on the inside—an "investment" in their future; in humanity's future. As for the rest—the sickly, the weak, the unskilled; those who were too devastated by the virus to recover emotionally; those who lacked the means with which to buy their way in—these people were kept out. They had nothing to offer, nothing to bargain with, and would have drained the city's resources. So they were forced to the outlying areas, mostly to the west.

And of course there were also those people who simply *chose* not to be a part of New Caelum. As I stared at the mountains just beyond our walls, I wondered what had become of those people. Would it be possible to reconnect with them and the outside world again?

"I'd like to listen to some music." My mother spoke over her shoulder. "Will you turn it on, please, West?"

"Music, Mother?" I studied the back of her head, her brown hair styled in a perfect short bob. She stood tall, her arms clasped behind her back. She hated music. Said it distracted her from her thoughts.

"Yes, music. It will relax me. Something happy, upbeat. Pop rock, maybe. And don't be stingy with the volume."

My mom was losing it. She hated rock music most of all. But I pulled my PulsePoint device from my pocket and began searching for the wireless connection to the room's speakers. I scrolled through the library of music on my device and chose something "happy" and "upbeat."

When the music started playing, Mother pulled her own device out of her pocket and began keying something into it.

Probably something related to the election—it was all that Mother had thought about the last several weeks.

"Mother, what does this mean for the election?"

She raised her head as the glass windows on the other side of the room darkened, giving us some privacy from the nurses and doctors observing us from outside the isolation suite. She was still able to control some of our privacy from her Pulse-Point despite the fact that we were officially quarantined. She walked over to me and spoke through the glass. "Listen to me, West." She urged me to look straight at her. "This is a setup. I don't know who would use Willow to hurt me, but it's someone who wants me to lose this election, and they didn't care who they had to sacrifice in order to do it."

"What are you talking about?"

"It is no accident that someone close to me has this virus."

"Why would someone do that? They're risking the entire population of New Caelum. And even themselves."

"I assure you, no one else inside New Caelum has the virus. And this isolation suite's air ventilation is cut off completely from the rest of the city." Mother threw her head back and laughed—but not out of humor, I didn't think. "Hell, this city was designed with the best air filtration and purification system ever devised. Even if the virus were to make it briefly outside this room, it would be near impossible for it to spread any further without direct person-to-person contact. No—this is an attempt to get me out of the way."

"Out of the way for what?"

"People are getting restless inside the city. There are a growing number of people who are ready to venture back into the outside world."

"But you think it's still too dangerous."

"I don't think we're ready *yet*."

I glanced toward Willow. Someone was willing to sacrifice my sister—for what? Political gain?

"Eventually, I think we should send scouts out to see what it's like out there," Mother said. "We know that there are survivors, and that they are flourishing in their own communities, but we don't know what kind of crime is occurring or if they're surviving all of the other illnesses that we've managed to overcome inside this city."

She continued, not letting me get a word in. "We organized this city because so many of the lower classes of our society were draining our resources during the outbreak. They were depleting us of supplies and medicines, but were unable to pay for them. And we were dying. Bad Sam had a one-hundred-percent fatality rate. We organized the city in order to save humankind—so that we could become a strong country again with hopes of rejoining the rest of the world some day."

"And you think someone wants to remove you from office in order to rejoin the outside sooner rather than later? Who?"

"Let me worry about who."

"So Willow is going to die because someone didn't want you to be president again?" There had to be more to it.

A tear leaked from Mother's eye. She quickly shoved it away. "I am not going to let that happen. But I need your help."

"Anything."

"Someone has successfully gotten me out of the way so that they can send out scouts tonight."

My back stiffened. "How do you know this?"

Mother cocked her head. "Please. I did not become president of this city based on popularity alone. I have spies and people who wouldn't dare cross me. I have arranged for Ryder to leave as one of those scouts. He's one of the newest and brightest coming up through the leadership ranks." She smiled at me. "He will serve you well in the future. He is very loyal, and has agreed to volunteer to be on one of the trucks leaving the city later tonight."

Ryder had said nothing to me about that. "What do you want from me?"

"I need you to be in the truck with Ryder. Your truck will go east, instead of west like the others. You will go in search of Christina."

"Christina?" I stared at the woman who had raised my sister and me inside this city. Protected us year after year. Given us everything we could possibly want. And I wondered if my own mother have lied about the single most devastating event of my life? "Christina, Mother? I don't understand."

"Yes. Listen to me, West. I don't have time to explain everything. Christina is with Dr. Caine Quinton. At least I hope she's still with him. They're in a settlement east of here."

"Christina's dead, Mother. You said she died." But even as the words came out of my mouth, I knew that Mother had deceived me.

Christina was the sole survivor.

....

chapter three

Cricket

I hiked two miles up the mountainside to one of the few places where I could see clearly over New Caelum's walls into the city. I found a tree stump to sit on. It was probably three or four o'clock in the morning, and people milled about outside the compound under bright lights like it was the middle of the day.

The grand city spread over a hundred acres of land, deep in the Appalachian Mountains. More than fifty buildings of varying heights had been joined together by airtight tunnels to create a fully functioning city, housing and accommodating the needs of more than a hundred thousand people, a population that was growing every day. Except for a few guards who checked the perimeter periodically and the people who hauled waste each week to the incinerator (the only building located outside the cluster of connected structures), it was also a population that almost never left the safety of the city buildings. Especially at night.

"Except for now," I whispered. I'd been watching New Caelum off and on at different times of the day for the past few years, and I'd never seen this much activity in the predawn hours.

I lifted binoculars to my eyes and was surprised to find that the people below wore red hazmat suits. They were rolling bins of garbage to large dumpsters, which were then lifted by forklifts and emptied into the incinerator. An orchestra of sounds disturbed what should have been early morning silence: the loud banging of metal dumpsters, the beeping of forklifts, and the industrial blowing of the incinerator, which bellowed white smoke hundreds of feet into the air.

Eight years ago, when the virus had crossed over—from a disease that could be transmitted only through contact with contaminated bodily fluids, to a deadly airborne illness—the world as we knew it changed forever. Not only did anyone who contracted the Samael Strain receive a death sentence, but there was no longer any way to hide from the fatal disease.

If the virus had been gone from New Caelum for six years now, why did those people feel the need to keep themselves covered up out in the open air? Did they think someone was going to walk inside the walls of their fortress and sneeze on them?

Or had a new virus been born?

"Why the incinerator, boys?" I directed my binoculars around New Caelum's perimeter—the area outside the airtight city buildings but still inside the tall brick and stone walls. A couple of guards stood at the gate in my line of vision, which was also rare. It had been years since anyone on the outside had tried to penetrate the city walls, and New Caelum had relaxed their security because of it. Also, *they* weren't wearing hazmat suits. "What's going on inside your fortress?"

Just as I was about to stow my binoculars, I caught movement next to a building on the eastern edge of the city. Two large rolling doors were rising upward.

And then everything around me seemed to go silent. The incinerator had stopped. The people in hazmat suits disappeared one by one back inside. I stared at the two doorways. The space just inside the rolling doors was dark. Time ticked by. I stood, my eyes glued to the empty spaces through the binoculars.

Suddenly, the roar of engines broke the silence, rumbling up the mountainside. The muscles along my spine and neck tensed. My knuckles turned white as my grip on the binoculars tightened.

The doorways lit up as if giant spotlights had been turned on inside.

Large army trucks came rolling slowly through the doors, two at a time. Four of them altogether, heading for the main gate.

In the years since New Caelum was built, when the elite people of this world, people who thought they had all the answers, holed up in an airtight complex behind their walls, not once had I ever witnessed people leaving the city.

They were protected inside the city. They had everything medical technology had to offer inside their own private cocoon. They didn't need or want the resources of the outside world. Or so they had said.

Yet here they were.

The trucks formed a single file. They approached the gate that would allow them to cross over from their elite world into my ordinary one. As the electronic gate in the stone wall vibrated to life, so did my heart, rapidly pumping blood to my head, making me dizzy.

I watched with anticipation to see where the trucks would go once they got outside the gate. It didn't matter that the roads outside the gates were overgrown with foliage and brush. The trucks would forge their own paths.

The·first truck made a right out of the compound. The second followed it. The third went left. And the last forged straight ahead. And as they sped up, so did my pulse. I tracked the motion of the headlights as the trucks eventually went in four different directions. They were on a mission, and I was helpless to know what that mission was.

As if suddenly slapped awake, I jumped up. I quickly stuffed my binoculars into my backpack and threw the bag over my shoulder. I slid several times on the wet foliage as I made my way back down the path toward the spot where my friends slept.

We, of course, always camped off the beaten path, but not because we wanted to be hidden from passersby. After all, no one ever passed by. And the only beaten paths were our own.

Twenty minutes later, as I neared the spot where I had left my friends, I slowed, listening for anything out of the ordinary. The forest was silent except for the shifting of trees and the blowing of crunchy brown leaves that hadn't yet fallen from the trees.

The leftover smell of campfire reached my nose. Of course my friends had thought I was insane for extinguishing the fire before I left, but they were used to my craziness.

Something stopped me from racing the rest of the way to the campsite. Something was... off. Allowing the trunks of the larger trees to shield me, I darted stealthily from tree to tree.

I spotted Nina as I took cover behind an overgrown rhododendron. She was standing without a coat, her pale-colored shirt almost glowing in the predawn light. I couldn't make out the expression on her face, but she didn't appear to be moving, and I could see the fear in her ice-blue eyes.

I saw no one else.

I couldn't see enough of the campsite to figure out what was going on, so I decided to take in the campsite from another angle. I moved right. I realized I would have to expose myself briefly in order to reach the next large tree that would cover me. I took in a deep breath, and just as I moved my foot, I heard movement behind me. I froze. I started to whip around to my left when the movement advanced on me too quickly for me to react.

An arm encircled my waist, and a hand covered my mouth. "Shhh. It's me. Don't scream," Dax whispered close to my ear.

Every muscle in my body ached with tension as I turned in Dax's arms, letting out the breath I was holding. "What happened? Something doesn't feel right." I kept my voice low.

"I woke about an hour ago and decided to go looking for you. When I returned, three men had cornered Nina and Dylan. I've never seen them before."

"They're from New Caelum."

Dax jerked back like he been punched in the gut. "What are you talking about? What are they doing outside the city?"

"I don't know. I watched them leave. Four trucks left the compound about thirty minutes ago, heading in different directions."

He held a finger to his lips, warning me to keep quiet. Grabbing my hand, he pulled me away from the campsite. We circled around a wide perimeter and came at the site from the opposite side.

From a spot well hidden in thick forest underbrush, we could see and hear three men questioning Nina and Dylan. Nina stood with her hands hanging to her side. Her fingers shook, and she shifted her stance.

"Who else was with you?" a man with short dark hair asked. He didn't appear especially threatening, despite Nina's obvious fear. "The two of you were obviously sharing this spot when we got here." He pointed to where they had slept. "Who do these two sleeping bags belong to?" He held up Dax's and my sleeping bags.

Nina and Dylan traded glances. I knew they wouldn't say a word about us. But I feared what the three men would do to my friends as a result.

One of them bent and sifted through Nina's bag. "Ryder, I think I found something." At the sound of the voice, my head popped up. Due to the lack of morning light, I had failed to notice that one was a girl. Her hair was short, and she was quite a bit smaller than the other two.

I squinted, studying the girl as she pulled what appeared to be the map Nina always carried around with her. We always teased that she'd get lost without it—which was true. I, however, had the entire area memorized—every tree, every body of water, every established community east and directly west of the city.

The one named Ryder grabbed the map and held it up to Nina's face. "What is this? What's it a map of?"

Nina remained silent. The third one, the one who hadn't yet spoken, stood back, appearing to take everything in. Though it was still dark, there was something about this one... a familiarity of sorts. I wanted so badly to get a closer look at him.

"You don't feel like talking? That's okay." Ryder opened the map and turned it in a few different directions until he decided on one. Almost as quickly, he folded it up. "We'll take this."

"Are we going to bring them with us?" the girl asked.

"I'll make that easy on you," Dylan said. "Over our dead bodies will we go with you. I don't know what you want, but you won't make it one day out here in the wild."

Ryder smiled. "What makes you say that, pal?"

Dylan stepped up to him. "Well, *pal*, you're obviously from the city. I'm going to guess you've been there a long time. The people on the outside won't take to you very kindly."

"Maybe they'll take more kindly to us if *you're* with us." Ryder raised a hand slightly and pulled a device from his waistband. Next thing I knew, he had stuck the device into Dylan's side, and Dylan collapsed.

Nina screamed and fell to her knees beside Dylan. "What did you do?" she yelled.

"He'll be fine," the girl said softly. "But we need you both to come with us. We have no intention of hurting you, but we need your help."

Ryder scooped his arms under Dylan's. The other man grabbed Dylan's feet. They carried him away, in the opposite direction from Dax and me.

By now, darkness was lifting. The sky was brightening. Through the trees, I followed the two men with my eyes until they reached one of the trucks from New Caelum. I could now see that they were younger than I had at first thought. Teenagers, probably. Boys.

The girl stood in front of Nina. She, too, was young. "I promise we don't mean you harm. We're looking for someone. A girl about our age. There are others from the city who are looking for other information, but we only want to find this person. You'll be more protected if you come with us."

Nina seemed to think about that. "Well, it's not like I have much of a choice. I'm not going to let you just take Dylan."

The nameless boy returned. "Ryder's waiting for you. You're going to go on ahead. I'll search the area for the missing companions. I'll contact you on the PulsePoint."

Nina smiled. "You'll never find them."

"Either way, you can either go willingly with your friend, or we can force you."

I could practically hear Nina's brain processing the choice. Finally, she sighed and followed the girl toward the large truck.

I cocked my head and watched as the remaining city boy bent at the knees and picked through the rest of our belongings, standing when he found something.

I squinted my eyes to see what he was holding. When the small item came into focus, my hand flew to my neck. It was my necklace—a leather necklace, with exotic beads from my parents' travels, and adorned with a small wooden charm, a gift from a friend.

He slid the necklace into his pocket, and my blood boiled. But I tried to hide my emotions, not wanting Dax to do anything to alert this guy to our presence. The city boy then surveyed the rest of the campsite, circling the fire, and studied the foliage. He moved toward the trees that I had squeezed through earlier that morning and disappeared into the forest.

I recognized a tracker when I saw one. This guy was tracking my moves from earlier. How the hell would he have learned to do something like that?

And why were we so important?

Dax stood slowly and motioned for me to follow him. We circled around the back side of the campsite, opposite where the mystery guy had disappeared into the trees.

The truck pulled away and continued making its way east, heading directly toward the community we'd left just the day before. I prayed Nina and Dylan would be okay. But we all knew and accepted the risks of going rogue, away from one of the established communities.

Slowly, Dax and I continued to circle the camp area. The mystery guy was gone.

Dax faced me. "He's tracking you." His tone came out in a harsh whisper. We'd both watched the guy studying the broken branches, the bent grass, and the impressions my feet had left in the moist dirt.

I smiled. "He can try. He won't be able to track me very far." I had learned long ago to cover my tracks.

Dax put his arm around me and pulled me to him in a playful hug. "That's my girl. Let's get our stuff and get out of here. We have to warn as many others as we can."

....

chapter four

West

I swore that discovering my best friend had contracted a deadly virus was the worst day of my life. That was, until the day Mother told me she was gone—dead.

We were both twelve years old, but we had a maturity level closer to that of experienced adults. We had to.

She never cried. Not upon hearing that she had the virus. Not when she became violently ill. Or so I was told. She had to have been in excruciating pain, but a nurse—Mother's friend—told me she had been brave all the way until the end.

The end...

I often wondered what "the end" entailed. Did she see a bright light? Was her body suddenly devoid of all pain? How much had she suffered? Were her parents there to greet her in some dream-like state? That's if her parents were actually dead.

Part of me had hoped her parents were dead so that she wouldn't be alone. But it seemed wrong to wish for someone's death. Even if it was for a good reason.

The day before Christina became sick, we spent time on the roof directly above the president's wing. That was one of the perks of Mother being elected president of New Caelum—we were permitted outside, but only on the roof.

Christina had long brown hair. Pale skin. Freckles. Her eyes were a light blue, the color of robins' eggs. She was the most beautiful creature I'd ever known. Would ever know.

She was just starting to develop a figure. I couldn't help but notice—and like—the way her breasts were filling out. Thinking back now, she was awkward. We both were.

What I remembered most was the way her lips felt that day. It was our first kiss.

And our last.

Her lips were hot. I think she had a fever, even then. I still wondered how I didn't contract the virus. For two weeks after that, I lived in acute fear that I would suffer through the illness that took so many of my friends, including Christina. If I was being completely honest, I would have admitted that I hoped the illness would take me, too. I found myself thinking often over the next six years that Christina had been the lucky one.

And now? Finding out she was alive somewhere? That she had fled the city years ago after surviving? That's what Mother had said—Christina had *chosen* to leave.

We were in love. Even at twelve, we knew we would be together forever. We were soul mates.

That thought seemed silly and naive, now that I knew the truth. Now that I knew that she had voluntarily left New Caelum. Voluntarily left *me*.

I held up her necklace in front of my face. A leather beaded necklace from her parents. It still held the wooden Tree of Life I had made for her, had given her when we were forced to move into New Caelum. The charm was meant to remind her that our life would be okay as long as we remained friends and together.

I pocketed the necklace again. I would find her. She would save my sister. She owed me that.

Then I would say goodbye to her forever.

Again.

....

chapter five

Cricket

Dax and I arrived at Boone Blackston just before dinner.

"They're not going to welcome us back every single time we up and desert them," I said in a low voice behind Dax.

"Especially when they find out we allowed some elite assholes to kidnap Nina and Dylan from right under our noses." Dax reached for my hand. The feel of his calloused fingers against my palm gave me the feeling of security I was craving. "Let's find Caine."

Boone Blackston was similar to an early settlement of the 1700s. The two hundred or so long-term residents of Boone had constructed a tall fence around the dwellings. Most lived inside the fence, though many of our resources—water, our extensive gardens—were located outside the fence. Everyone was required to pitch in, whether it was to grow food or to create the supplies we needed, or simply to search for items that had survived the past six years inside malls, stores, or wholesale clubs. The people of the community trusted each other, but they also looked out for each other. Though they mostly weren't related by blood, they felt a strong sense of family.

Dax and I approached a small door to the right of the larger steel gate that protected the entrance to Boone. Predictably, the small door opened and out popped a guardsman on duty— or, in this case, a guardswoman.

"Hi, Zara. It's so nice to see you." My words came out clipped and lacking sincerity.

Dax squeezed my hand hard. "That won't help," he said through gritted teeth.

I smiled oh-so-sweetly. Zara and I were not, and never would be, friends. She had tried to have me thrown out of the community several times, but Caine wouldn't hear of it. And she wouldn't be able to keep me out now, either.

Dax started to walk right past Zara, but she pulled a gun from her waistband and pointed it directly at his chest.

I tried to hide my surprise. Zara wouldn't have the nerve to hurt Dax. Me, maybe, but never Dax.

Dax stopped just short of letting the gun touch his heavy jacket. "Put the gun away, Zara."

"Why are you two back? You're not wanted here."

"Why don't I show you—" I began.

Dax squeezed my hand again, cutting me off.

"You should put a muzzle on her." Zara wore camouflage pants and a tight-fitting black knit top. She was military, and looked every bit the part. She did everything she could to be a necessity to Caine. And she hated that I, by contrast, didn't have to do anything to remain in his good graces. Even worse, in her eyes, I was constantly doing things to *not* deserve

Caine's fatherly affection—like leaving and taking his daughter with me.

"Let us through, Zara. We need to see Caine. Dylan and Nina are in trouble. Surely you don't want me to tell Caine that you played a hand in keeping us from helping his daughter."

Zara's lips lifted. "Seeing as Nina arrived several hours ago with some new friends, I don't think Caine gives a flying crap what you know. So why don't the two of you turn around and head on back from whence you came."

That was good news, but what did she mean by "friends"? Surely she wasn't talking about the guys who'd tasered Dylan and stolen him and Nina from our campsite. I wasn't about to ask. "Whence?" I laughed. "It doesn't matter how hard you try, or what fancy words you spout, you're still an idiot in Caine's eyes. Now get out of our way, or I'll move you myself."

Zara lunged at me, her arms flying, but Dax caught her in mid-air. She continued to reach, though, and she managed to grab and yank a handful of my hair.

I screamed, digging my fingernails into her arm and forcing her to let go.

"Give it a rest, you two," Dax laughed. "At least let me get you some white t-shirts and a pool of mud before you start this shit again." He shoved Zara backward. She was breathing hard.

My pulse didn't rise above sixty beats per minute.

Zara huffed, but allowed us to pass. "Why did you come back, anyway?" she yelled.

"We missed you." Dax blew her a kiss, and if we weren't walking away from her so fast, I was sure Zara would have spit on us.

Once inside the walls, I immediately felt claustrophobic. It was small-town living at its worst. A main street divided two rows of two- and three-story buildings on either side; these buildings had served different purposes prior to Bad Sam, but our people had managed to redesign them to our needs over time. There were other settlements like this out west, all having popped up gradually in the one to three years after Bad Sam was gone, but Boone Blackston was the only settlement between New Caelum and the ocean.

"You coming?" Dax called, getting ahead of me. He stood at edge of the sidewalk, and was about to head down the stairs to Caine's underground offices. Dr. Caine Quinton was Nina's father; he was also the doctor who had nursed me back to health and helped me flee the city once I was well enough. He had raised me from the age of twelve on.

When we'd left the community a few days earlier, I had made it clear to Caine that I wouldn't be back for a while. Yet here I was. "Yeah." I jogged to catch up.

We descended the stairs. But before we had a chance to knock, the door opened and laughter spilled out.

I followed Dax inside. Sure enough, Zara was right—Dylan and Nina were there with Caine. To my surprise, the two city kids were there too: Ryder and the girl. There were smiles all around.

"What the hell, Caine?" Dax stormed over and grabbed a handful of Ryder's shirt. "This guy tasered Dylan."

Ryder didn't seem the least bit bothered that a guy a third bigger than him was holding him in his fist. He looked at Dylan, and then over at Dax. "Wow, twins? How cool is it that a set of twins survived the apocalypse?"

I hated when people referred to what had happened as "the apocalypse." It sounded so end-of-the-world and made me picture zombies.

I made eye contact with Nina, raised a brow in question.

"We're okay," she said, for Dax's benefit more than mine. A vein was bulging from his neck.

"Yeah?" Dax's face reddened further.

I glanced toward Caine, who was leaning against a work table with his hands clasped in front of him, letting the scene play out. "Caine, you want to enlighten us?" I asked.

"Oh, I guess. This is so fun, though." He pushed off the table. Unbuttoning the cuffs of his shirt, he rolled up his sleeves, one and then the other, in a slow, relaxed motion. His dark hair, in need of a haircut, lay disheveled across his forehead. His eyes were a smokier blue than Nina's. "Dax, Cricket, this is Ryder and his friend Key. They've run away from New Caelum and have requested asylum."

"Run away," I deadpanned. "Why?"

"What Cricket means," Dax said, tightening his grip on Ryder, "is why would you leave your elite bubble and risk contamination from the likes of scum like us?"

"Let him go, Dax." Caine laid a gentle hand on Dax's shoulder. After a few seconds, Dax finally released Ryder. "Your questions will be answered in time. Their Tasers have been handed over to us. Their truck confiscated. We welcome visitors. Until they prove otherwise, we accept them as new friends."

Ryder and Key traded glances. Lines formed across Key's forehead as she opened her mouth to speak. "We have another friend. He chose to walk here after we found Dylan and Nina."

"Your friend will be welcomed as well," Caine said.

Dax chuckled under his breath and shook his head. It was clear that he wasn't going to be joining the welcoming committee any time soon.

"Thank you." Key moved closer to Ryder. She wore a silky, royal blue blouse, tucked into royal blue tight-fitting pants, and Ryder wore all black. They both had an air of polished sophistication about them. I couldn't tell if they were just friends or if they were a couple. It was funny that I'd thought she was a boy at first, because now that I saw her up close—her high cheekbones, her naturally pink-tinted lips, and her dark eyelashes—I had no idea how I could ever have mistaken her for anything other than a girl, and a striking one at that.

I also wondered why Caine was accepting these two into our community without further questioning. He'd always been very accepting of newcomers, but this was the first time any of those newcomers had come from New Caelum.

And would he be so accepting when he discovered that the virus might be back? Though Ryder and Key appeared innocent enough now, they had tasered Dylan, and they'd exited the city right on the heels of some kind of pre-dawn hazmat operation. Something didn't add up. I suspected they hadn't simply run away.

Nothing was ever that simple.

....

chapter six

West

Ryder and Key had successfully infiltrated the settlement where Mother claimed I was likely to discover Christina. Somehow, my friends played the role of "victims of the evil city" perfectly, and they had won the trust of the two outsiders we found camping in the woods.

I had yet to lay eyes on Christina, but according to Mother, I'd find her near Dr. Caine Quinton. I was skeptical. If Christina was so angry at age twelve that she ran from the protection of New Caelum, why would she remain this close? Especially if she had any idea that she might be hunted down one day if the virus were to ever surface again.

And who had taken care of her? She was only a child at the time. Had this Dr. Quinton nursed her back to health? Or was she already cured before she left New Caelum? I suddenly realized how little I knew .

I'd spent the day following the guy with a chip on his shoulder and the small blond-haired girl who looked angry at the world. They led me to the exact settlement Mom spoke about, the only one she thought existed east of New Caelum.

At the gate, it had been quite comical to see the tiny blonde engage in an argument with the butch-looking chick. This girl was twice her size and all muscle; she could have squashed the little one easily had Mr. Chip not protected her.

Now, in a tree half a mile from the settlement, I used my monocular to watch Ryder and Key. They emerged from the building they'd disappeared into over an hour ago—the same building Mr. Chip and Miss Blonde had run to the minute they arrived at the compound.

The air was cool and crisp and darkness was descending. I'd freeze if I didn't enter the compound soon, but I was hoping that Ryder and Key would tell me they'd found Christina before I made my presence known. What if she ran when she saw me? What if it was me she'd been running from all along? It seemed silly to think that I was the reason she ran from the city when we were only twelve, but I couldn't take that chance. I had to find Christina and take her back to New Caelum to help my sister. According to Mom, the antibodies living in Christina's blood were Willow's only hope for survival.

The girl they called Nina was showing Ryder and Key around. The three of them disappeared into a small house. I jerked the monocular away from my face, slamming it into my thigh. "Come on, Ryder." I needed them to call me on their PulsePoint, but I had no idea if they still even had their Pulse-Points on them. Were they taken when they relinquished the Taser? Did they leave them inside the truck?

After a while, I decided to give up on Ryder and Key for the night. I'd have to find a spot where I could stay warm until morning. If I still hadn't heard from Ryder by then, I'd enter the compound.

I hadn't seen anyone on the hike out of the mountains or on the deserted roads near the settlement, so I assumed I was mostly safe out here. I climbed out of the tree and decided to go in search of an abandoned building or some sort of shelter that would protect me from the cold wind.

I had only gone about a hundred feet when I heard what sounded like mild cursing. Under the cover of trees, I searched through the dark, thick shadows and barely made out the outline of a female form—it was the angry blonde I had been following all day, walking fast along the road. My luck had changed.

"Cricket," a male voice called out from the direction of the compound. "Cricket" didn't look back, and if anything, quickened her pace. It would appear that she didn't wish to be found.

I looked back in the direction of the voice; it was Mr. Chip, the guy who had hung close to Cricket all day. "You're going to freeze," he warned, then with a wave of the hand, he turned and headed back inside the compound. I was really starting to dislike him.

Cricket darted away from where I was hiding. I decided to follow.

She walked at a good clip. I found it difficult to keep up as it got darker out—especially since I had no idea where I was going, and I was trying to stay far enough back so as not to be heard.

More than a dozen turns later, not only did I have no idea where I was, but I realized I had totally lost sight of Cricket. I peered through my monocular, turned to night vision, but all I saw was the dead end of a gravel road. Overgrown shrubs lined one side of the road, and a crumbling stone wall the other.

I heard the sound of a howling dog in the distance, and in my mind it sounded very much like a hungry wolf. Leaves blew in the cold breeze, and limbs knocked together with an eerie crackling. I was growing colder. This had been a stupid idea.

Using my night vision monocular, I searched for Cricket again. She had vanished. How was that possible? Just as I was about to give up, I felt a hard jab in my ribs from behind. "Don't turn around," Cricket said with a low, but very girly, voice. "Who are you? Why are you following me?"

The muscles along my spine tightened, yet I smiled at the same time. I'd been had by a girl who was half my size and barely came up to my shoulders. "Cricket, I presume?" I tried to glance over my shoulder to get a good look at the blond beauty behind me.

She poked me harder. "And your name?"

"I mean you absolutely no harm. Can I please turn around so that I can introduce myself properly?"

"You tell me your name and why you're here, and then I'll decide if you can turn around."

I laughed. This was a girl who liked getting her way. "My name is West. I'm from New Caelum."

The moment of silence that followed was deafening. The pressure to my ribs lessened just long enough for me to turn on Cricket and see that she was holding nothing more than a rotten tree limb. She backed away, her eyes wide. She had just opened her mouth to say something when the silence of the dusk was broken by the roar of an engine, and a pair of bright headlights penetrated the dark, blinding me.

A large truck was coming toward us. I shielded my eyes against the headlights and saw the outline of two men inside the truck's cab. This was one of the scout trucks from New Caelum. And clearly not Ryder and Key, since their truck had been confiscated by the people inside the settlement.

I hadn't gotten the chance to discover the identities of the other scouts who had left New Caelum that morning. I had been too busy hiding, trying to keep secret the fact that the president's son (who was supposed to be in quarantine) had snuck out on one of the other trucks. But I knew that none of the other trucks were supposed to have come east, and I had no idea why this particular one appeared increasingly determined to run us down. It didn't seem to be slowing.

"Run!" I screamed.

Cricket and I quickly darted behind the stone wall. The truck slammed on its brakes, stirring up a large cloud of dirt, then beeped in reverse until it swung around and was once again facing us.

"This way." Cricket led me to an opening in a wire fence. She squeezed through, then turned and helped me, since I was much larger and didn't fit as easily. I followed her down some concrete stairs that seemed to lead nowhere, but at the bottom was a door in the side of a hill. She dragged me inside, then pulled out a flashlight and lit up a long hallway. I had no idea where she was leading me or why she was helping me. And as I stared down this hallway of darkness that led to who knows where, I wasn't sure I *wanted* her help

We walked, unhurriedly, to the other end of the hallway, passed through another door, then went up a flight of stairs. When we reached the top of the stairs, I was surprised to find myself inside a huge room with gigantic two-story windows. Many panes were broken, but they were still grand, elegant— unlike anything I expected to find outside New Caelum. I looked up to find a sliver of a moon hanging low in the sky.

"Where are we?" I asked. Of all the questions, that was the first one that came to mind.

"A large abandoned property—the Biltmore Estate." Cricket wasn't even out of breath. She walked to a table on the far side of the room.

After lighting a lantern, she turned, and the fire cast a soft glow across her pale skin. That was when I noticed the scars along her cheek. I couldn't tell what kind of scars they were; they could have been from a bad burn. Maybe she'd been born with them.

As if reading my thoughts, she shook her head slightly, letting hair fall forward to shield her scars from my view. "So, West from New Caelum, why are people of your city on this side of your protective walls? What are you looking for?"

I debated on whether to come clean and be honest with her. See if she knew Christina. But I couldn't tell the outside world that the virus was alive again. That information would be sufficient cause for the people of the outside to declare war on New Caelum. No one wanted to see that virus again, and the outsiders would likely care little about the fate of those inside New Caelum. After all, it was the citizens of New Caelum who had shut them out, deliberately kept them from the best doctors and medical supplies that could have helped many of them survive.

Finally, I decided that I didn't see the harm in asking Cricket if she knew Christina. But before I could speak, I felt a sharp pain to the back of my head. I fell to the ground and into a black hole of darkness.

....

chapter seven

Cricket

"You didn't have to hit him." I couldn't believe I was staring at the one and only Westlin Layne. My West. Six years had passed; he was a man. Yet I could still see the young boy that had kissed me on the day I'd developed the fever. What was he doing here?

Did he know I was alive? He *had* found my necklace, but he obviously hadn't recognized me.

And how could he? I didn't look anything like I did before. The virus had disfigured me. I'd still have the face of a monster if it hadn't been for Caine and the skin grafts. He'd saved me in so many ways. But I had died in others.

I knelt beside West. I wanted to rub the back of my hand against his face, to touch his skin, but not with Dax here. He didn't know about my past. No one but Caine and Nina knew.

Dax assumed I'd simply gotten lucky, like everyone else in this forsaken world. Everyone who remained in our country either successfully hid from the disease or was immune but didn't know it. I was the only one who had ever caught Bad Sam and survived it.

"What do we do now?" I asked. I hadn't gotten the chance to ask West who was in the truck, or why he ran from his own people.

"We wait until he wakes up, I guess," Dax said. "What were you two doing? You *brought* him here?" There was a bit of hurt in his voice.

I had never brought anyone to the Biltmore before. Dax had followed me here once, and ever since, he'd known to find me here when I disappeared. Which I liked to do from time to time. This was my place to escape. To clear my head. I liked to pretend it was my own mansion, that the piano in the corner wasn't caked with inches of dust and falling plaster from the ceiling. That the dining table in the next room was set for a feast. Music played anytime I felt like dancing. It was silly, but this was a place—the *only* place—where I allowed myself to dream. If only for a minute or two, before reality set back in.

"No, I didn't bring him here. I've never brought *anyone* here." My words came out harsher than I had planned. I stood and turned toward Dax. "I'm sorry. I didn't mean—"

He held up a hand. "Yes you did. It's okay. I guess I deserved that."

"No, you didn't." I glanced down at West. His fingers twitched.

"He'll be out for a while." Dax stepped to me, lifted a hand, and cupped my cheek. "When are you going to let yourself feel happy? I know that you come to this place to escape. This world is what it is. But you're not alone in it."

I cringed. Dax constantly asked me to run away with him. He wanted us to find an unoccupied house, one that we could call our own.

"Not a lot to be thrilled about these days." My stomach tightened as I spoke the brutal truth. I met Dax's unwavering gaze and tried to smile a little. "You didn't have to hit him."

He shrugged. "Meh. I'm not a fan of city boys." He dropped his hand. "Why do you think they're here?"

"I don't know." I pulled a dining room chair over and sat beside West. He was going to wake with a huge headache.

"You think it has anything to do with the increased activity at the incinerator?"

My head shot up, and I stared into Dax's eyes. "I have no idea." Fear pulsed through my veins like a raging forest fire. We both had to be thinking the same thing, but neither of us spoke it aloud. If the virus was back... How many were infected? *Who* was infected?

More than ever, I wanted to know why West ran from the other truck.

chapter eight

....

West

I heard the moan before I realized it had actually come from me. I squeezed the bridge of my nose, hoping to ease the pressure that sat like a blocked vessel behind my eyes.

Slowly, recent events slid back into my mind. I sat up—too quickly, because the entire room tilted when I did. "Where the hell am I?" I asked before I even looked to see if anyone else was there.

"Welcome back, Westlin." A tall, dark-haired man with a goatee approached. His sleeves were rolled to the elbows, and he crossed his arms as he eyed me with a lifted brow. His large size intimidated me, yet the partial grin counteracted that.

"Who are you? How do you know me?"

"I'm Dr. Caine Quinton." He handed me a small ceramic saucer with some liquid. "For the pain."

I eyed the cloudy liquid. "No thank you." I swung my legs around, letting my feet touch the ground, not quite trusting my balance yet.

"Suit yourself. You've got quite a bump on the back of your head."

I let my fingers graze the spot at the base of my skull. He was right. It was quite the painful knot, too. "I was with a girl." I looked up. "Cricket, I think she said her name was."

The doc smiled. "Yes. She didn't hit you, though. That would have been Dax. You don't get near Cricket without going through Dax first."

"He plays dirty. How good is he when his opponent's back isn't turned?"

Caine tilted his head to the side as if considering the question. "I'd say the end result would likely have been the same. Just not as quick."

"So that was a mercy hit?"

Caine laughed. "What are you and your friends doing here, West?"

"You first. How do you know me?"

"Your friends said you'd be coming. They told me your name." He walked over to a table across the room and picked up a picture frame. When he returned, he thrust the frame at me. "Plus, I knew your mother."

Inside a simple metal frame was a picture of my mom and the doc. Both looked younger. And happy. I couldn't remember the last time I'd seen my mom with a look of such contentment on her face. She had actual color in her cheeks. Her lips were glossy and red-tinted.

"When was this taken?"

"Eight years ago. You would have been, what... ten?"

"Sounds about right. Where were you?"

"At the hospital where she and I worked. We were on the first team to decide how to handle the possibility of a world-wide pandemic."

"And how'd that work out for the two of you?"

"I'm guessing you already have an opinion on that." Caine smiled while taking the photograph from my hand, but I saw the slightest twitch in a vein in his neck. "I've told you how I know you. Now... what are you doing here?"

"I'm looking for Christina Black."

"There's no one here by that name." Caine turned his back to me and poured amber liquid from a decanter into a small glass. His hand shook slightly.

Feeling steadier, I stood and began circling the room. "But you know her? She was here sometime in the past, right?"

Caine downed the shot of what I presumed was bourbon or whiskey. "You and your friends are welcome to stay for another day," he said, "but then you'll need to be on your way."

He was covering for Christina. Why?

"I mean Christina no harm," I said, and I meant it. As long as she could help my sister, I was happy to get what I needed from her and then never talk to her again. She obviously wanted nothing to do with me, or she wouldn't have run.

"Let's say I did know this Christina Black. What do you want from her?"

"She and I were friends once. I just want to see her." With my own eyes. See if she's the same person I remember. Only older. See with my own eyes that she's not dead.

I'd also need her to return to New Caelum with me, but the good doctor didn't need to know that just yet.

Caine Quinton turned on me so fast I didn't even see him coming. He grabbed handfuls of my shirt in both fists and held me so that our faces were just inches apart. "Listen to me, and listen carefully. Christina Black is dead. Gone. She can't help you. Now..." He took in a breath and let go of my shirt with a little shove backward. "I think you and your friends need to be on your way back to the city."

This was the man Mother wanted me to see? Was I really supposed to believe that the two of them had once been friends? He clearly knew something about Christina, yet just as clearly, he was determined to be as unhelpful as possible.

After another harsh look at the doc, I grabbed my pack and headed for the door. Just as I got there, it opened, and I stood face to face with Cricket. Her blond hair was pulled back into a ponytail, but strands of it hung loosely along one cheek, partially hiding the scars on the right side of her face.

"Good morning, West. Your friends are having breakfast with Dylan and Nina. You can meet them in our dining room. Just go up the stairs, turn right, and the dining building is two buildings down on your left."

She dipped her chin, turning her gaze toward the floor, but not before I saw a hint of how blue her eyes were against her delicate, pale skin.

"Thank you, Cricket." I stepped to the side to allow her to pass. "I assume I also have you to thank for stopping your friend from pummeling me further."

"Dax only meant to protect me. He thought you meant me harm. You shouldn't follow people in the dark around here."

"Are you *sure* I didn't mean you harm?"

She walked past me, still not making eye contact, then stopped, turning her head only slightly in my direction. "No, but I didn't need Dax to protect me, either. If I had felt threatened, I could have knocked you on your ass myself and left you for your friends in the truck to pick up."

I smiled. "Good to know." Then I turned and headed up the stairs as directed.

I decided I was sorry I wouldn't have more of a chance to get to know this Cricket.

....

chapter nine

Cricket

"The virus is back," I said without looking at Caine. I climbed a small wooden ladder to pull a shoebox from his highest shelf.

"I suspect you're right. West isn't talking, though." Caine sat in a wingback, drinking Kentucky bourbon from a crystal lowball glass. He only drank bourbon or used the fine crystal to celebrate really good news—or when he was depressed. "He doesn't trust us."

"Mmmm. He didn't recognize me." I said it as a statement, but there was a hint of uncertainty in my tone. I carried the shoebox over to one of Caine's work tables.

"No. You're nothing like the old Christina. And it's been six years. But if the virus is back, the city could become desperate. Maybe they already are."

I opened the box and pulled out the PulsePoint device I'd learned to use before I'd developed the fever. I hadn't used it since leaving New Caelum, though—hadn't even turned it on. Not once. But I had wanted to. I'd wanted to see West's face, talk to him, and know that he was all right. Let him know that I was alive.

I had missed West the minute I was out of the city—and his sister, Willow. She was younger than me and West, but the three of us had spent many hours exploring New Caelum together. Still, as hard as it was to do, I had decided that it was best for everyone to think that Christina Black was dead. Because even at twelve years old, I wanted nothing to do with the people who had sentenced my parents to die.

I had not forgotten—would never forget—the loss of my parents, and who was to blame for the fact that they were shut out of my life. During the initial stages of the pandemic, my parents had gone abroad, had taken their medical expertise where it was most needed: to poorer countries with few doctors and little advanced medicine. But then the bureaucrats had banned all international travel, had grounded all flights in and out of the USA. And in so doing, they left my parents for dead in the country where they had graciously given of themselves to help others.

That was back when world leaders—West's mother included—thought they could actually contain the virus.

I stuffed the PulsePoint in my bag, then closed the box. I was tempted to rummage through it, but there was no point. I knew what it contained. Keepsakes, mementos. A special rock, a gift from Dax. A small case of beads from my parents, brought back from one of their trips—the same beads my necklace had been made out of.

The necklace that was now in West's possession, I thought, and scowled.

I turned to study Caine. He had leaned his head against the back of the chair, and his eyes were closed tightly like he was in pain. Stress was evident in the deep troughs that formed across his forehead.

"You're excited to see him," he said without opening his eyes.

"I'm glad to know he's okay. I don't like what seeing him means."

I pulled a stool over and sat in front of Caine—my father, for all intents and purposes.

"Caine." He opened his eyes and focused on me. "Are we prepared if the virus is back?"

"As prepared as we can be." He leaned forward and scooped my hand into his, a fatherly reassurance that only he would know I needed. "We are not prepared, however, for the virus to be inside New Caelum."

I cocked my head. "Why is that? What do you mean?"

"If the virus breaks out inside New Caelum, close to a hundred thousand people will flee the city in search of a new way of surviving."

I understood. "They'll overcome us," I said. Especially if they could be reassured that those surviving outside the city were living well.

"That's right." He took a drink. "And it's probably the reason West is looking for you. You have the antibodies that might help battle the virus if it has, in fact, reared its ugly head again."

Would West hurt me? I wondered. Six years ago, I'd have answered that with an emphatic "no."

"I told West to get his friends and leave, but..."

"But we need to know what's going on inside the city," I finished.

He nodded. "But Cricket, I don't want you anywhere near him. Nina and Dylan are already getting close to Ryder and Key. They'll fish for all the information we need."

I wasn't sure I could stay away from West. I needed to know the truth of why he was here. And to be honest, I was just plain curious about his life. But I also knew that Caine was only trying to look out for me. "Okay. I'll be in touch." I stood and started for the door again.

"Cricket, if you decide to disappear for a while, I'll understand."

He was giving me permission to flee. It was what I was good at, after all.

"Protect yourself. West's mom and any doctors she's told inside the city must know that you're alive—and they know that you're their best hope of survival if the virus becomes a problem." Caine knew this because he had once been one of them himself—before he helped me to flee New Caelum. He had been an infectious disease doctor for New Caelum, and one of the best of the best. Yet, like me, he'd ultimately chosen not to be locked inside.

"Then we'd better hope it doesn't become a problem." I took a look around Caine's living quarters. The fact that he chose to live in a basement apartment said a lot about his personality, his own desire to hide in darkness. "Do you have enough samples from me?"

Caine directed his tired eyes at me, but said nothing.

"You need more." He hadn't taken blood from me in a while.

He stood, walked toward me, and placed his hands on my shoulders. "We'll find a way."

"I'll meet you at the lab. It's going to be harder to sneak away, though. Dax is watching me closely. He's worried I'll leave again."

"He knows you well."

"I was always destined to hurt him."

Caine nodded. "Take the south exit. I'll make my way to the lab by midday."

I lingered by the door, debating whether to question Caine about the problem that haunted us every time we began working on a treatment.

"What's on your mind, Christina?"

I squeezed my eyes tight. He never called me by my real name. "What if the virus mutates again?"

"A definite possibility. Let's hope that never happens."

~~~~~

I snuck away while Caine sought to distract and delay the others. I passed by the vegetable gardens, which were thoroughly picked over; the settlement had harvested every vegetable and grain we could, and having experienced the first frost last week, a month earlier than we had hoped, the growing season was over. As in years past, we could only hope and pray that we'd stored up enough food and resources to get us through the winter—especially since our winters had gradually become more and more harsh.

In the park across from the gardens, children played hopscotch and swung on swings—some made of wood, others made of tires. All of the rusted metal structures had been removed the year before, after being deemed too dangerous for the small children. It struck me funny how the adults in our community considered some old piece of metal dangerous, when more than ninety-nine percent of our population had been wiped out by a single illness. If we had survived that, you'd think we could survive a rusty swing. Why didn't we just live as the invincible people that we apparently were?

I stopped to watch one girl who was swinging by herself. Her dark brown hair blew in the cool breeze as she leaned her head against the rope with a look of melancholy. She was about the same age I had been when I was told I would never see my parents again. Twelve was too young for that kind of loss. To never again see the two people who loved me more than any others, who made all of my important decisions, who held me when I had even the slightest scratch.

There had been no one to hold me when I was struck by an illness that would forever change who I was.

Just when my feet began involuntarily walking in the direction of the sad little girl, a woman passed in front of me. The girl smiled up at her, then climbed off the swing and into what I presumed to be her mother's arms. I stopped myself, realizing that this little girl was not me. She had someone—and hopefully she always would.

I could see my breath as I turned and made my way down the broken street and out through the back gate, looking back several times to make sure I wasn't being followed. Caine had long ago given up on trying to keep me caged inside the settlement. And since all the other settlements were out west, on the opposite side of New Caelum, the area we called home didn't see a lot of crime. Except for a random incident here and there, there just weren't enough people in the area for anyone to cause any serious trouble.

That was, until the New Caelum people showed up. Now, I wasn't sure what was the bigger threat—the visitors, or what their presence meant.

I still hadn't gotten to hear the story of how Dylan managed to forgive Ryder for tasering him. But Dylan had never been one to hold a grudge. In fact, we were a pretty forgiving society by nature. Most of us, anyway. I probably would have knocked Ryder unconscious the first chance I had—and if not, then Dax would have done it for me.

I smiled briefly at the thought before a tinge of guilt took over. It was my fault Dax had become so attached to me. We had both taken advantage of each other's vulnerability and loneliness.

It was a quiet morning as I strolled through one of the warehouse districts on my way to the hospital; it was several blocks from Boone Blackston, outside the settlement walls. Caine had managed to set up a completely sterile lab there, dedicated to studying the virus, a possible vaccine, and treatments. For some reason, he continued to act like we were still fighting a disease that had been gone from our society for six years.

Of course, who was I kidding? Caine's behavior was no odder than my own. Since the world had been altered so drastically, we'd all developed our own particular obsessions and insecurities. I spent most of my nights listening for New Caelum's incinerators. Even last night, I'd snuck out of the Biltmore Estate, leaving Dax and West asleep on the floor, climbed up to the roof, and stared up into the mountains, listening for any sign of movement outside New Caelum. And for any sign that the city was once again awake in the middle of the night, burning all evidence of the return of a deadly disease.

Fortunately, I'd heard nothing. No incinerator, and no additional trucks leaving the east gate.

I knew Caine and I were feeding each other's paranoia. I wanted to believe that the likelihood of the virus being back was ludicrous; maybe West was simply here because his mother finally told him the truth—that I was alive when I fled New Caelum. But why would she do that? Why now? And why would he and the others risk exposing themselves to the outside world without good cause? Surely they knew they were putting their own immune systems at risk by leaving their sterile environment and mixing with the poor communities on the outside. What was so important that they would take that chance?

My thoughts ping-ponged all over the place, racing through so many questions that I would never be able to ask West. I couldn't tell him who I was—I knew that much. No one could know. But I did miss him. He had been my best friend once. He had stood beside me when the only other important people in my life were stripped from me.

Questions assaulted me. What kind of person was West now? Who was he becoming inside the city? A politician like his mom? He had always been into computer programming. Had he continued down that path? Maybe he—

Voices echoing off the sides of buildings stopped me mid-thought. I froze. No one from the community should be out here; they rarely ventured this far beyond the walls.

I moved forward quietly. At the next corner, I poked my head around. Just down the street was one of the trucks from the city—it could have been the one Ryder drove, or maybe it was the one that had chased West and me the night before. No one was in it, but I could still hear the voices. They seemed to be coming from a building directly beside it—a warehouse with a large open door. Whoever it was, they weren't making any effort to be quiet.

I inched closer, my back up against the side of the building. There were two male voices. They were yelling at each other. "Let's just go back to the city. We have to get help. She *needs* help." The voice sounded panicked. "What do we do, West?"

I moved closer, edged right up to the open doorway. Ryder and West were facing each other, arguing. Obviously Caine hadn't found them.

"I don't know!" West sounded just as desperate as Ryder. "I can't reach Mother on the PulsePoint—she's not answering. I don't know what to do. We can't chance how security will react when we pull up to the gates with her like that." He clasped his hands behind his neck and paced. Then he turned back to Ryder. "When did you first see signs?"

"This morning after breakfast."

"How about you? How are *you* feeling?"

"I'm fine." Ryder sucked in a deep breath. "I feel fine." He was starting to sound even more hysterical. "You don't think—"

"I don't know *what*—" he yelled, then stopped himself. "I don't know what to think," he said in a much lower voice.

They both turned away from me. They still hadn't noticed me standing in the doorway.

Then I saw what they had turned toward. It was Key. She was lying on her side on the ground, curled up on top of some sort of blanket or sleeping bag. And she was shaking uncontrollably. *Oh no.*

I stepped inside and cleared my throat. The warehouse was one of those buildings that reminded me of old movies where the mob ran stolen car operations. It smelled of damp mildew, and it was large and drafty. And currently, it was completely empty, so Ryder's and West's voices echoed off the walls.

"What's wrong with her?" I said. I crossed my arms and leaned against the opening. My heart was gradually picking up speed, like a marathoner looking for a pace to settle into. I knew exactly what was wrong with her.

"Oh, great. Just fantastic." Ryder turned and tried to cover Key with a blanket, but without getting too close to her or touching her in any way.

"Cricket, you can't be here." West stormed toward me, but stopped more than ten yards away. "Caine told us to leave, and that's what we plan to do."

I stepped forward. "Is that right? You plan to leave?" I nodded toward Key, who was shivering in the fetal position. "Is she sick?" I knew she was, but maybe it was a simple flu. Maybe, although I suspected not. I knew the signs better than anyone. Not only had I suffered through the illness myself, I had nursed so many others through it. I had watched them die right in front of me.

West held a hand out, stopping me from advancing and blocking my view of Key. "She's just tired. She hasn't slept well since leaving the city. She'll be fine when we get where we're going. You need to leave."

"West, maybe she can help," Ryder said.

"She can't!" West answered quickly. His face was cold, hard.

My head spun out of control trying to remember the exact steps for quarantine that our entire settlement had memorized. Time was of the essence. We needed to isolate any and all people who had potentially been exposed to the virus, and then block off all locations where these people had been.

I stared at Key's quaking body. She would need medical care before her fever escalated to the level of seizures. "I can help," I whispered.

"No, you can't," West insisted.

How was I going to convince him I could help without exposing my identity? I had to take drastic measures if we were going to isolate the disease and have any chance of helping Key survive.

I lowered my backpack to the ground, then dug through it until I found a bottle of simple fever-reducing medication. I pulled the bottle of water from the side pouch and held out both the water and the pills to West.

"Just set the items down and step away," he ordered.

I started to do as he instructed, but then I realized that I was the only person in the room who couldn't get the virus. I looked up at West, and I almost lost my breath when I saw the fear etched in the grooves of his forehead, the redness in his eyes. "No," I said quietly.

He cocked his head. "No? What do you mean, 'no'?" He studied me, and I resisted the urge to turn the scarred side of my face away from him.

"My pills. My water. I'll give them to her. And you're going to let me help the three of you."

"Why would you do that?"

"Because I'm trained for this. I know how to deal with the possibility of an infectious disease infiltrating our society again." I was lying, but if I could do something to keep this disease from spreading—keep West from getting sick... "Besides, she might just have the flu. The three of you have been inside a world devoid of most bacteria and all viruses for six years. Your immune systems probably aren't prepared to fend off what for us would be a common cold."

"She has a point." Ryder crossed his arms, his hand shaking like a junkie, distraught with the possibility that his girlfriend was dying. "Please let her help us, West. You said yourself that you think the doctor and others inside this settlement know where your stupid Christina is hiding. Maybe Cricket can help."

I narrowed my stare at Ryder. Who was he calling stupid? But I remained silent while West assessed the situation. It seemed like he was taking forever to make up his mind, and I knew I was running out of time. Each minute that ticked by increased the risk that our settlement would be exposed to the possibility of another outbreak. And this time, perhaps no one would be left.

"What's it going to be, West?" I wiggled the bottle of water in front of him. "Let her suffer more than she needs to, or let me make her a bit more comfortable while we assess what we're actually facing?"

"Fine." He stepped aside. "Set the pills in front of her, and then step away. She's strong enough to reach for them."

I walked a wide path around the two boys, then knelt beside Key so that I could see her face. Her teeth chattered. She looked up at me as I set the bottle of water close enough for her to reach. "Hey, Key. Can you open your hand? I'll drop the pills."

She did as I instructed. She awkwardly put the pills in her mouth, then grabbed the water bottle. Too weak to raise her neck, she simply squirted some water in her mouth and rolled her head backward to swallow. She choked slightly, but managed to swallow the pills. Water ran down her cheek and into her hair. "Thank you," she managed.

"I'm going to get you help, Key. Do *not* let yourself think the worst. You might just have a nasty bug." I rose and faced Ryder and West. "I need for the two of you to tell me why you're so sure this is the Samael Strain." When they just stared at me, I repeated, "Tell me why you think Bad Sam has returned."

They traded glances. Caine was right: West didn't trust us. Why would he?

"Why did you come here?" I asked. "You risked our lives and your health when you left the safety of New Caelum. And now you're taking a huge gamble just staying in the same room with Key."

"So are you," West pointed out. "Why would you do that?"

"I'm the one asking the questions now, because not only have you risked your own lives, but now I have to tell *my* people—mothers, fathers, their children—that they must put themselves into quarantine. We have to watch each other in fear and paranoia while we wait out the incubation period of a virus that those people hoped to never again see in their lifetime." My voice grew louder and more panicked with each word.

"I'm sorry," West said softly, looking down at his feet. I was confused by his sudden retraction.

"You're sorry? For which part?"

He lifted his head, and his eyes narrowed in on me. And in three quick steps, he was on me. He fiddled with something at his waistband, and before I knew what was happening, he'd pulled a Taser from his holster and jabbed it into my side. The electric jolt immobilized me, and I collapsed into his arms.

He slid a hand to the small of my back, and another under my neck, supporting my head as he lowered me to the ground. "I'm sorry, but I can't let you tell your people."

chapter ten

West

The look on her face when I drilled the Taser into her ribcage would haunt me for a long time. And apparently, I had overdone it, because now she lay unconscious. What had this scarred girl ever done to me except try to help me and my friends? And I had rewarded her with a fifty-thousand-volt electric shock. What kind of person was I becoming?

"Grab her feet." I slid my arms under hers and lifted her upper body while Ryder grabbed her feet. "We need to relocate before her friends discover us."

"What about Key?"

"There's a hospital a few blocks away. I passed it yesterday. We can hide the truck, and hopefully there'll still be some supplies to help keep Key comfortable. We'll try to call my mother again from there, and we can go out at night to hunt down some food and water." I needed to reach Mom. I had to know how Willow was doing and find out if the virus had spread. I glanced at Key over my shoulder as we carried Cricket. God, I hoped she didn't have Bad Sam.

Ryder and I put Cricket in the front cab of the truck. When we went back inside the warehouse, Key was pushing herself up, first to her hands and knees, her arms having obvious trouble even with her lightweight frame. "I've got it." She stood and held her hands out to the side, trying to gain some sort of balance. Her eyes were watering. Her face flushed. "I can ride in the bed of the truck. As long as I can lie down, I'll be fine."

"Key, let me help you." Ryder stepped closer to her.

"No! Don't come close. We have to minimize your exposure." After grabbing Cricket's water bottle, she limped weakly outside, and was barely able to lift herself into the back of the truck before she collapsed.

I scooped up Cricket's backpack, and Ryder and I climbed into the cab.

At the hospital, we found an underground garage and parked the truck. The hospital looked to be in even worse shape than most of the rest of the buildings: windows shattered, doors busted open. I figured the hospital must have been ravaged by desperate looters during the outbreak. The odds that there were any supplies left weren't good.

I carried Cricket to an exam room and lay her on a bed. It wasn't the cleanest spot, but it would have to do for now. I checked her pulse; it was slow. Too slow. Why hadn't she just turned around and left when I'd told her to?

I had never intended to hurt her. But the longer she'd stood there, the more I'd wondered if she, too, knew something about Christina. I was already sure that Caine was hiding something; was this girl in on it? She looked to be the same age as Ryder and me, and therefore she was the same age as Christina. Could they have been friends?

74

She moaned; she was waking up. I began sorting through her bag. I found the bottle of pills, a jacket, some binoculars, and a PulsePoint. I paused, staring at the device carried by all residents of New Caelum.

I moved to stand over her. "What the hell are you doing with a PulsePoint?" I asked her, even though she wasn't really conscious yet. It didn't make sense.

I searched the room for supplies. Nothing, as expected. I'd have to venture deeper into the hospital. Maybe we'd get lucky.

Two exam rooms over, I discovered some padded hand and ankle restraints. I returned to Cricket and strapped her to the gurney. She moved her head from side to side, her hair falling away from her face to reveal the scars on her right cheek and neck.

Unable to stop myself, I traced my fingers along the textured skin. Her eyes popped open, and I stepped away.

"What are you doing?" She jerked her head left, then right. "Where are we?" She took in her surroundings. "We're at the hospital. Where's Key? You need to move her to the infectious disease wing. It's locked, but Caine has a key. We can help her, West." Only after her ramblings did she finally try to move— and discovered her restraints. She tugged at them before turning her shocked gaze on me.

I had stooped to new depths. I reached in her backpack and pulled out the PulsePoint again. "Where did you get this?" I asked calmly.

She looked from the PulsePoint to me, and her eyes widened further. I could almost see her mind racing through a hundred possible answers, none of them the truth. She leaned her head back and stared up at the stained ceiling, and her breathing quickened.

Ryder entered the room. "Key's all set up in a bed down the hall."

Cricket remained silent. Her blue eyes pointed to the ceiling while I inwardly berated myself. I glanced over my shoulder at Ryder. "Cricket says there's an infectious disease wing, but that it's locked. Caine has a key." That's where they must have stored all the supplies.

Ryder walked over to Cricket and looked down into her face. "Is this true? Why would you need such a place? It's not like you people on the outside have any real doctors, or any idea how to treat the sick."

Cricket laughed under her breath. Ever since I had met her, she'd seemed quiet, shy even, except with the GI Jane gate guard. But this time when she spoke, she seemed confident, self-aware. "You two are a couple of real heroes, aren't you? Why did you leave the city? You obviously didn't do it because you thought it was better out here. Although I must say, that was a nice act you put on to get Dylan and Nina on your side. But now what? What are you going to do when Key's fever gets so high that she has seizures? Or when she becomes dehydrated because the fluids in her body are evaporating? What will you do when she starts to bleed from the eyes and other not-so-pleasant areas of her body?" She jerked her hands and feet against the restraints. "What are you going to do when the two of you become infected too, and you can no longer help her? What, exactly, is your plan?"

Ryder's face paled. His mouth hung open. I moved to stand in front of him, blocking Cricket from his view. We needed to focus.

"The plan is..." I moved toward Cricket and waved the PulsePoint in her face. "The plan is for you to tell me where you got this." When she didn't answer, I placed a hand on her shoulder, leaning in close to her face. "You stole this, didn't you? You know Christina. What did you do to her?"

She refused to answer. She wouldn't even look me in the eye. I tucked the PulsePoint into my waistband. "Fine. Don't answer. But you'll stay restrained until you tell us what we need to know." Finding Christina was our only hope to save Key and Willow.

I turned and motioned for Ryder to join me in the hallway. Just as I reached the door, Cricket said, "Get Caine, let us help Key. And then I'll tell you where Christina is."

chapter eleven

Cricket

The last conversation I'd had with my mom and dad occurred the day before I moved to New Caelum with West and his mother. I still remembered Mom's voice, even now, over a sketchy telephone connection. She was tired. I asked her if she was crying, but she denied it.

She knew then, as I would find out a day later, that she had been cut off from her home country—from me—forever.

She told me things like, "Keep up your studies, and work hard always." And, "Do something nice for at least one person, even someone who might not deserve it, every single day."

I didn't know what she meant at the time. But now, thinking back, I realized that my mother and father had done nice things for people they didn't know every day of their lives— even when doing so meant risking their own lives in a foreign country.

My mother said goodbye to me that day. And I have wished for the opportunity to tell her I loved her ever since—because I don't remember what my last words to her were.

What if my mother died and didn't know how much I loved her?

The lump in my throat was almost too much to swallow past. I choked against it. Tears fell from my eyes with nowhere to go but down my temple and into my hair. I wiggled my wrists against their restraints, wanting badly to wipe all evidence of emotion from my face.

I must have eventually drifted off to sleep, because I woke to the sounds of various distinct noises—the distant sound of voices, the echo of many footsteps, and doors slamming against walls, loose on their hinges.

I was watching the door like it might explode, and it did when Dax blew through it. "What the hell!" He ran to me, cupped my face. "Are you okay? Which one did this to you?"

"I'm fine. Calm down." As angry as I was at West, I didn't need Dax playing the hero at the moment.

West and Ryder entered the room behind Dax, followed by Caine, who seemed to be assessing the situation.

Dax began unbuckling the restraints. His breathing was coming at breakneck speed. "*Calm down?* Are you *kidding* me?" He pulled at the leather with increased frustration. "Tell me who did this."

As soon as he had freed one of my hands, I grabbed his arm, my hand gripping the rough fabric of his heavy coat, and tugged him toward me. He leaned his face in and stared into my eyes. I pinned him with my best listen-to-me-or-else gaze. "Dax, don't do anything. I mean it. There will be time for consequences later."

He searched my eyes like a crazed lunatic. "West did this, didn't he?"

"Dax, look at me." But I had lost him.

He turned and charged at West.

Caine stepped in front of him and pushed him backward. "Listen to Cricket. Help her remove the other restraints."

Dax reluctantly returned to me, then smoothed my hair back. "I *will* kill him," he said, not caring that everyone standing there heard him, including West himself.

Dax didn't mean what he said in the literal sense, but I'm sure he *did* mean to hurt West. I would make him understand. I'd have to. "No, you won't, because that would hurt *me*. Please don't do anything until we've had a chance to talk, okay?"

He took deep breaths in and out while he continued to free my limbs from the leather straps and rusted buckles. By the time he helped me off of the metal exam table, his breathing was finally slowing a bit.

With Dax directly behind me, I took three steps toward West and looked up into his eyes. "You will live to regret strapping me to that table and not letting me help Key."

"Maybe. But as long as you keep up your end of the bargain, I don't really care what I have to live with."

I analyzed the desperation in his expression. Did he mean my promise to help Key, or was he that determined to find Christina Black? Though I had promised, I wasn't sure I could produce Christina for him. "Why is finding your friend so important to you?"

He tilted his head, considering the question. "I have my reasons."

"You're so desperate to find her that you were willing to hurt someone you barely know?"

"You might not believe me, but I *am* sorry. I didn't mean to hurt you. I panicked."

"Actually, I do believe you."

"You do?" Dax asked behind me. When I didn't answer right away, he ran a hand through his hair. "Unbelievable."

"Like I said, he'll regret it. We're wasting time." I looked at Caine. "What has West told you?"

"Not enough. That he left you here at the hospital, and that I needed to come. Dax was nearby and overheard. Obviously, there was no stopping him."

Dax scoffed behind me.

I nodded in understanding. "Key has a high fever. I don't know what it is. Could be the flu. Their immune systems are most likely compromised from being locked up inside that airtight facility. I gave her fever-reducing meds, but that was hours ago."

Caine turned to West and Ryder. "You two have been exposed to her. You'll need to stay here at the hospital—but away from her."

"Like hell we will," Ryder said. "If you think I'm turning her over to you, you're crazy."

Caine stared at Ryder for a full ten seconds in silence. Then he pulled a weapon from behind his waistband and handed it to Dax. "Fine. Dax and Dylan will escort the three of you back to the entrance to the city."

Dax cocked the gun and held it in the air, just looking for an excuse to use it.

I held up a hand, urging him to stand down. "Wait. Just stop." I stepped up to West. "You don't want this. Key will die if she has the virus. So will you if you get it." I looked back and forth between West and Ryder. "And if my suspicions are correct, the virus is already in your city. They won't take you back, which is probably why your PulsePoints stopped working. You've been cut off."

West stared into my eyes. I wanted to turn away, but I didn't dare.

Finally he turned to Ryder. "She's right. We need their help. For Key's sake, and for Willow's."

I gasped at the sound of his sister's name. West lifted a brow; he heard me.

What's wrong with Willow? I wanted to ask, but I couldn't. Did she have the Samael Strain?

Ryder let out a huge sigh. "Why should we believe that you guys can help us?"

Caine turned to me. I closed my eyes for a brief moment, then opened them and said, "Because if Bad Sam is back, I can produce Christina Black. That's why you came, right?"

Ryder looked from me to West, who didn't stop staring at me. "Fine. What do we need to do?"

"Dax," Caine began. "You will return to the settlement and alert the town that we are in quarantine status until further notice. Everyone is to go into lockdown mode, and they are to know that this is not a drill. Bring Dylan and my daughter back with you. They'll need to be monitored and tested for the virus. Let's just hope that if this *is* Bad Sam, we can contain it."

Dax nodded at each instruction. I couldn't help but think about what Caine didn't say: *If we can't immediately contain the virus, our settlement most likely won't survive.*

"West, you and Ryder will follow me." Caine grabbed the gun back from Dax. "And if you give me any trouble whatsoever, I won't hesitate to send you back where you came from, and I will have no problem using force to protect my people." He led West and Ryder from the room while I stayed back to speak with Dax.

Just before West disappeared, he looked back at me one last time, like he wanted to say something to me but wasn't quite sure what.

It wouldn't be long before he figured out who I was. One way or another, I knew he'd put two and two together. How could I have been so careless with the PulsePoint?

When they were gone, Dax started in on me. "What the hell, Cricket? Do you realize what kind of danger you've put yourself in?" He faced the window while running a hand through his sandy blond hair.

Not as much danger as he thought, seeing as I was immune to Bad Sam. "Yes," I said simply.

"Why would you do that? What were you thinking?"

"I was thinking that a girl needed my help, and I was able to provide it."

The look on his face softened. "Have you given up? Is that why you keep disappearing and constantly putting yourself at risk? Are you planning to leave?" He touched my cheek gently, then slid his hand around to the back of my neck, holding my gaze with his chocolate brown eyes. "Sometimes I feel like... like you're always just a day away from leaving me—from leaving Boone Blackston. Like you're just going to walk off into the sunset and never return."

I blinked up at him. "I'm not going anywhere." Not yet, anyway.

He pressed my head to his chest and wrapped his other arm around me. "Don't leave me," he whispered. "If you go, I go with you."

~~~~~

Dax unlocked the bell tower in the center of town. We raced up the six flights of stairs, and Dax entered the code to signal the alarm for a mandatory quarantine. The quarantine alarm—a verbal message over loud speakers—would continue to play for one hour from the time it was started.

I looked Dax in the eye, searching for a sign that he was virus-free. I didn't think he had been exposed to Bad Sam, but I couldn't be sure. He hadn't been around Key since she'd gotten sick, but he'd been exposed to all three of the city folk on several occasions now, and had spent the night in the same room with West, back at the Biltmore Estate. We'd learned years ago that it didn't take much to contract this virus—casual contact, breathing the same air as someone with symptoms. Key wasn't coughing yet, but that didn't mean she was safe to be around. Her temperature was climbing quickly, and other symptoms would soon follow.

My heart squeezed at the thought that either Dax or West would come down with the disease. My heart couldn't handle seeing either of them sick with this fatal fever. They had both meant too much to me at different points in my life.

Dax crossed to me. "Let's leave. Get away from here." There was fear in his voice.

My heart felt tight, knowing I couldn't leave with him. "I can't. Caine needs my help." I cringed inwardly at my choice of words. How would I explain to Dax that Caine needed my blood in order to continue working on the antibodies for a cure for Bad Sam? Dax and I had agreed a long time ago that we didn't need to rehash every detail of our past—and I had decided that that included my intimate history with Bad Sam.

"Caine doesn't need you. If this is Bad Sam, we both know our best chance of survival is to leave the settlement. Caine will understand that."

Dax was right about one thing: his best chance of survival was to flee. Most of the people who had survived the initial Bad Sam outbreak did so only because they lived in isolated areas far away from the cities, away from the people who spread it. It wasn't until after the virus had died out that settlements started popping up, formed by survivors who craved community.

But if the virus was back and the people dispersed, we'd be starting all over again.

I knew I couldn't promise to leave with Dax, but the look on his face was desperate. "Let's at least let Caine test us to see if we have the virus now."

He nodded in agreement, though reluctantly.

Footsteps thudded on the stairs below. Nina popped her head through the opening in the floor. "What's happened? Where's my dad?" She climbed up, and Dylan followed.

"He's at the hospital. It's Key."

Nina gasped. Her hand flew to her mouth.

"You don't think—" Dylan grabbed Nina's hand and pulled her closer. Exactly the way they shouldn't react.

I shook my head. "I don't..." I crossed to the window and looked out over the south side of town. "I don't know." I faced them again. "The four of us need to get to the hospital. We were exposed to them more than anyone else. We have to think of the townspeople."

They all nodded silently. Nina moved toward the exit.

I started to follow, but Dax put a hand on my arm. "Who is Christina Black?" he asked, and for a moment, it felt like the Earth stopped moving on its axis.

Nina's head snapped around to look directly at me, her eyes wide.

I turned to look out the window again. There were times when Christina Black had been gone for so long, I wondered if she had ever existed at all. "Christina Black was a little girl who came down with the Samael Strain. She was twelve years old, already an orphan, and by some grace"—*or curse*—"she survived the unimaginable disease. She was forced to start her life over with no family, no friends, no one to care about, and no one who cared about her in return."

"She survived Bad Sam?" Dax asked. "I thought that was impossible. Where is she now? Why is this West looking for her?"

"Christina disappeared a long time ago. Before you and Dylan came to town." I spun around, not making eye contact with any of them. "We need to go. Caine is expecting us."

....

chapter twelve

West

Finally, Cricket returned to the hospital. She had not yet looked my way. On purpose? Maybe. I wouldn't look at me, either, after what I did to her.

The isolation unit I was in was obviously state-of-the-art, and I was impressed that Dr. Quinton had been able to keep it in such good shape. Pretty much every hospital in the country had built one of these units eight years ago, back when Bad Sam looked to kill everyone in its wake.

It was actually nine years ago when we first heard about the new deadly virus—one year before it reached our country. But it was across the ocean then, and no one thought for a second the disease would affect the privileged in a country with infinite power and money and the best health care in the world.

But of course it did. And when the first cases popped up, our government dismissed fears and ignored concerns. Hospitals built small quarantine and decontamination centers like this one, but that was mostly to appease the Centers for Disease Control.

And these small units proved to be not nearly enough.

But before these decontamination centers were even built, the future people of New Caelum had already formed a secret society of sorts. Some of the most influential, powerful, and richest people in the country, led by my mother, came together and decided to build their own city. A city with state-of-the-art scientific labs, medical facilities, and living conditions fit for royalty.

And many believed one had to be near-royal to secure a spot inside the city. The people who built New Caelum predicted the world as we knew it was going to end, and they felt it was up to them to stop it—or, failing that, to at least ensure that our species survived.

Those who weren't invited to join New Caelum—which was virtually everyone—thought they could control the spread of the disease with things like this infectious disease unit. Those poor souls thought they would survive the pandemic, just like they had survived every other crisis before it—with protocols and guidelines handed down from government powers.

And a few people who were invited to New Caelum—like Dr. Caine Quinton, a well-respected doctor according to my mother—declined. They chose to live outside of the city.

Most of them were dead within a year.

I fiddled with the PulsePoint I had found in Cricket's bag. Caine had been nice enough not to take my belongings from me, and Cricket hadn't asked for it back—not that it mattered. She probably knew as well as I did that it was useless without the owner's fingerprint. And Cricket was not the owner.

No, this PulsePoint belonged to Christina. I knew this because I recognized the worn butterfly stickers on the back. She and I had been kids when we were first given these devices, and of course Christina had immediately taken to decorating hers—evidence of just how young we still were.

Critical questions swirled through my mind: Where was Christina now? Why did Cricket have her PulsePoint? And since it was useless to her, why was she carrying it around?

I tucked the PulsePoint back in my bag and looked out through one of the glass walls of my unit. Ryder was in the unit next to mine, and I could see Key shivering in a hospital bed two units over. Caine was with her, covered head to toe in a complete hazmat suit in surgical blue. Of course, the world had learned that even the most conservative precautions didn't guarantee that health care workers wouldn't contract Bad Sam. Yet still, the same man who had pulled a gun on us earlier today was now risking his life for Key.

Ryder stood against the glass that separated him from Key, monitoring Caine's every move—and watching the suffering of the girl he'd loved since they were kids.

At least the isolation units were built with lots of glass. Patients didn't go as crazy when they felt they were still around people.

Outside in the hallway, Cricket talked with Dax, Dylan, and Nina. As they spoke, she played with the hair on the right side of her head so that it covered her scars. Did she know that the scars didn't stop her from being attractive?

I gave my head a shake. What the hell was I doing thinking of this girl as pretty?

As if hearing my thoughts, Cricket turned her head slowly toward me. Dax had a hand firmly planted in the small of her back. Were they an item? He treated her like she was his property, but I didn't sense her reciprocating that same level of affection toward him.

I couldn't help but smile at that. There was something about her that made me want to get closer to her. And there was something about the way he touched her that pissed me off.

Maybe in another life I'd get the opportunity to know someone like her.

When Cricket saw me smiling, she quickly turned away. What *was* it about her? She was a puzzle.

But it was one I didn't have time to solve. I was here for one purpose only—to find Christina and get her back to the city. Mom seemed to think Christina had the answer that would save my sister from an ugly death. And if the girl who'd deserted me all those years ago could do that, then I'd find her.

Caine exited Key's isolation room and entered the short hallway that connected our three iso units. Then he stepped into some sort of decontamination chamber, similar to the ones in New Caelum, and was sprayed head to toe with a sterilization substance. After a few minutes, he stepped out on the other side, minus the hazmat suit.

It was then that I noticed that Cricket and Nina had begun scrubbing in as if they were surgeons.

What are they doing? I felt the start of a panic attack building in my chest.

When their scrubbing was complete, Nina proceeded to help Cricket put on her own hazmat suit. Nina suited her up, double-gloved her, and checked to make sure she was covered from head to toe. Dax watched all this with a worried expression, which didn't do much to calm my building nerves. Why was I feeling so protective of this girl?

Because I need her to help me find Christina, I reminded myself. She'd be of no help to me if she got sick.

Then Cricket walked toward the decontamination chambers. So, she was coming in. Was she headed for Key's room? I rushed over to the window and was about to bang on it. I didn't want her further exposed to Key.

But when she emerged from the decontamination chamber, she didn't turn toward Key's room. She turned toward mine. And with the press of a few buttons, she entered.

"Hi, West," she said through the filtration mechanism of her gas mask. "I need to take some blood from you, if that's okay."

"What if it's not?" I asked.

She raised her head, not hiding her face the way she had only moments ago, but her scars were now covered by the mask. "Then you'll stay in this room for the twenty-one or so days it'll take to prove you're free of the Samael Strain."

"How will giving you my blood keep me from that?" I had no intention of staying in this room for twenty-one days; Willow didn't have that long. If Cricket couldn't, or wouldn't, give me the information I needed about Christina, then I'd be leaving this place and searching elsewhere.

Cricket moved closer to me. Stared straight at me. "I have what you need to take back to your city doctors. It will help Willow." She spoke so low, I could barely hear her.

I grabbed her arm. She pulled back slightly, but then stopped herself. She glanced over her shoulder toward the others.

"They're not watching," I said. It was true; for once, something had distracted Dax long enough for him to take his eyes off of her for more than a second. I yanked her even closer, breathing steam against the plexiglass of her mask. "I let you help Key—now it's your turn. Tell me about Christina. That was our deal."

Her eyes didn't have the fear I was expecting. "Christina is dead." Her voice didn't waver. She didn't flinch. She didn't struggle against my grip, which grew tighter as she said the words. "But I have what you need from her."

Christina was dead. I had suspected it for so long, but to hear it spoken aloud... it still sent me reeling. Cricket's words sounded strange and muffled in my head, like they were traveling through a tunnel with no end. Her eyes were stone cold, and she didn't dare look away from me. She truly believed what she was telling me.

Or she wanted me to *think* she believed it.

"What is it you think I need?" I released her arm and held mine out so that she could take blood from it. Fighting her now would serve no purpose.

She tied a rubber tourniquet just above my elbow. "You want a cure for your sister." She stuck a needle in my arm with zero warning.

I flinched. "Ow."

Her lips lifted at my expression of pain, and she attached a collection tube. "Your doctors are missing a key ingredient they need in order to come up with a treatment for the virus."

"And you have that?"

She didn't answer right away; she collected the blood she needed, then proceeded to place the tube back into the carrying tray and dispose of the other biohazard waste.

Finally she turned back to me and spoke. "Yes, I have what your doctors inside New Caelum need." She turned and exited the room.

chapter thirteen

Cricket

aine had been peering into a microscope for ten minutes, grunting and sighing. Then finally he said, "He's immune."

"Are you sure?" I trusted Caine's expertise, but my fear of Bad Sam was just so great.

He raised his head. "I've tested his blood multiple times. It doesn't contain the antibodies that yours contains, but like Nina and me, he has the gene that protects humans from Bad Sam. He cannot contract this particular virus."

I breathed a sigh of relief for my childhood friend. Even though he had strapped me to a table earlier that day, I couldn't stop the feeling of gratitude. He would never know the fear of a fever that would put him in his own private hell. It was a hell I had lived through, a hell I would never wish on anyone.

"Good. That's good. So West is immune, like you and Nina. That's good." I repeated "That's good" as if I needed extra convincing. "What about Dax and Dylan?"

Caine simply stared at me. The way his cheeks drooped told me that Dax and Dylan were at risk. My heart sank.

A thought struck me. "But wait—how can West be immune when his sister isn't? Like you and Nina—you both have the gene."

"That's true. But just because a parent or a sibling has the gene doesn't necessarily mean another family member will have it, too. We're all a mix of our parents' genes. And who knows, maybe this is a mutation."

"Well, thank you," I said, touching Caine's arm in a rare instance of affection between us. "For the extra testing." There had never been reason to test anyone for the "immunity gene" before, but now that Bad Sam was back, it was important to know who could tend to the sick. And besides, he knew that I would want the extra assurances.

Boone Blackston was fortunate to have Caine as a doctor—fortunate that he had refused to be a part of New Caelum's medical team, fortunate to have on their side perhaps the only infectious diseases specialist in the world who was immune to Bad Sam. But I felt even more fortunate to have him as part of my life. He'd been like a father to me

"What about Key? Is it Bad Sam for sure?"

Caine frowned. He began removing West's slide from the microscope. "Won't know until morning. The test takes a while for me to run."

"And you're testing Dax and Dylan for the virus?"

He nodded. Dax and Dylan were now in isolation units on another floor.

So, though I was relieved West was in the clear, I still had to worry about Dax and Dylan.

~~~~~

Caine left to inform West that he was in the clear, while I ate dinner with Dax. I sat with my legs tucked under me in a chair while we both picked at peanut butter and jelly sandwiches. Nina was with Dylan in the next room. She was in charge of monitoring both Dylan and Dax for any signs of fever or sickness.

"What are you thinking about?" Dax asked.

I sighed and looked at my plate. "I just can't stop wondering what will become of our world if this virus is back. Our community of people has finally begun to trust each other."

Dax shrugged. "Please don't get mad at me when I say this, but why do you care?"

I snapped my head up. "What is *that* supposed to mean?"

"Come on, Cricket. You've always had one foot pointed straight out of town. I've lost track of the number of nights I've fallen asleep thinking you'd be gone when I woke up. That you'd leave without saying goodbye."

"I would never leave without saying goodbye." Would I?

"Do you think you could ever love me?"

I tried to hide the surprise from my face. "Dax, I—"

He placed his fingers over my lips. "Just think about this. If Key turns out to have this virus and I don't, and if it looks like we can't contain it ... Will you consider leaving with me? I would do everything in my power to make you happy."

"I know you would."

"Just think about it."

I smiled. "Of course I'll—"

"Hey, Cricket." Caine entered the room, cutting me off. "I need your help." His lips tugged downward, and his voice was somber.

"Okay." I touched Dax's hand; I could see that he was disappointed by the interruption. "I'll be back later. Don't go stir crazy." I flashed him the most sincere smile I could muster, knowing it wasn't good enough. He wanted so much more from me.

Then I followed Caine into the stairwell. The infectious disease unit was up one floor from where Dax and Dylan had found rooms. "So, what's wrong? Why did you come get me?"

We were alone, but Caine kept his voice down anyway. "We have a problem with the treatment."

"What do you mean? I thought everything was finally going well." I knew that Caine had been using animals to test treatment options for Bad Sam over the past few years, and he'd told me that his latest approach showed a great deal of promise.

"I'll show you."

He led me to his lab, down the hall from the isolation unit, and we both slipped into protective gear, including gloves. Though neither of us was afraid of contracting the virus, we still had to be careful not to get the virus on our clothes or bodies. We couldn't risk tracking it outside the controlled confines of the lab.

Caine unlocked the door to the animal testing area and pushed the door open. "Take a look."

When I stepped inside, my heart fell to my stomach, and I swallowed against the bile that rose in the back of my throat. "What happened?"

"They're all dead."

I glanced from cage to cage at the small animals that gave their lives so that we might study this disease. "I can see that, but why?"

Caine circled the room, almost frantic. I'd never seen him this upset. He grabbed a clipboard and started flipping through it. "Mostly, it's their hearts and kidneys. I simply can't stop the vital organs from shutting down." He kept flipping. "I thought this time I had found the right formula." He then turned to a miniature computer laptop and began typing something into it.

"Are you sure you didn't just miss something?" I asked. "Something fixable?"

"I didn't miss anything." He stared at his computer screen. "I really thought I had it this time, Cricket." He shoved a metal stool across the room. I flinched at the noise it made. "Something in your blood helped you fight the infection that shuts down the organs of everyone else who contracted the virus. I just don't understand it."

I walked over to him and urged him to look at me. "You need a break. I'll stay with the three patients up here. Why don't you find somewhere where you can get some sleep. We'll need you at your strongest if anyone else gets sick." That was an understatement. "Maybe after some rest, you'll think of something that might have gone wrong."

He nodded and wordlessly headed toward the door. Anger and disappointment weighed heavily on his slumped shoulders.

"Caine?" I said.

He turned back to me.

"Dax still doesn't know that I survived Bad Sam—that my blood has antibodies. I need to be the one to tell him."

"He won't hear it from me." He stood there a few seconds longer, and then he made a confession of his own: "I didn't tell West that he was immune."

"Why not?"

"I guess I'm more than a little pissed that he's partly responsible for bringing Bad Sam—or whatever this is—to our settlement. Thought it could wait till morning, when I get the other test results."

It was a little heartless, but I couldn't blame him. And hopefully, it meant West would stay put for now.

When Caine was gone, I stared at the caged dead animals for another ten minutes. What if Caine had exhausted all of his options for finding a cure? Until now, he had never been under any deadline to find a treatment. But now, staring the possibility of the virus in the face? We suddenly seemed out of options.

~~~~~

The main hallway lights were dim, and being late fall, it was already dark outside, though it was still early in the evening.

I had decided to check on our "guests" from New Caelum. More specifically, I was ready to talk to West and convince him to open up about New Caelum and Bad Sam's return. One thing that had bothered me ever since Ryder, Key, and West had arrived was how little they'd told us about New Caelum. Among other things, if Bad Sam really was infecting citizens of New Caelum, why had West and Ryder seemed so genuinely surprised that Key was sick?

In the quarantine area, the smell of bleach from the decontamination chamber lingered. I checked on Key first, eyeing her through the glass. Caine had given her something to help her sleep, and she seemed to be doing just that, although her head thrashed about restlessly. Just beside her, in the next room, I saw Ryder. He had pushed his bed up against the glass, close to Key, and was sleeping soundly.

Then I walked down the row to West's chamber.

It was empty.

My heart immediately sped up. I flipped on the light.

Nothing. He was gone.

Crap. I hurried back to Ryder; maybe he knew something. Maybe he'd seen West leave. Maybe they'd even talked about it.

I was just about to bang on the glass when I realized that something wasn't right. Ryder's skin was flushed. His breathing was shallow and raspy.

No longer worried about bothering the patients, I flipped on the lights in Ryder's and Key's units so I could get a better look at both of them. Key was no longer thrashing; she had stilled. From this distance and through the glass, she even appeared peaceful. But as I peered closer, I noticed a dark shadow around her eyes.

Although my heart was speeding out of control, the sight of her made me stop breathing altogether. And then a shot of adrenaline sent my limbs into action.

I flew to the scrub room, washed my hands and arms until they were almost raw, dried them, and slipped into a full hazmat suit and triple gloves. I went through the decontamination chambers as quickly as was safe, then went straight to Key.

Her short, brunette hair was matted to her head. A layer of oils gave her skin a faint glimmer. And the shadow around her eyes...

... was blood.

"This is not the flu." My whispered words echoed inside my head like the wind of a tornado; then the air fell still, leaving behind a ringing in my ears. I backed up slowly until I bumped hard into the far wall. I gasped, trying to catch my breath, and my hand flew to my heart in an attempt to coax it into continuing to beat.

Until that moment, something deep inside of me had still hoped that this would be the regular flu. That we would chalk it up as a successful drill, nurse the few who had caught the treatable virus back to health, and that our settlement of people could go back to their normal, mundane lives.

But no. There was no doubt now.

For the first time in six years, I was standing in front of someone with a near one-hundred-percent unsurvivable disease. Assuming it was the same virus strain I had fought my way through six years ago, we had only a matter of days to try to save her life. And if Ryder was already coming down with it too, our limited resources were quickly going to be spread thin.

I entered the decontamination chamber, waited for the sanitation spray to do its work, then entered the next room and stripped off my contaminated layers. Then I quickly scrubbed up all over again and suited up a second time. This time, armed with another triple layer of gloves and a thermometer, I raced to Ryder's bedside.

His heart rate had slowed to an alarmingly sluggish pace. After pressing the thermometer to his forehead, I simply stared at it. *102 degrees.* My feet felt heavy, like they'd been nailed to the floor. I was paralyzed.

It was back—the nightmare I had hoped would never happen again—and it had been brought to us by the very same people who'd deserted the rest of the world during our time of need. The same group who'd thought that their way of fighting the disease—hiding—would be the best way to save the world. Or at least the best way to save themselves.

A loud banging interrupted my panicked thinking. I spun toward the noise. Was it West? Had he returned? Was it one of my friends? I couldn't let them come up here and risk further exposure.

Once again I raced to the decontamination chamber, went through the process of ridding myself of any traces of the virus from my body, and stripped off my outer protective layer.

When I entered the outer hallway, the banging noise got louder, and I heard voices I didn't recognize. I immediately shut off the lights in all the iso rooms, and with the push of a button, I was able to lower the shades across the interior windows of the isolation rooms, blocking them from view.

Then I made my way toward the stairwell—toward the voices.

"We-est! Ry-der!" a male voice sang, followed by more banging. "You can't hide forever!" The voices were definitely coming from the stairwell, from somewhere below, and they sounded like they were coming closer.

I glanced down the hallway to the opposite stairwell. That's when I saw Caine and Dax. I ran to them, and we slipped into a room at the end of the hall and closed the door. Caine went immediately to a set of drawers and pulled out a gun.

I raised a brow, wondering just how many weapons Caine had hidden around the hospital. "Where are Nina and Dylan?" I asked.

"They're locked in a room on the floor below, armed with a tranquilizer gun." Dax peered out through the window in the door. "Who are those guys?"

I shook my head. "I don't know. But I bet they're the same guys who chased West and me last night."

A loud commotion erupted in the hallway. I froze; Caine cocked a gun behind me.

I eyed Caine over my shoulder. "Don't we have enough problems already without worrying about gunshot wounds?"

"I won't use it unless I have to."

"Well, I'm not one to hide from whatever this is." I pulled open the door.

"Cricket!" Dax tried to stop me, but I was already out the door.

A short way down the hall, West was lying on the floor against the wall, blotting at a bloody lip. I raised an eyebrow. West was no small man to be thrown about.

A guy dressed in a red fleece jacket was facing him, daring him to get up, while another—a tall, lanky one with glasses and dressed in light gray—turned at the sound of Caine tapping the gun against the doorframe.

"Well, who do we have here?" Mr. Eyeglasses asked, stepping toward me.

His friend threatened West with a Taser. I knew firsthand how those things felt. Perhaps West did too, because he wasted no time getting to his feet. Mr. Fleece Jacket put him in a chokehold, and they turned to face us.

"Want to tell us what the three of you want?" Caine asked, stepping up beside me. Dax followed just to the other side of Caine. His fingers stretched, then curled into tight fists; he was just biding his time before he would charge, I was sure.

"We'd love to tell you. We're tracking a couple of friends, and their PulsePoint signals tell us that they're somewhere in the vicinity of this hospital. In fact, it appears"—he looked down at his own PulsePoint—"that they're on this very floor."

I shot a sideways glance at Caine, then looked back at Mr. Fleece Jacket. "What do you want with your friends?"

He cocked his head and then walked right up to me. Using his Taser, he lifted the hair off of my right cheek, causing my breath to catch. "Oh, look, Dale, she's scarred. Who burned you, little girl?"

West struggled in his captor's arms. "Don't touch her," he grunted.

Dax inched closer. I glanced sideways and gave my head a little shake, praying he would hear my silent pleas and not get involved. We couldn't know how many people from New Caelum were infected at this point, and I didn't want Dax coming into contact with any other people from the city.

Eyeglasses turned to West. "You feeling protective of one of *them*?" he spat. "What's gotten into you, West? What would your mother say to find out you've fallen for outsider scum?"

"It's you I'm trying to protect," West said. "Do you really want to risk catching the diseases they carry?"

I flinched, but tried to hide how much West's words sliced at me. How had I ever been considered one of these people?

"Good point." Eyeglasses backed up a tiny step as he turned back to me. "All right, Scarface, I'm going to ask you this once:

Where are Ryder and Key? Once we find them, we'll be out of your way."

"Oh yeah? I'm supposed to believe you'll just leave once you have your friends?"

"What? Are you deaf *and* stupid, Blondie?"

I smiled, then brushed past the three of them. "Fine. Follow me."

I led them to the quarantine units down the hall, then smacked the button on the wall to open the shades. "Be my guest. Go get 'em. Take them back to your people. We'll be happy to give you a personal escort back to New Caelum."

Caine cocked his gun again for effect.

"What did you do to them?" Fleece Jacket asked.

"They arrived this way. They apparently have Bad Sam."

Eyeglasses turned to West. "Is this true?"

"Yes."

"Oh, man!" Eyeglasses quickly backed away from the iso units. "You think we could have caught it just by being up here?"

"I don't know." I shrugged. "Maybe. Didn't the people at New Caelum tell you that Bad Sam was back?" I began biting at my fingernails to show them how boring this was.

"What? Of course not. This came from you guys. *You're* the ones with the virus."

"Afraid not, my friend," I argued.

"That's not possible—they would have said something. We were just told to scout out the various settlements and see what was going on—nobody said anything about Bad Sam. Then, after we visited the settlement west of here, we got a call from New Caelum telling us that these three needed help." He thumbed his hand in the direction of West and the isolation chambers. "We're supposed to get them and report back to the city. And we're supposed to be on the lookout for this girl." He pressed a few buttons on his PulsePoint, then held up a picture of a brown-haired teenager.

Leaning closer, I cocked my head. Studied the picture. It resembled me from when I was a child, except the girl in the picture was older. The three of them watched me for any sort of reaction. I stepped back. "Never seen her before."

"Are you sure? This is a computer-generated model from an old picture. She should look similar to this, but maybe not exactly."

I felt Dax's presence beside me; he was trying to get a closer look at the photo. But I was safe. Neither Dax nor West were going to think I was the girl in the picture.

"I'm sure. Now, unless you plan to use those Tasers, and give Caine a reason to fire his real gun, I think it's time for you to go. And you can take your friends with you."

Eyeglasses glanced at Ryder and Key, then back at me. Smiled. Stepped closer. He pushed the button on his Taser. A distinct buzzing sounded, and I flinched.

I matched his step forward and, being quite a bit shorter, looked up at this bully. "Careful. If they *do* have the virus, then that means that West, my friends here, and I have *all* been exposed."

It only took a second for that information to sink into Eyeglasses' thick brain. He took two quick steps backward and spoke quickly. "We've seen enough. We'll let President Layne know that we didn't find her son."

Fleece Jacket, who had released West the second I'd suggested that West may have been exposed to Bad Sam, grunted, then charged his Taser and slammed it into West's side as a last-ditch effort to show him who held the power.

A low but loud growl rumbled from West's chest, up through his throat and past his lips. I squeezed my eyes tight, not wanting to witness the pain, even though West himself was the one who had subjected me to that same pain.

Fleece Jacket removed the Taser, and West fell to his knees. Then Fleece Jacket and Eyeglasses left the way they'd come in.

~~~~~

"Key and Ryder have the virus." I leaned against a counter next to Dax. He'd been quiet while Caine had doctored the skin below West's lip with butterfly bandages.

By the looks on Caine's and West's faces now, they weren't surprised by my declaration. West pressed an ice pack gently to his wound.

"How can you be sure? Did the test results come back?" Dax asked.

I shook my head. "I don't need the test results. Just look at them." I gestured toward the iso rooms where the two patients slept. "Key is bleeding from her eyes. Ryder is now running a fever."

Dax locked his hands behind his head and took deep breaths in and out.

I reached up and grabbed one of his arms, brought it down, and let my fingers wrap around his forearm. "Listen to me, Dax." I squared my shoulders to face only him, attempting to block out Caine and West behind me. "You need to return to quarantine. You shouldn't be up here at all."

He searched my eyes. "What? No." He shook his head. "You and I need to leave, Cricket. We should all disperse. That's how we survived the last outbreak. We can survive again."

I ignored his pleas. I was only going to hurt him. One way or another, I was key to a treatment for anyone with Bad Sam. My friend—West's sister—was dying inside New Caelum as we wasted time, and who knew how many others would contract the virus. If anyone had any hope of surviving this...

"As soon as we confirm that you and Dylan don't have Bad Sam, I want you to get far away from Boone Blackston until we know the virus is contained."

Dax stared into my eyes, raging with the desire to run away with me. He searched for the truth that was hidden in the ashes, way down deep where I had burned some former version of myself long ago. "Why are you saying this? Why won't you leave with me?" He glanced uncomfortably over my shoulder at West. "What are you not telling me?" He raised his hands, his fingers hovering near my cheeks. But then he abruptly backed up and dropped his hands, knowing he shouldn't touch me.

I looked to Caine for help—help he couldn't provide—then back to Dax. "I can't run away with you. I'm needed here. West came to Boone Blackston for a reason. I have to help him."

"Do you love me, Cricket?"

My heart constricted. I could hardly breathe as I prepared to deliver a fatal blow to our relationship. I loved him. Besides Nina, he was my best friend. In time I may have developed something even deeper for him, but I guessed I had always known that my life's purpose would drive a wedge between us. And saving him from catching a deadly disease was more important to me than anything else I could do for him right now.

And then there was West, whose presence behind me was like a raging fire on my back. I glanced down at my feet, unable to meet Dax's stare.

"Look at me." He touched my chin with a gentle finger. "Do you love me?"

I swallowed hard. "I love you, but..."

"No. No buts. You love me. You don't owe these city people anything."

"You're wrong." I shook my head. "I'm sorry. I love you, but it's not enough. I need you to take care of yourself while I help West."

Emotion turned his eyes to glass. He leaned in, and knowing I was incapable of contracting Bad Sam, I let him place a gentle kiss on my lips and then pull back.

"It's okay," he whispered. A sad smile touched his lips, and he turned and left.

~~~~~

When I finally got up the nerve to face West, I was shocked to discover an expression softened by compassion and warmth. "Why did you do that?" he asked. He sat on the floor, leaning against a wall while still holding an ice pack to his face.

I didn't owe him an explanation. He didn't need to know why I'd sent Dax away, or why I was about to give him exactly what he and the people inside New Caelum needed. "How many people inside New Caelum have Bad Sam?" I asked.

"Only one."

"That you know of."

His lips stretched into a thin line before he agreed with a single nod.

"How did Key and Ryder contract the disease?"

He lowered the ice pack, resting his arm on a knee. "I haven't a clue."

I took a deep breath while staring briefly at the ceiling—for what, I had no idea. "West, Caine was close to having a treatment for Bad Sam, but something's wrong with it."

Caine and I traded knowing glances. We had few options, unless we planned to watch Key and Ryder die.

"Wait here," I ordered and then turned to Caine, who shrugged. Wordlessly, he followed me down the hallway. We made our way to the lab, suited up, and entered.

"There are doctors inside New Caelum who could possibly be closer to a cure than I am," Caine said.

I closed my eyes. I wasn't surprised by his admission of defeat. We both knew that when those rats died, it had proved that he was no closer to a cure to Bad Sam today than he was last week or last year. And before he could figure out the problem, Willow, Key, and Ryder might die, and others might contract the virus.

"How do you know this?" I asked.

"Because the best infectious disease doctors and research specialists the world has ever known are inside New Caelum. I would go myself, but—"

"Someone has to take care of Key and Ryder."

"I can send you with samples of the antibodies I've extracted from you, and with vials of the treatment I thought was helping the rats. Who knows what they've been working on inside the city? But we know one thing: they've lacked at least one major ingredient."

"Me," I said. "My antibodies." I closed my eyes, sucking in a deep breath and letting it out slowly. "I have to go. I can't let

Willow die. And if I can help stop this virus from making a comeback—"

"Are you sure about this? It's not your fault that their citizens have come down with a virus that should have been long gone from our world. I mean, those people are responsible for turning their backs on *millions* of people."

I cocked my head. "What are you saying, Caine? One minute you're telling me they're the best doctors in the world, the next you sound like you're trying to talk me out of going."

Though we were garbed in thick hazmat suits, he closed the distance between us and folded me into a fatherly embrace. "I just want you to be sure. I wouldn't blame you for not wanting to go."

I pulled back from him. "Those people killed my parents. It took me a lot of time to get over that. I'll be going to them with my eyes wide open."

Caine's shoulders drooped. "You're like a daughter to me. I couldn't be more proud of you." He pulled out a padded black case and began loading it with the things I'd requested, including the vials of the live virus and my antibodies, and surrounded them with dry ice. He then folded some papers from his clipboards and stuffed them inside an outer compartment of the same case. When he was done, he handed me the case and said, "You don't have to do this."

"Yes, I do. I survived Bad Sam for a reason." *Do something every day for someone who doesn't deserve it.* Or, possibly, for a whole *lot* of people who might not deserve it.

Caine placed a palm on the outside of my mask next to my non-scarred cheek. "You'll need to find Dr. Hempel. Of all the doctors who joined the people on the hill, I think we can trust him. And before they closed New Caelum up for good, he was the go-to person for studying the Samael Strain."

"Dr. Hempel. I'll look for him." I tried to smile.

After ridding ourselves of our protective outerwear and armed with the supplies I needed, Caine and I reentered the hallway and came face to face with Nina. Her face was pale. She stared straight ahead, not really focusing on anything.

"Nina, honey," Caine said.

"Dylan's sick."

My hand flew to my mouth.

She redirected her gaze to me. "Dylan's sick, and Dax is gone. As soon as Dylan spiked a fever, he picked a fight with Dax. Dax left, Cricket."

I nodded. But I knew that wasn't the sole reason Dax ran.

I placed my hands on her shoulders. "It's going to be okay, Nina. I'm going to make sure we get a treatment. Count on it."

chapter fourteen

....

West

"Where are we going?" I followed Cricket through the streets past Boone Blackston and toward the abandoned estate at the base of the mountain. I still felt the effects of the jolt of electricity that the asshole from my own city had given me.

I watched for any sign of their movement, using the knowledge of tracking I'd learned in survival classes at New Caelum. It was gratifying to find that I could apply these skills in the outside world; our classes had always been held inside simulation chambers.

Either Cricket also knew these signs to watch for, or she simply got lucky with the route she took.

"Are you not going to answer me?" I asked when she ignored my first question.

She had barely spoken to me since we'd left the hospital, except to tell me that I was to come with her if I wanted her help. I figured she had the things she promised—the things that Willow needed—inside the case she'd slid into her backpack, but I also suspected that she had information I wanted, locked up inside that head of hers.

I had never expected her to send Dax away like she did, clearing the way so that she could come with me—wherever it was we were going. Though I didn't care much for the guy, I had to admit to feeling sorry for the poor chap when she crushed his heart.

When she still didn't speak, I said, "So I guess you're not talking to me? Why? What did I do to you? I'm going to keep talking just like this until you speak to me. I will annoy you to death before any virus could ever get you. Well, I suppose the virus could get me first, so you can hold out hope for that, but I will keep talking until it does. Kill me, that is. Is this working—"

"It won't kill you." She interrupted me without a hint of humor.

"So, she *does* talk. What do you mean? What won't kill me?"

"Bad Sam. It won't kill you. You're immune. Caine was supposed to tell you, but..." She shrugged. "I guess he never got around to it."

I stopped walking. Cricket didn't. I had to jog to catch back up. "How do you know this?"

"We tested your blood. You're immune to the virus."

We walked in silence the rest of the way to the estate. I might have been in shock. Immune? Was that possible? That would explain why I hadn't come down with the virus after I'd kissed Christina. We had been inseparable back then, and I'd never understood why I hadn't caught the virus from her.

I followed Cricket down a set of stone stairs, different from the ones I'd followed her down before. For a while we made our way through overgrown brush on a path that was well worn, but then she cut away from the path, weaved around a crumbled brick sidewalk, and led me through a large door that was barely hanging on its hinges.

Cricket pushed a few stray strands of hair behind her left ear. The complexion on the left side of her face was smooth, her cheek naturally tinted, flawless. "Watch out for the boards here." She pointed to an area of flooring to our right. "They're rotten. If you step in the wrong place, you'll be in the swimming pool below. And the pool is empty, so that would kinda suck for you."

"Good to know," I said, then mumbled, "I'm surprised you warned me." Out of the corner of my eye, I thought I caught a glimmer of a smile from her. I walked in a larger circle than was probably necessary around the area she'd pointed to.

We climbed the grand staircase, then another smaller set of stairs, and finally exited the building onto a grand balcony that was in a sad state of disrepair. There we stopped. At least I now knew *where* we were going.

"Do I get to know why we're here?" I asked.

"I needed to be able to hear New Caelum." Cricket nodded to the forest we now overlooked. Beyond that was New Caelum. "We can rest here tonight. We'll head toward your city in the morning."

"I'm sorry. Did you say *hear* New Caelum?"

"Yes. Your city has been active at night lately. The sounds give me a clue as to what might be going on."

Cricket marched over to a dark corner of the porch and returned with a handful of twigs, which she proceeded to pile inside some sort of metal contraption. She then grabbed some dry brush from another pile and placed it in the middle of the sticks. From her backpack, she pulled out what appeared to be a fire starter. A quiet girl, refusing to explain many things, but definitely resourceful.

"I'd be glad to help you if I knew what it was you were doing," I said. She'd obviously done this before. I'd venture to guess regularly. "How often do you come up here?"

"Quite a bit." She stood and started to walk away again, but I grabbed her arm, stopping her. She stared at my hand, wrapped around her forearm. "If you want my help, you will not touch me."

I slowly loosened my grip, but pinned her with my stare. "What are we doing here, Cricket? I'm starting to lose my patience."

"You're welcome to leave. You can try your luck at walking through New Caelum's gates in the middle of the night, but I'd venture to guess your arrival wouldn't be welcome, given that your PulsePoint seems to be reaching no one." She grabbed some larger logs and threw them on the fire she'd quickly and efficiently started. Then she stood up straight and faced me directly. "Since you're in such a mood to talk, why don't you tell me why you think New Caelum isn't communicating with you?"

I stared into her eyes—eyes she so seldom showed me. They were a deep shade of sapphire. I was mesmerized by the darkness in them; I suspected it had been left there after years and years of surviving in a broken world.

"I don't know why New Caelum isn't communicating with me," I said. Or why my mother hadn't been in contact. I desperately wanted to know how Willow was doing.

"What happened before you left, West?" Cricket sat down on the ground, then pulled some sort of sweatshirt or something out of her bag. Curled up and facing the fire, she used it as a pillow to prop her head up on the hard ground. The fire cast a warm glow across her face.

I also sat, facing her. "My sister was diagnosed with Bad Sam. They quarantined my family."

There was no surprise in her face. "If they quarantined you, how did you get out?"

"They were sending scouts out to survey how the closest settlements were doing. We made sure a couple of the scouts got reassigned, and Ryder and Key took their places. Mother sent me out with distinct instructions to find Christina."

Cricket closed her eyes. "Why?"

"Why find Christina? Well, because apparently she miraculously survived Bad Sam six years ago." I couldn't help the anger that seeped into my voice. In an attempt to calm my nerves, I lay back, propping my head on a bent arm. "And then she left New Caelum, never to be heard from again."

"You seem angry at her."

"At Christina? Hard to hold a twelve-year-old responsible for a decision she made when she was dying of a fatal disease."

"Then why do you sound so angry?"

"Why do you care?"

Cricket fell silent, staring into the fire.

"That was harsh. I'm sorry. But you couldn't possibly imagine what it was like to mourn the death of your best friend, to think of her every day for six years, then discover that she's been alive all along. And that she *chose* to leave New Caelum." To leave *me*.

Cricket's voice lowered, almost to a whisper. "Maybe it wasn't her choice. She was only twelve."

"Maybe, I guess. But it was certainly her choice to *stay* away, and it's her choice to stay hidden *now*, isn't it? That's why you and Caine seem so hell bent on keeping her from me. She wasn't dead then. And she's not dead now, is she?"

Cricket ignored my accusations, and when she spoke, her voice was quiet. "Try to see things from her point of view. She carries the antibodies that will help an entire species fight a disease that threatens their very existence. That disease is trying to make a comeback, and you and your friends show up with your Tasers and your elitist attitudes, your belief that whatever drivel you spout is the gospel. Can you blame her for not falling all over herself to help New Caelum?"

"But it's not New Caelum who's asking. It's me." But even as I said the words, I realized that Cricket was right. I hadn't shown up with kind intentions, but with anger. I had tasered Cricket, for crying out loud. She had said I would regret hurting her and restraining her, but I'm not sure I ever did. I did what I had to do. And if I thought I could force Cricket to tell me where Christina was, I'd do it again.

As I watched this mysterious girl beside me settle into sleep, I wondered why she had become so involved with Dr. Caine Quinton and his quest to find a cure for Bad Sam. She and Caine had said they thought they'd developed a cure, but that they'd come up short. They were hoping that Dr. Hempel could help. But would New Caelum simply allow her to enter the city? Would they treat her kindly, or would they treat her like a diseased piranha? Could I protect her inside? Did I want to?

The answer to the last question was easy. It didn't matter that our meeting had started out somewhat rocky. I was being groomed to be one of New Caelum's next leaders, and I would not let harm come to a guest I brought into the city. Especially one that had done nothing but be gracious with her help.

As her breathing evened out, I lay down and tried to get some sleep myself. As I did, something in Cricket's words nagged at me, but I couldn't figure out what it was.

....

chapter fifteen

Cricket

I managed to sleep for four hours. More than I'd slept at one time in months. When I woke, I immediately dug for my binoculars. I peered through them, searching as much of New Caelum as I could from the estate's balcony. The part that was lit anyway. The city seemed quiet. More importantly, the incinerator was quiet.

In the bag beside me, I carried enough Bad Sam to kill off all the remaining members of our race. At least, all who weren't lucky enough to carry the gene that made them immune.

I checked West's breathing. It was slow and even; he was sleeping soundly. I moved quietly over to his bag, pulled out my PulsePoint, and slipped it into my backpack.

I was closing up his bag when I noticed my necklace; it was attached to a tether just inside the bag. As much as I wanted to take it back, I knew I couldn't—not yet anyway. He recognized that necklace, knew it was Christina's. If I wore it, or even acted possessive about it, he might put two and two together. So I reluctantly left it there, then put his bag back where I had found it.

I looked back at West. His face had changed so much. He'd filled out, and tiny hairs had now grown into a light beard. I let my fingers hover along the shadow forming along his cheeks and chin. I longed to lean down and press my lips to his, to prove that the memory I had of him was real. Even though he'd said some unkind things to me, I missed him. And he didn't know he was actually speaking to the very friend he longed to find.

Seeing that our fire was close to going out, I tossed some branches on it to keep it going for a couple more hours. That should give me enough time to find Zara, get what I needed, and get back.

I snuck off into the night. Since I suffered from chronic insomnia, my eyes had gotten pretty good at adjusting to a soft moonlight, and I'd gotten pretty good at recognizing and reacting to the sounds of night. Not much spooked me anymore.

Of course, the streets were quiet. The settlement was under lockdown. Few people inside our little town would be bold enough to go against its mandatory quarantine. In doing so, they would not only risk contracting Bad Sam; if they were caught, they might be cast out of our community forever.

When I reached the front gate, a figure appeared in front of the small door to the right, just like clockwork.

"Who's there? Stop, or I will have great pleasure in shooting you in your tracks."

"Zara, it's me, Cricket."

"What the hell, Cricket? Do you not understand what mandatory quarantine means?"

"I don't understand mandatory anything." I walked closer. "I need your help."

"Why would I help you? And you can stop right there. How do I know you don't have Bad Sam?"

"To answer your first question, you'll help me because you'll get to test your bomb-building skills. And as for your second question? Because I don't. Feel free to take my temperature. But if you're worried about it, you can always stay three feet away from me at all times."

Zara smiled, wiggling her fingers together. As I'd expected, the prospect of bombing something had overcome all other concerns, including her dislike for me.

"What are we blowing up?" she asked eagerly.

~~~~~

Zara and I wore gas masks and three layers of gloves as we placed the live Samael Strain into the box. Zara twisted and cut various different colored wires every which way. Then she added an additional container into the box.

"What's that?" I asked.

"*That* is what will blow the lid off of the box and break the containers of virus. And *this*," she said, pointing to what looked like a tiny digital clock, "is the timer. It'll be synchronized with this larger timer." Zara handed me a slightly larger digital clock. "Now—you said you wanted to set up a way to deactivate it remotely?"

"Yeah."

"Then you'd better give me your PulsePoint. I assume you still have it?"

I took a step back, stunned. "How do you—? How do you know I—?" I stammered. "How do you know about the Pulse-Point?"

Zara smiled, but didn't answer. She turned and began messing with an old computer.

"Zara, I know you and I have never been close, but—"

She raised her brows. "Don't get sentimental on me."

"I'm not. But I *am* wondering who the hell you are, and where did you come from. How do you even know what the PulsePoint is—much less know that I might have one?"

Zara grinned widely then; clearly she had been keeping a huge secret from me all these years, and just as clearly, she was quite pleased with herself for having done so. "Let's just say that although I wasn't lucky enough to have *the president of New Caelum* help me flee the city, I *did* manage to escape before they sealed up the doors to the outside."

"What? How did I not know this?"

"You never asked."

"And you've known who I was all this time?"

"You mean, did I know that you were Christina Black, survivor of Bad Sam? Yeah, I knew. Why?" she asked coyly. "Was that supposed to be a secret?" Zara was enjoying this far too much for my liking.

"Please tell me you said nothing to anyone." I'm sure my mouth hung wide open as I stared at this girl I barely knew—this girl I'd chosen not to know.

Zara shrugged. "It wasn't my story to tell."

I suddenly had a newfound respect for the girl in front of me. She could easily have used that knowledge against me.

"Now, hand me your PulsePoint." I reached into my bag and pulled out the handheld machine. "You can't turn it on, though. They'll be able to—"

"Track you, I know, I know," she interrupted, taking the PulsePoint from my hands. "Don't worry, I've got this."

I watched as she removed some kind of small device from the old computer and plugged it into a socket in the side of my PulsePoint. "And that's it. Everything is set up to synchronize as soon as the timer on the Bad Sam bomb is activated. When that timer runs out, the bomb will release Bad Sam into the air, and your PulsePoint will release a computer virus into New Caelum's system that will shut down their air filtration system."

"A virus? I thought we would just—I don't know, blow up the filtration system."

"That would be way more fun, but it's not so simple. The system is too widespread; you'd never get to it all. But this'll take the whole thing down. The bomb releases the virus into the air, the computer virus takes out the filtration system, and the whole city is flooded in minutes. You know," she said, cocking her head to the side, "you're lucky we're such good friends."

I couldn't help but laugh. We were anything but "friends," but I *was* lucky to have Zara on my side. What she'd designed was so much more sophisticated than anything I'd imagined.

"Thank you, Zara," I said sincerely. "You're... amazing."

For a moment, Zara looked genuinely touched. But she quickly got her old swagger back. "So listen," she explained, "assuming you don't *actually* want to infect a hundred thousand people with Bad Sam, you *have* to deactivate the virus before the timer runs out. The deactivation option will be in the control menu. Because the timer is attached to *your* PulsePoint, only you can stop it."

"But what about the bomb? How do I deactivate that?"

"No need, really. As long as the air filtration system is working, that'll prevent the virus from infecting anyone." She must have seen the shocked look on my face, because she added, "Or you could just tell them where the bomb is and let them toss it in the incinerator."

I raised a hand and drilled my fingers into my chest, massaging the area over my rapidly beating heart. "What if I find I need more time? Can I reset it?"

"Cricket, you came to me because you didn't want to get trapped inside New Caelum. You said this is your insurance policy to make sure you can get back out, right? So no resets—no stalling. If those people want to live, they have to let you go. Only then will you disengage the timer. This *is* what you said you wanted."

She was right. I'd asked for a 96-hour timer. Four days. From what West had told me, and from what I knew about the course of the virus, that was about how long Willow had left to live. I would do what I could to help her—I would give them Caine's research and my antibodies—and then I would get out. There was no point in staying longer.

Zara continued. "I'll plant the bomb tomorrow. Hopefully before you've even entered the city."

I shook my head. "What? No way. You're not planting this. I'll get it in there."

Zara sat back in her chair. "Oh yeah? You really think Westlin Layne is going to help you plant a weapon of mass destruction inside his own city?"

I squeezed the bridge of my nose. "No, you're right. What am I thinking? This whole idea was crazy. I can't go through with this."

"What? Yes you can. That's not what I meant. Getting leverage over them was a great idea; you just need help to pull it off. You don't want to get trapped inside that city, Cricket. Do you know what they'll do to you when they discover that you are, in fact, the sole survivor of Bad Sam?" Just in case I was living in denial, she went ahead and told me. "They will hook you up to an IV and drain you of your blood."

"I know. I know that. You're right. This is the only way I can be sure to ever come back out of New Caelum." And I would never let that bomb detonate. No matter what. I wasn't capable of such destruction.

I just needed to make the people inside believe that I was.

"So we agree that I'll plant the bomb?" Zara said.

"Fine," I agreed. "How do you know so much, anyway? And how do you know all these systems? You couldn't have been much older than me when you left, and you weren't there for very long."

"I'm a few years older than you. And my parents were on the original team who designed the PulsePoints and the computer network that runs everything inside New Caelum. I knew my way around those systems before they even existed."

"What happened to your parents? Are they still inside?"

"They're dead."

~~~~~

The plan seemed cruel, but as long as no one tried to hold me hostage against my will, they'd have nothing to worry about. And the threat of spreading the virus throughout New

Caelum was an incredibly powerful insurance policy if things went wrong.

On my way back to West, I pulled the PulsePoint from my pocket. Staring at it, I thought of the many times I'd wanted to turn the device on and see the picture of West and me from the day before I got sick—the day before everything changed. That was the day West took me to the roof above the president's wing.

The day he kissed me. We were only kids. But I felt very grown up that day. And like nothing bad would happen to me ever again as long as West was in my world. God had taken my parents, but He had given me West.

That's what people had told me... that God sometimes took the good ones to be angels in His kingdom. Of course, the problem with that was that my parents weren't dead—at least, not that anyone knew. God hadn't taken my parents to be angels to look over me; my parents had been cast out by the people of New Caelum, forever shut off from their home—and from me.

I had kept the PulsePoint with me all these years. I never thought I would have a reason to use it, but I had kept it anyway, knowing it was my link back to West. And it was my link to the city I had tried but failed to leave behind.

Now West was here, and the feelings I'd had for him way back then and the feelings I'd imagined over the last six years were real again—maybe even *more* real now that we were adults. But they couldn't be. I couldn't let the feelings I'd had as a child resurface now. We weren't children anymore. My mission was to help Willow and then get out. Give the city a way to cure the virus, so they wouldn't have a reason to exit the cocoon they'd built for themselves. And so I could exit with a cure of my own.

~~~~~

As soon as I reached the estate, I knew that something felt off. The sounds of the area were different—more awake than they should have been at that hour. I scanned the area, but saw no signs of anyone following me.

The sky was just starting to show glimmers of light on the horizon. "West," I whispered. He was probably awake and thought I had left. Not to mention he wouldn't know his way out of the estate without falling through some of the traps set by Mother Nature during six years of neglect.

I picked up my pace. Down the stone steps, through different overgrown paths, always changing the routes I took to get to my various hiding places.

When I arrived at the balcony, my heart plummeted. West was gone.

I let out a breath, staring at the blankets left beside the fire. Only embers were left now. I fell to my knees. West was used to Christina leaving him. Why should Cricket be any different?

Now what? I buried my face in my hands and massaged my forehead with my fingers, thinking. Could I enter New Caelum without West? Why not? It wasn't like I had given him any reason to protect me inside the city. I would have been on my own anyway, with or without him. So if I didn't need his help, why did his disappearance bother me so much?

Because I would miss him. I had longed for my best friend over the years, and seeing him now...

It had made me feel things I never thought I'd get the chance to feel again in this lifetime.

....

chapter sixteen

West

When I woke, Cricket was gone. I had obviously misjudged her. I had been sure she was planning to willingly help me; she wanted a cure to Bad Sam as much as I did.

I tracked her steps all the way back to the settlement gate. There I found her speaking with the same ill-tempered girl I'd seen her fight with the first day I arrived here. Just as I arrived, the two of them turned and disappeared inside the settlement. I waited, not knowing what else to do. To say I was relieved when she reappeared would have been an understatement, and when she started heading back toward the Biltmore, I breathed a lot more easily.

At one point, she stopped and pulled the PulsePoint from her back pocket; she stared at it like she might turn it on. But Christina's PulsePoint would only work for Christina, I reminded myself. There was no way it could work for Cricket. Not even the best computer geeks could hack that device.

So why did she carry it around with her? Not to mention that if she *did* turn it on, New Caelum would immediately know where she was. Or rather, they'd know where Christina's

PulsePoint was. And they would undoubtedly send someone after it, assuming that Christina was the one operating it.

I'd rather that didn't happen. Though we were headed for the city, anyway, I wanted to be in control of when we arrived and how we approached them, not ambushed by another search party.

Cricket replaced the PulsePoint inside her back pocket and took off toward the estate again. I followed, at a discreet distance, as she went all the way back to the balcony. Still hoping to gather more information about what she was up to, I hung back in the shadows and watched.

To my surprise, she fell to her knees by the cooling embers of the fire and buried her face in her hands.

Why? I thought she had deserted me, but it seemed she was upset that I was gone. Why would Cricket react that way? I had tasered her, tied her up, and questioned her unkindly about someone she was under no obligation to hand over to me. She had protected Christina, and a part of me admired her for that.

I thought about how Cricket had shown up and offered to help Key, even when Key clearly had a fever that could have been—and, we now knew, was—Bad Sam. Why would she have done that? Why would she have risked exposure, unless— did she already know she was immune? She hadn't mentioned it, though, and she *had* suited up any time she'd entered the quarantine chambers.

And what had made her suspect that I might be immune to the virus? I didn't remember her taking blood from Ryder before he came down with the fever. I was the only one she tested, so she must have had some particular reason to suspect what she'd find.

Why me?

As I stared at the back of this girl and thought about the selfless things she'd done for me and my friends in the past day, I remembered one more thing she'd said to me. She'd told me that she had what I needed to cure my sister. That was right before she stuck me with a needle and distracted me.

But now her words sank in. Ryder and I had mentioned Willow.

But we had never mentioned that Willow was my sister.

The world around me began spinning out of control. My eyes focused on the back of Cricket's head—her blond hair. It couldn't be...

I ran through a mental list of Bad Sam symptoms: high fever, excruciating headaches, joint pain, and bleeding sores...

... especially on the face and neck.

My heart was beating out of control as I stared at Cricket. I couldn't catch my breath. *"You will live to regret strapping me to that table and not letting me help Key,"* she had said. Until now, I didn't understand why she'd thought I would regret carrying out my mission and doing whatever I had to in order to protect my friends and locate Christina.

My backpack slid from my arms and hit the ground.

At the sound, Cricket started. She stood, and turned to face me. "Oh—I thought you had left." Her voice came out soft and slightly shaky.

"No... I..." I stepped to the side and looked out over the balcony toward New Caelum. The sky was becoming lighter, but the cloud cover still made it difficult to actually see the buildings. I couldn't think, and I couldn't look at her.

"Are you mad? I'm sorry. I didn't mean to worry you. I've suffered insomnia ever since..."

"Ever since what?" I asked quickly, turning to face her, because even though I couldn't look at her, I couldn't *not* look at her, either.

"Since... well... for a long time. Since I stopped sleeping inside the settlement."

"Where did you go?"

"Um... I just took a walk. I needed the air and time to think. I can't believe I'm truly going to go inside New Caelum today and breathe your stale, recirculated air."

I studied her face. Her eyes were pointed to the ground, hidden from me, and she was hiding her scarred cheek with her hair again.

She was lying to me about where she'd gone. Of course she was; why would she trust me after I—

Oh my God, I'd tasered her and tied her to a hospital bed. What kind of monster was I?

I stepped closer to her, placed a crooked finger under her chin, and lifted.

She jerked away and stepped backward. "What are you doing? Don't touch me."

I retracted my hand. "I'm sorry. I..." Though she pulled away, I saw something in her eyes: she was in there, deep within those dark blues. How had I not seen it before?

Because she was constantly hiding her eyes and her face from me. Except now...

"Your hair... it was darker."

She squinted up at me like she was trying to solve a puzzle, then her face morphed into some sort of understanding. She backed up another step. "You know."

I don't know how much time passed with us just standing there staring at each other.

"I don't know what to say," she said in the softest of voices. "Somehow, I think I'm supposed to apologize."

"What do you have to apologize for?"

She looked away while hugging her arms across her stomach. "I'm sorry we led you to believe Christina was dead, but..."

"But?"

Her hard gaze met mine again. "Christina *is* dead. The naive twelve-year-old you knew is gone forever. She died when she faced the worst fight of her life."

"How did you..." I could barely speak it. I had tried to imagine what it had been like for her, but I couldn't. "How did you survive?"

"Caine. I wouldn't have survived without him."

"Where did you go? Have you been here just outside New Caelum all this time?"

"I bounced around some. But yes. Mostly here."

I took a step toward her and raised a hand—then I dropped it to my side again. I so badly wanted to touch her. The vision of her lying motionless in my arms after I'd tasered her flashed in my head. I closed my eyes. "You were nothing but nice to us, and I hurt you." When I looked at her again, she only stared back at me. "Will you ever forgive me?"

"I will help your sister. You don't need my forgiveness." Her voice was emotionless, cold. Had I hurt her beyond repair? "I will make sure New Caelum is virus-free. That's what they must want. And you will make sure I leave New Caelum with the same cure for my friends."

"I will help you." Although I wasn't sure how. I had no idea how I would be received when we returned to New Caelum. After all, I was supposed to be under a mandatory quarantine. Is that why they had cut off my PulsePoint? Would they even let me back inside the city? They might lock me up when I returned, even if I *was* being groomed to govern New Caelum.

I looked back at the girl standing before me. The Christina I had known had been full of light. But the Cricket I was learning to know now was shadowed by darkness. What kind of life had she witnessed during the last six years?

She was wrong about one thing, though. I did need her forgiveness.

chapter seventeen

Cricket

I had to focus. It didn't matter that West knew who I was. He didn't *know* me. We had been kids the last time we were together. He didn't know how the illness had changed me. He had no clue what I'd gone through. Sure, he could see the scars on the outside of my skin, but he had no idea about the extent of the scarring I'd suffered on the inside.

The air was still, cool, and crisp as we left the shelter of the estate that morning. We had a purpose, but it was a purpose that had little to do with getting to know each other again. Darkness hung around West and me and it had nothing to do with the clouds blocking the sun.

We followed the paths leading into the mountains—paths I'd hiked many times before with Dax, Dylan, and Nina. Some were well worn, while others—ones we hadn't frequented— were thick with overgrown brush. I wondered where Dax was now. I knew he could take care of himself. But this outside world made us all vulnerable, each in different ways, and I hated that I had hurt him.

A nervous sweat broke out across the back of my neck from a combination of our fast pace and my anxious thoughts. I removed my outer layer—a black wool winter pea coat I'd found in an old department store a year ago after one of my final growth spurts. Dax had been with me the day we'd gone on a spree to find some new clothes for the people of our small community. And now he had run, which is what he and I seemed to do best—run from trouble, run from discomfort, run from each other when times were tough.

"You're quiet. Are we going to talk at all?" West glanced over his shoulder at me. His brown hair flipped up at his ears—he was in need of a haircut—and I mentally squashed my initial urge to play with it. He'd grown into a good-looking man, and I found myself wanting to know more about him. I didn't know him any more than he knew me.

Though I knew that he was desperate enough to save his sister that he'd taser a girl he'd just met.

What was I supposed to say to him? Nothing sounded good inside my head, so I stuck with the basics. "What's it like inside New Caelum?"

"It's okay," he said. "It's sleek and clean, and at times, it's like growing up in a hospital. The people inside feel safe. But I think we like that clinical feel, because it assures us that Bad Sam is kept out." He laughed a little, but I suspected it wasn't because of something funny. "All citizens are required to re-port their temperature twice a day through their PulsePoints. There's very little sickness. But by taking temperatures, the medics are able to catch many illnesses before they spread."

"Sounds cold and controlling." And exactly why I was thankful I had escaped that world the second the opportunity had presented itself.

"It can be, but it's been all right. I've been happy enough. I'm with Mother and Willow." He cast me a sideways glance. "I'm sorry. I shouldn't have said that. I wasn't thinking."

"It's okay. You were lucky to grow up with family. Tell me more."

"Well, everyone has their own responsibilities inside the city," he continued. "Once children reach seventeen or eighteen, they're steered toward what their permanent job will be within the city."

"What are your responsibilities?"

He turned and walked backward, facing me. "I'm the president's son. I'm responsible for behaving the way my mother expects me to, and walking a straight line." The beginnings of a smile touched the corners of his lips, but faded.

I cocked my head. I could see in his eyes he wasn't telling me something. "And do you? Behave the way your mom expects you to?"

This time, he gave a full-on grin. And it was exactly the smile I remembered. Six years hadn't taken away the dimple on one side of his face, nor had he lost the mischievous glint in his eye that he got when he wanted to cause trouble. "Let's just say I learned how not to get caught."

I wanted to return his smile, to laugh like this was some sort of game. "And what happens this time? When you get caught? What happens to you when you walk back into New Caelum?" Could he really just walk back into a city that monitored every move and change of temperature in its citizens?

His cheeks fell. "You're right. Things are different. And I'm not even sure *how* they're different, since I've had no communication with anyone on the inside."

"You still haven't told me how many of your citizens have Bad Sam. The truth this time."

"What do you mean? Only one. Willow."

This time I stopped. "You're not serious."

"Dead serious. After Willow came down with the virus, our family was quarantined, and Mom figured out a way to get me out of New Caelum so that I could find Chris—I mean, you."

"And Key and Ryder?"

"Based on the timing, I'm guessing Key caught the virus from Willow before she was quarantined, and Ryder must have gotten it from her."

I could almost buy his argument. Almost. But I suspected he was dead wrong. "Let's pretend for a minute that you're right. How do you think Willow came down with the virus?"

We approached a fallen tree, and West gestured toward it. "Let's take a break."

We didn't have time to take much of a break; but I needed more information if I was going to successfully get in and out of this facility. So I climbed up on the trunk. With one leg bent in front of me, I faced West, who straddled the log.

"I have no idea how Willow contracted it," he said simply. With a stick, he dug at the bark in front of him.

"None?"

He cast the stick aside and stared into the woods over my shoulder. He wasn't telling me something. "Mom was terrified when she suggested I leave and find you. She knew it was a risk to send me out with the scouts leaving the city."

"I bet she was," I whispered.

"What do you mean by that?" When I stared blankly at West, he breathed an exasperated sigh. "You know... you act like we *asked* for Bad Sam to infect our lives again."

"Your words, not mine." My voice took on an edge I couldn't hide.

West raised an eyebrow. "Yet here you sit with your judgment already formed. It's all over your face. So, tell me: why do *you* think my mom was terrified?"

"Besides the fact that your sister has been given a death sentence? Because she knows that a virus now threatens the empire she helped build." I played with the shoestrings on my boot as I gave West a minute to think. He'd been so hell-bent on finding me, and terrified at the prospect of leaving the inner sanctum of New Caelum, that I didn't think he'd ever really taken the time to process what was truly going on here. "Willow is not the first person inside New Caelum to contract the virus," I finished.

West sat up a little straighter. He rubbed his hand back and forth across the stubble on his face. "And what makes you say that, you who knows nothing about New Caelum?"

I remained perfectly still, reminding myself that I didn't have to convince this boy—who might as well have been a stranger to me—that New Caelum was an evil place to live and that I knew plenty. As a matter of fact, I should have been doing the opposite. What I wanted was for the people of New Caelum to continue to believe that their way of life was the right choice for them, now and always, so they would stay right where they were. The outside world didn't need a hundred thousand or so people flooding out into our tiny communities. We didn't need New Caelum taking over our lives. Especially if we were facing another virus epidemic.

"You're right," I said. "I know nothing about New Caelum or the people in it." I slid off the fallen tree and pulled my coat back on. Sitting for even a few minutes had reminded me that winter was approaching. "We're still about two hours away from the outer walls of New Caelum; we should probably get a move on."

West didn't move to join me. And when he finally looked up, his lips tugged down. "What makes you think this virus outbreak didn't start with my sister?" He stood and stuffed his hands in his pockets. I didn't answer, so he urged further, "I need to know what makes you think that."

"Your city is covering up instances of Bad Sam."

"Not possible," West said, but his face didn't reflect confidence.

I paused, thinking about how to explain. I decided I needed to back up a bit.

"About a year ago, I noticed a change in Boone Blackston. A change in attitude. The people were finally starting to build a life that didn't include things like... like taking their loved ones' temperatures every day. Or staring accusingly at anyone who looked flushed. The paranoia was finally starting to drop away."

"If there's so much distrust in your community, why do people live there? Why don't they continue to live in rural areas, where they know they're safe from the virus?"

"Some people do. They live off the land and stay away from the established communities except when they need something they can't get on their own. But for the most part, I've found that people need community. They crave it."

"But, wasn't there a lot of crime early on? Didn't people break into the malls and stores and forage any and all supplies? We were taught that life out here was horribly difficult."

I couldn't really do anything but stare at West. Here he was, describing my world to me, a world he'd seen nothing of while living in his castle of comfort.

"What?" he said.

"I'm shocked at your people's ignorance," I replied in the kindest way possible. "There weren't enough people left in the country for there to be any kind of crime wave. I'm not saying that only good people survived the virus, but there were more than enough resources to go around for those of us who did. We didn't need to fight or kill for supplies. And those who wanted to be left alone were left alone; they collected necessities and returned to their homes."

West considered this. "How many active towns do you think exist across the country?"

"Not sure. I've ventured out a bit. Farther, once I taught myself how to drive, but there's not much gas left—the initial panic saw to that. There were small pockets of people here and there, as far as I went."

"I guess things are a bit different out here than we were taught."

We walked in silence, for a while before West spoke again.

"You were going to tell me why you think there's more of an outbreak inside New Caelum."

"Right. Like I was saying, about a year ago, people became more relaxed, less suspicious. And as they grew more comfortable, I kind of became the opposite. It occurred to me that if *we* were settling into a certain comfort level, then so were the people of New Caelum."

"And that made you uncomfortable?"

"Very."

"What does this have to do with Bad Sam?"

"Well... I've always liked camping up in the mountains. I like hearing the hum of electricity running outside your city. So I go up there kind of regularly, sleep under the stars, listen to the hum. And one night, when I was camping alone, I heard a sound in the very early morning hours that I had never before heard at night. Your incinerators."

"So? We use the incinerators all the time. That's how we get rid of trash."

"Not all the time. You never used them at night until recently—two to three times a month for the past six months. And I've watched them, West—the men working the incinerators. During the day, the incinerator workers are wearing normal outer clothing. But on those rare occasions when the incinerators ran at night... they're wearing hazmat suits. The very night you and your friends left New Caelum was one of those nights. And there were a *lot* of hazmat suits that night—more than I'd ever seen before."

"I agree all this is a bit curious, but it doesn't exactly prove anything."

"Maybe not. But can you explain how a city that built itself on the principles of complete sterilization—a city that views itself as some sort of Noah's Ark meant to save the human race from extinction—suddenly has an outbreak of Bad Sam? And the first patient just happens to be the president's daughter?"

chapter eighteen

West

I couldn't even stomach the thought that Cricket might be right. Mother had said the same thing, and I hadn't believed her. She, too, thought Willow was purposely infected with Bad Sam as a way to get to her, to keep her from being reelected as president by the council.

But Cricket and Mother disagreed on the larger implication. Mother thought Willow was targeted alone, that no one else inside the city was infected with Bad Sam. Cricket clearly believed the outbreak was more widespread.

What would it mean if Willow wasn't the only person to be infected inside New Caelum?

We hiked the rest of the way to an area high in the mountains, where we could actually look down into the city. I turned in a circle and watched as Cricket pulled a couple of large duffels down from the trees.

"What is this place?" I asked.

"A safe spot, where I can watch New Caelum—and escape Boone Blackston when I need to." So this was the spot where she liked to sleep and listen to the hum of the incinerators.

Cricket began pulling stuff from one of the bags. "These are supplies I've collected over the years. Clothing, extra socks, various survival items, knives, cooking and eating utensils... weapons."

"Wow, you've turned into quite the Girl Scout. Funny, I always remembered you as somewhat of a princess type."

She didn't even crack a smile. "Lucky for you, I've changed." She stopped sorting and stood. The determined glint in her eye was a new look on her, and it was unbelievably attractive. She walked over to me and held out her hand. In it was a knife and sheath. "Just in case." She stared down at the weapon instead of making eye contact with me. "I don't know what we're going to face, but you might want this if they don't welcome you back. It might give you half a chance of escaping."

I'd never had any need for a weapon before I'd left New Caelum. The guards had carried Tasers, but I'd never felt the need. However, Mom had given me one before I left, also for "just in case."

I reached out, and as I grabbed the weapon, I let my fingers graze hers. Her eyes shot up to mine. Without dropping my gaze, I secured the knife and sheath to my belt. I let my eyes wander from her eyes to her lips. They were dry and chapped from the cold air.

"We really need to get inside tonight." She stepped away, dropping her gaze. I'd obviously made her uncomfortable. "Our friends and your sister don't have much time. Willow's been sick for—what? Four or five days now?"

"Yes." Under any other circumstances, I'd force Cricket to spend another night with me back at the estate, out of the elements, and convince her to open up to me. I'd have given anything to break through the barriers she'd so masterfully erected around her and get to know her. If I could have, I'd have tried to convince her to return to New Caelum with me and live a more comfortable life. But the circumstances were what they were, and my sister was dying. I didn't have time for any of that. "You're right. If we're going to give Dr. Hempel time to look at what Caine has done and come up with another solution, we need to get inside New Caelum soon."

Cricket pulled a bundle of heavy rope from the duffel. She held it in front of her face for a few seconds, then stuffed it in her bag. She picked up her pack, carefully slid her arms through the straps, and began heading back down the mountain. "Let's go," she called over her shoulder.

As I followed her, I couldn't help but wonder about the possibility of an outbreak in New Caelum, and what it would mean for Christina when we got there. If she was, in fact, the only person to have ever survived the disease that had killed so many—the only person to carry antibodies that could possibly cure others—they might well lock her up and never let her out.

With a sudden urge to protect her, I caught up to her and grabbed her arm. "Wait." She stopped and looked at me. "When we get to New Caelum, you can't tell anyone who you are."

"I'm not sure it'll be possible to hide it, but I'll try to keep it a secret." She pulled her arm from my grasp and began walking again. "Don't worry about me. You need to worry more about getting us inside. A city that hasn't let new people inside for more than six years is not going to just let you waltz back in now that you've been in the contaminated world. And me getting in... that's going to be even harder."

"I've got to figure out a way to call my mother. New Caelum isn't heavily guarded around the outer walls, because it hasn't needed to be in recent years, but getting inside the actual buildings could still prove tricky."

"We'll try your PulsePoint when we get closer to the city. If that doesn't work, we'll use mine. Something tells me mine will do the job."

"What? No. We turn on your PulsePoint, they'll know who you are."

"You have any better ideas?"

"As a matter of fact, I do."

~~~~~

By the time we reached the city, it was late in the after-noon. It would be dark in an hour, and the temperature was already dropping. A wind was coming in from the north and making the air almost unbearably cold.

We gave up on calling my mother on my PulsePoint after several more failed attempts. However, I did notice that the PulsePoint was ringing differently now. It seemed to at least be connecting, whereas before I had gotten nothing but silence on the other end.

I led Cricket around to the backside of the fenced area. Thanks to the earlier-than-usual below-freezing temperatures, much of the brush had died back, making it easier to fight through the thick foliage.

"How often have you watched New Caelum?" I asked.

Cricket shrugged. "Mostly at night during the warmer months, but only for short periods. My friends pretty much accused me of going crazy, especially lately when I'd panic any time I heard the incinerator, so I had to pull back a bit, or at least pretend to. I'd sneak away if I ever wanted to truly spy."

"How often have you seen people leave New Caelum?"

She stopped for a second and looked at me then. "Never. Not until you and the other three trucks left."

"Mom said there were people inside who were starting to suggest that it was time to leave the inner sanctum of New Caelum and venture into the outside world."

"I assumed they would eventually. I'm guessing you're wondering, why now?"

I nodded. "And I'm wondering who would dare go against my mother in that way. I don't know, but I plan to find out. It will definitely cause a divide among the people."

We hung back, hidden behind some dense trees. We couldn't see over the walls of the compound, but I knew the incinerator was located just beyond the gate.

Cricket pulled two ropes from her bag. She tied a grappling hook to the end of one of them, then tossed it over the wall, pulling until the grappling hook took hold. Then she took the second rope, tied it to the trunk of a tree, and tossed the rest of it over.

She glanced at me. "Here goes nothing." She stuck a foot up on the wall, preparing to climb.

Before she could start, I grabbed her gently by the waist. "Wait! Let me go first."

She cocked her head and puffed some strands of hair out of her face. "Fine. But hurry. I'll be right behind you."

I grabbed on to the rope, and with all the strength I could find, pulled myself up and to the other side, doubting the whole time whether Cricket had the strength to do the same. I was quickly silenced when she showed up right behind me. She easily hiked her leg over the top of the wall, then lowered herself down the second rope. I smiled. She was definitely everything I would have hoped my Christina would have turned out to be.

When she got closer, I reached up and gripped her hips with both hands. "I've got you." She slid the rest of the way down, against my chest, until her feet were firmly on the ground.

"Now what?" Cricket asked.

"Now, we wait."

······································

chapter nineteen

Cricket

We didn't have to wait long. The large rolling doors began to lift, and out came a forklift carrying a dumpster piled high with large garbage bags. I'd witnessed this purging of the trash often over the last few years.

"Stay here." West looked like he was about to venture from behind the dumpster and approach the forklift—when suddenly the large gate to the outside world began to open. West froze in place.

The forklift stopped, too, and its driver turned toward the gate. He gawked like he was watching a ghost descend from heaven. Then he quickly threw the forklift in reverse, trying to get back to the safety of the New Caelum building.

Before he got far, a truck raced through the open gate and into the compound. I glanced up at West, who was staring at the truck's driver-side door.

"Who is it?" I asked.

"I don't know." His head twitched, and his line of sight shifted to the right.

I followed his gaze—and gasped when I saw two people slink down from the back of the truck and sneak away to the right, running low to the ground and away from the forklift.

"Oh no," I whispered. "It's Zara and Dax." Zara had assured me she'd find a way inside the outer walls. I'd never doubt her again. And Dax was back. "He didn't leave," I whispered to myself.

I was about to run after them, but West stopped me with a hand to my wrist. "What are you doing?"

"They'll get caught. I have to help them."

"They chose to come inside these walls. They obviously knew what they were doing and the risk they were taking."

I doubted that. But he was right. Drawing attention wouldn't help.

The driver side door of the truck finally opened, and out slid one of the two guys who had pushed West around at the hospital. The forklift driver approached Mr. Eyeglasses with a Taser held out. Eyeglasses raised his hands to show he was unarmed. "Hey man, it's me, Garrett Jenkins. I was sent out from New Caelum on orders from the president and the council."

I looked up at West. "Could that be true? Did your mom send the trucks out on some sort of mission?"

"No, not her. The council, maybe, but not my mother. Mother vowed to always protect the people inside this city, and she swore that we were only safe by staying on the inside. She knew about the scouts, but she never approved the mission."

"What's wrong with you?" the forklift driver asked.

I looked closer. Garrett swayed on his feet. "He's barely standing," I whispered to West. Behind Garrett, I could see his friend in the fleece coat still sitting in the truck. "Oh no," I whispered.

"What?" West asked. He stared ahead, trying to see what I was seeing.

"They're sick. Garrett looks like he might pass out, and the other one is bleeding from his eye."

To the right and behind the truck, I saw Zara and Dax running low to the ground again, ducking behind some sort of machine. They appeared to be out of the line of sight of the city men.

The forklift driver shifted back and forth on his feet. "You guys need to get back in the truck and go back the way you came."

"What?" Garrett asked. "No. We need help. We're sick, man. You need to get the president. Or better yet, we need to get inside to the hospital."

"I can't let you do that." The forklift driver stepped in Garrett's path. Garrett's friend in the fleece jacket still sat behind the wheel of the vehicle. His head dangled forward.

"You don't get to decide." Garrett made a move forward, but the forklift driver was fast. He took off in a full sprint. Garret limped after him, but was way too slow.

The forklift driver ran inside the garage door, staring out at Garrett and Fleece Jacket.

"No. Don't—" West started.

His words were cut off when the forklift driver hit a large red button with the palm of his hand. A loud honking sound erupted, and large spotlights drenched the entire backside of New Caelum in light. West and I moved farther back into the shadows of the dumpster.

I began mumbling to myself, "Run, Dax. Run, Zara." This wasn't good. They had to get out of there.

As if they heard me, Dax and Zara darted from behind a section of the building and began a full-on sprint toward the back gate. I began chanting "Go, go, go" inside my head.

Then the second rolling door began to open. When it was halfway up, a dozen or so men in hazmat suits appeared, armed with rifles. Garrett's hands shot up. Fleece Jacket's head fell against the steering wheel, apparently passed out.

Without warning, one of the men in hazmat suits shot Garrett three times.

I jerked at the sound of each shot, grabbing West's arm for support.

Garrett fell forward onto his knees, then face-planted into the dirt.

The shooter calmly walked over to the truck, still idling behind the forklift, raised the rifle, and shot Fleece Jacket in the head.

I closed my eyes, but then heard the muffled sounds of people yelling through the hazmat masks. I looked up to see Dax and Zara sprinting through the gate to the outside, four men racing after them. Dax and Zara disappeared out of view—and then the men stopped and opened fire.

I opened my mouth to scream, but West circled my waist with his arms and pulled me back into the darkness. "Shhh. Don't make a sound," he ordered close to my ear.

My heart was racing. "Did they make it?" I asked in a panicked breath. My eyes were closed tight. I couldn't look.

"I don't know. I think so." West turned me around and shook me. "Open your eyes. Look at me." After I did, he said,

"We have to go. We have to climb back over the wall. These guys are not asking questions. We won't even get the chance to tell them what we have in our bags before they shoot us."

He was right. We needed to escape. We needed to come up with another plan.

We ran the short distance back to the wall, and West helped me get started up the rope. When we were both on the other side, I stomped off in the direction of the gate.

"Where are you going?" West grabbed my shoulder, forcing me to turn.

"I've got to know that they're okay."

He placed his hands on my shoulders and pinned me with a hard stare. "You can't help them right now. You'll only get yourself shot or captured, most likely killed."

I breathed hard, my eyes glued to his. I wanted to kick him in the shin. Instead, my body relaxed just slightly, and I leaned my forehead into his chest. "They were here to help us." Or at least me, anyway.

West's arms came up and circled around me, holding me tight. "We can't stay here, Cricket. They'll send out drones to scan the outer walls."

I nodded, then I let West lead me directly up the mountain, forging a path away from New Caelum and back toward my campsite.

~~~~~

It took us twice as long to get back to my camping spot high above New Caelum as it had to get down. We took as many extra precautions as we could to cover our tracks and throw anyone off who might decide to come looking. That's if they found evidence that we had penetrated the outer walls of the city in the first place.

By the time we arrived at the campsite, the weather had turned, and the wind was whipping through the trees. The temperature had plummeted. Neither West nor I uttered a word about the frigid air. This was the kind of cold that could kill someone unprepared. Which I was not.

I pulled the duffel bags from the trees, threw them in the center of a small clearing, and began digging out the necessities. West caught on pretty quickly and started looking through the bags as well.

Over the past couple of years, I had smuggled lots of supplies to this spot: a small tent, a sleeping bag, a battery-powered lantern, flashlights, extra batteries, nonperishable foods, tarps, ropes.

"We have to block the wind," I said, handing West the tarp. "We'll secure this in the trees to the northwest."

"What about a fire? Do you think they'll see it if we build one?" Worry rattled though West's voice.

"Even if they didn't, they'd definitely smell it if they wandered anywhere nearby. And they're probably on high alert with the activity inside their walls tonight."

I watched as West began tying a corner of the tarp to a tree. His hands shook. He didn't even have gloves. It dawned on me that he hadn't been in these elements in more than six years. His body was in no way acclimated for the weather we might experience tonight.

After securing my two corners of the tarp, I began sifting through the extra clothing I had stashed away. I had never been picky about sizes, especially when it came to coats and gloves. Finally, I found a pair of thick, hot pink ski gloves. "Here," I said. He turned to me, and I tossed the gloves to him.

"Thanks." He struggled to tug them over his shaking, already ice-cold fingers. "Nice color." He smiled.

The tarp was secure, and it did a decent job of blocking the wind. I unrolled the tent, and after sliding the poles through the sleeves with West's help, I staked the corners into the ground.

"That's an awfully small tent," West said, his implication obvious.

My face must have turned several shades darker as I stuffed the only sleeping bag into the tiny tent. When I was done, I faced West. "You won't survive without the shelter of the tent and the warmth of the sleeping bag. Your body's not used to these low temperatures."

"You're not suggesting that I sleep inside the tent with the sleeping bag and leave you out here in the cold? I've not once thought you'd grown into an idiot over the years—until now, if that *is* what you are suggesting."

I glanced into the woods away from the campsite, then back at him. "I don't sleep much. I'm going to hike back over to the lookout and watch New Caelum for a while. I'll slide into the tent when I get tired or cold." *After West falls asleep,* I added in my mind.

"So, you *are* stupid."

I jerked my head and narrowed my eyes at him. "Look, asshole. There's no need for you to tear me down. You and your friends are the ones who entered the outside world unprepared." Something inside of me had definitely snapped. "On top of that, you brought Bad Sam with you. We were virus free!" I raised my hands in frustration. "You know what? Never mind. I don't want to fight with you." I pulled some hand warmers from a duffel, then ripped them from the outer plastic wrapping. "Here, take these. You shake them and squeeze them, and they heat up. They'll do wonders for your fingers. You can even put them down in your shoes after they're warm."

Then I turned and stormed off.

I approached the spot in the trees where I liked to sit on top of an old tree stump and stared down into the city. The spotlights were still on, keeping the area between the buildings and the outer walls on display. Yet New Caelum was quiet. Hopefully, they'd decide that the threat was over and they could relax, let their guard down soon.

I thought of Zara and Dax, and a heavy pressure clamped down on my heart. Hugging my legs up to my chest, I rested my forehead against my knees and prayed they were okay.

"Christina," West said softly behind me.

The muscles along my spine tightened at the sound of the name I had laid to rest years ago. "Please go away." I tried, without success, to keep emotion out of my voice. Being near him again was starting to affect me in ways I didn't understand.

He walked around the tree stump and knelt down in front of me. "I'm sorry."

I raised my head. "For what? For calling me stupid? For bringing the virus back into a world of people that was finally feeling safe? What, exactly, are you sorry for?"

A hint of a smile touched the corners of his lips. "You're not stupid. I'm sorry I called you that. That was just my insecurities talking."

I set my feet back down on the ground, and West rested a gloved hand on my thigh, taking my gaze from the curve of his lips to where his hand touched me. Though the heat of his skin was far from reaching me through the layers of clothing, my leg tensed, and I let my eyes roam upward to his intense stare. A small fire erupted in the pit of my stomach. "Well, don't bother being sorry about the virus, because I know you had no way of knowing what New Caelum was up to."

"No, I didn't. You have to believe that I only left the city with the hope of finding a way to save my sister. I never would have knowingly exposed others to Bad Sam. But now that this nightmare is back, I'm begging you to help me get back inside New Caelum. We need to figure out a way to put a stop to this disease."

As I sat on the stump, West's hands rested on either side of my thighs. He pinned me there with scared, vulnerable eyes. He had spoken like a true leader of New Caelum.

And he was right. This was exactly why I had stayed close to New Caelum all these years, wasn't it? I had always known that Bad Sam still existed in the world. Caine had taught me that this was what doctors and scientists did: they kept things like Bad Sam and smallpox alive. For souvenirs, in the name of science and medical advancement—to study vaccines and how to treat the illnesses. The public ignorantly assumed that doctors and scientists had protocols in place to keep the public safe from future outbreaks of the same diseases.

And Caine had also taught me that, without my antibodies, innocent people would die in the next outbreak. That, because I was the only human to have survived the deadly virus, my blood was crucial to a possible cure. So I stayed.

But that wasn't the only reason I stayed near New Caelum. I also stayed because of West. I knew he—my Westlin—was somewhere inside the city that I studied night after night, day after day. I had been only a child when I knew him, but Westlin was my first love, the boy—and, eventually, the man—I dreamt about.

Now, as I stared into his pleading eyes, I knew I would help him. Even if all of the people inside New Caelum didn't deserve it, I would do what I could. Because that was the legacy my parents had instilled in me.

"I will help you," I said with a shaky breath.

He didn't smile when he heard my answer. He didn't even look happy about the decision. He only nodded, knowing neither of us had a choice about what came next.

....

West

Finally, after Cricket's teeth began to chatter, I convinced her that we needed sleep if we were going to figure out a way inside New Caelum the next day. And to get sleep, we needed warmth.

I crawled into the tent. Cricket followed. We both removed our cold boots, stuffed in some foot warmers, then set them aside. There was very little room to move around, but we had just enough room to sit up. Cricket had brought a large Mag-Lite flashlight, good not only for illumination, but for knocking someone over the head if we needed to.

She was shaking, as was I, but unlike me, she barely had any fat or muscle on her body for warmth. I rubbed my hands up and down on her arms, trying to generate some heat. When neither of our sets of teeth would stop clicking together, I realized I was going to have to take drastic measures.

I unzipped the sleeping bag and slipped inside. "Cricket, look at me."

She turned in the tight space. Her eyes followed the length of my body, noticing that I was now inside the unzipped bag.

"There's only one way we're going to survive this night without going into hypothermia."

She took in a cold, shaky breath. Her shoulders slumped forward. "You're right. This is ridiculous. We're old friends, right? We're going to need each other if we want to survive this."

I was pretty sure she was talking about surviving more than just this night, but for now, we both knew what we needed to do.

Cricket wiggled out of her jacket and tucked it behind her. I followed her lead, discarding my coat. Next, she pulled her sweater over her head, leaving herself dressed in nothing but a black tank top and her cargo pants. I reached for the flashlight, and was about to turn it off when I noticed the scarring that extended down her neck, disappearing beneath her top, then reappearing on her arm. Pulling my glove off, I reached my fingers out and traced the markings on her cheek. Thanks to the hand warmers, my fingers weren't ice cold as they ran along her pocked skin. "This was from the disease?"

She glanced down, and I wanted to hit myself. She certainly didn't need me reminding her of what the virus had left behind. She raised her eyes back to mine. "Don't feel sorry for me." She grabbed my hand and rubbed it between hers. "I survived. Now, come on. We need to zip up into the bag before we freeze."

We stripped down until she wore nothing but socks, a tank top, and underwear, and I wore socks, a T-shirt, and boxers. We had no choice but to hug close. I tucked her into my arms, her back to my chest, and zipped us in tight. We both continued to shake and shift uncomfortably.

Though at first I thought we were too late, and there was no way we were going to generate enough heat to survive the night, after ten minutes or so, I noticed a gradual increase in temperature. Slowly, sensation returned to my fingers as Cricket held my hands in hers. Her back started to warm against my chest.

Despite how much I wanted to hold this vulnerable girl in my arms, I also wanted her to *want* to be in my arms—to forgive me for how I'd treated her when she'd found Key with Bad Sam. Maybe that would come with time. Maybe after we found a way into New Caelum and did what we needed to do there, we'd also find a way to stay in each other's lives, get to know each other again. Maybe she would stay with me inside the city and find happiness beside me.

"West?" Cricket's voice, still a bit shaky, was soft in the silence of night.

"Yeah?"

"What's it really like inside New Caelum?" Where she had been rubbing my hands, she now absentmindedly played with my fingers, intertwining hers into mine. "I mean, you described what it looked like, but what kind of life have you had?"

"I'm luckier than some. I've been privileged as the president's son. I've continued to go to school, though it did change somewhat this past year. Now that Ryder, Key, and I are over eighteen, we're expected to work. Key works in the labs. Ryder is being groomed to work in leadership, near me actually. I work in my mom's office." I didn't bother to tell her that I was being groomed to take over running New Caelum eventually, and Ryder was being trained to be my right-hand man.

"Are you happy?"

"It wasn't easy to settle into a life on the inside, but it's what I know. It was difficult at first to accept never getting to run through the forest or feel the rain on my face. It was like how I imagine living in outer space might be. But yeah, I guess I've been content." Talking about life inside New Caelum took my mind off of the cold. Cricket was shaking less, but I didn't dare loosen my hold on her. I leaned my head into her hair. It smelled fruity, heavenly.

"Do you ever go out on the roof?"

I stiffened a little. My fingers stilled in hers. "Only once after you were gone. It just wasn't the same." Cricket grew silent, but I wasn't ready to let her stop talking. This might be the last opportunity we had alone for a while. "So, you remember being on the roof?"

"I remember," she said, her voice low, almost a whisper.

"Mother thought you would become like a sister to Willow and me, but I already knew we'd be so much more than that."

Cricket sniffed. She let go of my hand, and though I couldn't see what she was doing, I was afraid she was wiping at her eyes.

"Hey," I said, reaching for the flashlight. I flipped it on, but pointed it away from us so that the light wasn't in our faces. "Turn to me."

Though she hesitated at first, she eventually turned in the tight space to face me, but kept her chin tucked so that I couldn't see her face. One of my arms was stretched out under her. With my other hand, I touched her chin and forced her to look at me. Moisture pooled in her eyes and spilled over. "Why are you crying?"

I could guess, but I wanted to hear her say it. I swiped my thumb across her cheek, clearing some of the tears away. Her cheek was silky smooth, cool to the touch. My fingers tingled as the cold air hit my tear-drenched skin.

She swallowed hard. "I didn't want to leave you. You were my best friend."

"Why did you?"

"I was sick and dying. I didn't want you to see me die." She sucked in an uneven breath. "And I was so pissed off at your mother for what she did to my parents." For the first time, Cricket raised her hand and touched my face, tracing an imaginary line from my forehead down to my chin. "But I loved you."

I closed my eyes, squeezing them tightly at the sound of her words. I'd loved this beautiful girl since I was a young boy, and now she was a woman and here in my arms. Even if it was only for one night, it was a gift. I was about to lean in and kiss her, when she continued speaking.

"I promised God that I would let you go, and I would leave the city, if He would save you from Bad Sam."

"You didn't have to leave, though. Turns out I'm immune." I offered her a smile, attempting to lighten the mood a little.

"Maybe you're immune because of my promise."

I didn't believe that, but it was silly to question it now. I touched her hair and moved it off of her forehead. "You look so different from what I remember, but your eyes... now that I'm truly seeing them... they're the same. You are beautiful." I tapped her nose playfully.

She immediately looked down.

"Don't look away."

After a few seconds passed, she raised her eyes again, peering through a veil of dark eyelashes. "You look almost exactly like I pictured you would. Well, except for a few extra whiskers," she laughed. "I've dreamt of seeing you again." A playful grin spread across her face, reaching all the way to her eyes. "Maybe not quite like this, but..."

"But you'll take it?" I laughed. I slid my hand behind her neck, letting my eyes drift toward her lips.

Her smile faded. "West—"

I leaned in and cut off her protest with a gentle kiss. She didn't resist. Her lips were soft and cool to the touch. I knew I should pull back, but I simply couldn't. As I deepened the kiss, her lips warmed. She snaked her arm around my back, and I did the same, pressing her body closer to mine. Her feet hooked around my calves, our legs intertwining and getting tangled.

When we broke the kiss, I refused to let her turn away. We lay in silence for a while after. Many unsaid thoughts lingered between us—thoughts that threatened to change everything all over again.

The sounds of leaves rustling in the wind and tree limbs clacking together were the only things we heard for a while. Then, eventually, Cricket's eyes closed, her breathing slowed, and her body relaxed. Tension seemed to fall away as she fell into a deep sleep in my arms.

I was terrified to fall asleep—terrified I would wake back up, and this dream would be over.

···

chapter twenty-one

Cricket

The familiar sound of the incinerator woke me sometime in the middle of the night. I was completely disoriented. The warmth of West's arms around me comforted me at first, but then I remembered why I was facing him, and the feel of his lips on mine. The claustrophobic effects of being confined in a tight space soon crept in, and the sound of the incinerator, though far away, thundered inside my head.

I slowly eased out of West's arms, hoping not to wake him. He was finally warm, and I was certain he hadn't slept much since he'd left New Caelum.

I quickly dressed and, after stuffing new warmers inside my boots, slipped out of the tent and hiked over to the lookout to stare down into New Caelum. The activity at the incinerator was no mystery to me tonight, though. I knew exactly what the people in hazmat suits needed to rid New Caelum of—the diseased bodies of Garrett and his fleece-jacketed partner.

I lowered my gaze to the ground. I didn't even know Fleece Jacket's name. Would the people inside even tell the two boys' families what had happened? Or were they simply human sacrifices to whatever New Caelum was trying to do?

I glanced over my shoulder in the direction of our little campsite, making sure West hadn't awoken. The wind had died down finally, but it had brought much colder temperatures than we'd had in recent weeks.

As I watched the activity around New Caelum, I thought about each time they had run the incinerator in the middle of the night. The first time was three months ago, and I'd heard it three times in one week. Two weeks later, I'd heard it three more times. After that, I was so paranoid that I camped closer to New Caelum each night, sometimes allowing Dax, Dylan, and Nina to come with me. Dylan and Nina thought I just needed time in the great outdoors, but Dax knew I was building conspiracy theories surrounding anything the city did. He just didn't know why.

And he knew me well enough not to press, or I would have shut him out.

Once I moved closer to the city, the incinerator stopped for a while. In fact, it didn't run again for three weeks. Then it began to run on exactly one night every other week, almost always on a Thursday or Friday.

Though the frequency with which the incinerator was run had changed, it followed another predictable pattern. It soon became my favorite obsession to predict the incinerator's activity? What night would it run? What time of night? For how long did it run each time?

Even now, as I parsed through the statistics I'd gathered, it continued to nag at me, until it hit me—

I sat up, staring straight ahead. "They're conducting a scientific experiment," I said to absolutely no one. "They're running a controlled experiment, complete with exact, identified parameters."

I climbed off my tree stump and ran over to the campsite. I carefully unzipped the tent, and crawled in, trying to be as quiet as possible. But when I got there, I couldn't bring myself to wake West. I just sat there and stared at his face, the only part of him that stuck out of the sleeping bag, and I couldn't help but smile. For a moment, I was taken back to when we were kids. I couldn't see much of his face, which was partially covered, and it reminded me of how he slept with a pillow over his head when we were kids. On the first night I slept inside New Caelum all those years ago, Willow, West, and I camped out on the floor in the president's room. We were all a little scared, so West and Willow's mom let us sleep on the rug at the foot of her bed. That's when I learned how he liked to cocoon inside blankets and sleep with pillows over his head.

Now I listened to West's rhythmic breathing and wondered what was waiting for him back at New Caelum. Would he be welcomed back in, or would the people shoot him on sight now that they knew the others who'd left had contracted the virus? Was his life in danger?

My stomach tightened into a knot, and a lump formed in my throat. I didn't know if Dax or Zara was dead. West's friends, Key and Ryder, were dying in one hospital, and his sister, Willow, was dying in another. Dylan was now sick. It was happening all over again. The people around me were sick and dying or somehow being cut off from me. And no matter how many ways I tried to look at it, I kept coming back to the same conclusion—the return of Bad Sam and the killings were the fault of the people inside New Caelum. Just like it had been President Layne's fault that my parents were cut off from our country during the initial stages of the pandemic. She'd been the one to give the order to shut down all air travel in and out of the country. West's own mother had insisted that we cut our country off from the rest of the world.

And with that ice-cold order, she also cut off my desire to have anything to do with the world of New Caelum. My chance to grow up with West—for us to be together—was over. Even at twelve, I had thought we'd be best friends forever—in fact, I'd thought we'd be more than best friends. And now, I knew he had believed the same thing. But we had been so naive.

Was being here with him now a second chance? And if so, a second chance at what? What if he'd been raised to be just like his mother? No, I refused to believe that. Besides, his PulsePoint wasn't working. Had his own mother cut him off?

I came to a decision. I wanted West to live, and I knew they would kill him if he returned to New Caelum. They sure weren't taking names last night when they began shooting at will.

And that meant I would have to leave him behind.

I leaned down and placed a kiss on his lips, letting the warmth of his breath feather across my face before I pulled back. After leaving his PulsePoint where he would see it, I crawled back out of the tent, thankful that he was both ex-hausted and a heavy sleeper.

I gathered my backpack, loaded with only the few things I needed: the vials of virus antibodies, the beginnings of a cure that Caine had started, and my PulsePoint. And, of course, the countdown timer at the bottom of the pack.

I had very little time. If Zara successfully planted the bomb inside the walls of New Caelum last night, I had barely three days.

I hiked down the mountain at a good clip, attempting to cover my tracks the best I could as I went. But with only the moon to light my path, I stumbled a few times. Finally I was forced to slow down; the last thing I needed was a broken bone or spilled vials of viruses and antibodies.

When at last I reached the gate into the city, I pulled out my PulsePoint and typed a message to West that he would hopefully find when he woke.

Then I scrolled through my contacts, found the president's private line, and pushed "call."

The video call was answered on the third ring. "Hello," said a man with dark hair and dark facial hair, trimmed short in almost a full beard. "Who are you?" he asked.

It was strange that this person didn't automatically think it was Christina Black. Would my name not have popped up on the screen of the PulsePoint he was holding? Of course, I looked nothing like the Christina they were expecting.

"I need to speak to President Layne," I said.

"I am the acting president. Who are you?" He narrowed his eyes, looking beyond me. "You're outside." His voice grew more concerned. "I demand to know who you are. I'm starting a track on this device."

Without even giving me the chance to answer, the man covered the PulsePoint and began to issue a muffled series of what I assumed were orders. When he reappeared on the screen again, he said, "Who are you, and why do you have Christina Black's PulsePoint?" Now he was getting closer to knowing who I was.

"I am with Christina Black, but by the time you reach me, she will be gone. If you would like a cure to Bad Sam, you will allow me to enter your city unharmed, and you will guarantee my safety while I'm there."

The man smiled, and not in a way that made my heart rate slow. "What should I call you?"

"I'm Cricket, and I am your only hope for saving the president's daughter and anyone else who has contracted Bad Sam."

"Well, Cricket, I'm Justin. I think we can accommodate your wishes... if what you say is true."

It didn't take long to hear the scrambling of vehicles and feet. The outer gate of New Caelum clicked, then slowly began to open outward.

A truck pulled through. Headlights blinded me. From around the truck came twenty or so people dressed in red hazmat suits, holding firearms pointed directly at me.

chapter twenty-two

·······································

West

The fact that my arms, feet, and nose were ice cold eventually rose to the forefront of my subconscious. It took several more minutes for that irritation to jolt me awake. And as I woke, I realized why that freezing sensation had come back:

Cricket was gone. And she had taken the warmth with her.

My eyes sprang open. Not only was Cricket missing, so were her winter coat and the backpack that she never let out of her sight.

I sat up and felt around for my clothes. When I reached for my coat, my hand fell on my PulsePoint. I knew I hadn't left that out.

I scrambled to get dressed and pull my boots on. I climbed out of the tent and secured the camping gear the best I could, then quickly scanned the area for any sign of where Cricket had gone. It was still very early, and only a little light filtered through the trees.

Had she left me sleeping in order to enter New Caelum alone? How could she possibly think she would survive without my help?

177

And she had left my PulsePoint out. Had she left me a note?

I started to turn it on and check, then remembered how Cricket warned me that she was careful not to leave any tracks that might lead anyone to the campsite. I wouldn't want to activate the PulsePoint here and risk bringing people to her sacred spot.

So I started down the hill, and waited until I was far enough away before I turned on the PulsePoint. And as I feared, she had sent me a note:

Westlin,

In another life, I would have loved the fact that you found me again. But this is not that life. I don't know what's happening at New Caelum, but for some reason they cut you off, and after witnessing their murderous acts last night, I hope that you will decide to stay away from there. I will do what I can to save your sister, and to make it back out.

Please understand that I, with the help of Zara and Dax, have already ensured my safe escape. Please don't interfere. You've been given a chance at a completely different life, if you want it. I hope you'll go back to Caine and your friends and wait for me there.

I asked you if you had been happy inside New Caelum. Content is not good enough. I hope you'll take this chance I've given you to stay on the outside and find happiness. Maybe, just maybe, we'll get the chance to get to know each other again.

Love,
C

"You've lost your mind!" I shouted. I was a second away from shattering my PulsePoint against a tree trunk, but stopped short, knowing I might yet need this one connection to the inside.

How had I given her the impression that I desired any sort of life on the outside? I had no intention of living out here, and I had every intention of one day leading New Caelum into the next era.

I rounded a bend in the path and faced New Caelum's outer gate. Had Cricket truly gone in there without me? How did she get past the gate without being shot?

I stared down at my PulsePoint. She'd obviously turned her own PulsePoint on in order to message me—and that meant she'd alerted anyone watching for it to the fact that Christina was, in fact, alive. That was a big risk, and I knew she hadn't made that decision lightly.

Maybe it was time for me to take a risk, too.

Since I'd left New Caelum, the only person I'd tried to contact had been my mother—because, of course, she was the only one who knew I had left the city. But she wasn't answering, and it was a safe bet that everyone else had figured it out by now anyway.

I scrolled through my contacts and pressed on the one name I was sure would answer.

A faint ring sounded through the PulsePoint several times before I heard a voice on the other end.

"Well, well, well. If it isn't the president's son."

"Hi, Justin. Something seems to be wrong with my Pulse-Point. Mother sent me out to scout out a nearby settlement, but when I tried to call her to let her know—"

"Don't bother lying, West."

I made a fist and tried to keep the anger off of my face. "What are you talking about?"

"We know you found Christina. Your travel companion, Cricket, is here, inside New Caelum. We know she left you behind. You will be allowed back inside under one condition."

A sweat broke out across the back of my neck, immediately turning cold in the frigid air. I couldn't decide if he knew Cricket was Christina, or if he simply knew Christina was alive because of Cricket. "And what condition would that be?"

"You will stick with the government track so that you can join your mother and me in the governing of New Caelum. And you will convince Christina to join us inside New Caelum as well."

"Or what?" There was no way I would convince Cricket to do anything against her will. And given the amount of hate I had for Justin Rhodes, my mother's vice president, I wasn't especially motivated to try.

"Or I will make sure this Cricket thinks that you were the one responsible for Bad Sam being sent out into the outside settlements."

chapter twenty-three

Cricket

The enclosed sanctum of New Caelum was drastically different from the outside world I had come to know. The hallways were brightly colored. Lighting was placed strategically along the floor and on the walls near the ceiling, making me feel almost as if I were on a spaceship. The sleek, clean interior contrasted greatly with the run-down, and often dilapidated, buildings that I'd come to know over the last six years.

But despite the colorful atmosphere, I wasn't welcomed to New Caelum with open arms. As soon as I walked through the gate, I was escorted to a tiny white room by armed men dressed in red hazmat suits, then told to wait.

Hours later, I still waited. I sat on the edge of a bed that was covered in crisp white sheets, perfectly folded back and tucked under the mattress. There was nothing to do, nothing to look at. There were no exterior windows, and the blinds on the interior windows were closed from the other side.

On my arrival, I had been given a change of clothes and pointed toward a bathroom—with "everything I needed" to take a shower and "sanitize" myself—but I had chosen to remain in my cargo pants, black tank, and tattered, oatmeal-colored sweater. My heavy coat, dirty and torn, was draped over a silver metal chair in the corner, and crumbles of dried dirt fell off the bottom of my boots onto the tiled floor every time I moved them.

When at last the door to my room opened, I stood and faced it. In walked a man in a dark gray hazmat suit.

I cocked my head. "You're scared I'm sick?" I asked.

"We can't be too careful," the man said through the speaker in his mask.

"Whatever. I need to speak with Dr. Hempel."

"What makes you think there's anyone inside New Caelum by that name?"

"Because Dr. Caine Quinton sent me." I decided I wasn't playing games with these people. Maybe if I shot straight arrows, I'd hit my mark faster. "He says Dr. Hempel is the only person who can help me."

The man shifted and looked around the room. "Why have you chosen not to shower?"

"Because I like my clothes, and I don't plan on being here longer than I have to."

The man smiled. "You'll be here long enough. You'll see no one until you've properly sanitized and been tested for Bad Sam, as well as a few other diseases."

So, he obviously knew about Bad Sam and its reappearance. "Is Willow still alive?" I asked.

Through the mask, I saw the man raise both eyebrows. "Yes." The tone in his voice did very little to convince me though. "She's alive," he added, as if the additional words would reassure me.

182

I took a couple of slow steps toward him. "Look, whoever you are, I brought several vials of the Samael Strain with me. I also brought information that will help Dr. Hempel find a treatment for Willow and a cure for Bad Sam. But we're running out of time." I could only hope Dr. Hempel was capable of doing what Caine claimed he could do.

The man leaned away from me. "We have your bag. Why would you bring samples of the virus here? Don't you realize the danger you've put yourself in, not to mention everyone else inside New Caelum?"

I stared through the mask into his eyes. "Are you not listening to me?" My voice escalated. "I'm here to see Dr. Hempel. Give my bag to him, and when he's ready to hear what I've come here to tell him, tell him to come see me. If this stupid city has any hope of surviving another outbreak, you'll take me seriously."

Perhaps it was the crazed look on my face, but the man's eyes suddenly widened, and he backed up toward the door. As he reached for the handle, I stepped even closer to him. Then I sucked in the biggest breath I could and blew it all over the front of his mask.

When he finally managed to open the door and practically fell through it, I yelled, "I want to speak to the president, too!"

He pulled the door shut behind him.

I turned and walked back toward the bed. I didn't even hear the door open again behind me.

"Hi... Cricket, is it?"

I whipped around. Justin stood just inside the door—and without a hazmat suit.

I cocked my head. "You're taking quite the risk, aren't you?" I asked.

"I'm immune to Bad Sam."

I raised an eyebrow. So, some people inside New Caelum knew how to test for immunity? Interesting.

"And I'm pretty sure you're immune as well, am I right?"

I didn't answer.

He walked over and picked up the clean clothes from my bed, then thrust them at me. "If you want to see Dr. Hempel, you will shower and put these clothes on."

"And if I don't? I'd like to see the president first."

"Funny. I don't see how you're in any position to make demands. You're inside *our* city now; you'll do what we tell you. And if you cooperate, we'll see about allowing you to *live*... inside our city walls." And if I didn't cooperate, the threat of death was clear. He spoke like New Caelum was some sought-after prize, like I had *chosen* to come here.

I knew I wouldn't be welcomed, especially since they didn't know who I was. But I also knew that they wouldn't understand the timer at the bottom of my backpack. Not yet. And even if someone did figure it out, they wouldn't be able to stop it without my help. Nor would they locate the bomb that I hoped Zara had successfully put in place. "Fine, but if you don't come back and get me soon, not only will you risk Willow's survival, but you will put all those not immune to the virus inside New Caelum at risk of contracting the disease."

He narrowed his gaze, pausing with one foot outside the door. "What do you mean by that?"

I crossed my arms, attempting to hide the shakiness in my hands. "You didn't think Caine and Christina sent me here without a well-designed insurance policy to make sure I got back out, did you?"

chapter twenty-four

....

West

After agreeing to Justin's terms, I was granted entrance to New Caelum and delivered directly to a decontamination chamber, where nurses ensured no trace of a virus could have survived anywhere on my body. And as I waited for the shower to scrub me clean, I could think of only one thing—Cricket. Was she close by? Were they treating her kindly? Had they put her through a more rigorous decontamination than me? Though they were treating me like a diseased outsider, I was still a member of leadership, so they knew better than to act abusive. But Cricket had no such protections.

If anyone has laid one thoughtless hand on her, they'll suffer. Why couldn't she have just waited and let me bring her in? Now I had no control over the situation.

Once I was decontaminated, showered, and dressed in my normal black and charcoal gray government clothes, I was covered in a full hazmat suit and escorted to the Presidential Suite, my home for the past six years.

Mother was waiting for me when I arrived, sitting on the edge of a chair. Her feet were crossed at the ankles, and her hands fidgeted in her lap. Her face and eyes were void of any emotion. She, too, wore black pants and a gray sweater.

"Mother?"

She stood. "Remove that suit. I know you don't have the Samael Strain." The guards behind me left without comment.

Once I had cast the hazmat suit aside, Mother crossed to me, sliding her arms around my neck and gripping me in a tight hug.

I peeled her away and held her at arm's length. "Where's Willow? How is she?"

I had been forbidden from entering the isolation wing where I presumed Willow was still being held. Given that Willow's disease had probably progressed to a more advanced state, I wasn't surprised by the restricted access.

Mother smoothed the collar of my gray shirt. "She's doing as well as can be expected, but she's very sick." She dropped her eyes and seemed to sniffle. "They're taking good care of her."

She backed away from me and fidgeted with a ring on her right hand. She seemed unusually unsure of herself. When she looked up, her brows lifted in question. "So, you found her?" Her lips lifted at the corners like she was excited about something.

"Found who?" For some reason, I felt the urge to play dumb.

"Christina, silly." She slapped at me playfully, a gesture I'd never known her to do in the past. "Tell me all about her. Was she beautiful? Did you recognize her? Did she recognize you?"

I cocked an eye. "What is wrong with you?"

"What do you mean?" She pursed her lips. "I want to know more about Christina. Willow will be so excited to see her again."

The more Mother spoke, the more I suspected something was off. Her voice was almost gleeful. She was happy, airy. Nothing like a woman worried about her only daughter dying.

"I never found Christina, Mother, but I did find someone who could help us. Someone who knows Christina."

"I don't understand. Justin told me—"

"Since when do you speak to Justin about anything?" Though he was technically her vice president, she had stopped communicating with him months ago, and had even talked of taking on a new vice president. She had been pretty confident the council would support such a change.

Now she backed up and returned to her uncomfortable chair. She stared down at her feet, muttering something under her breath.

I kneeled in front of her and slid a hand up to her cheek. "Mother, what is wrong with you? Did someone give you something? To help you relax, maybe?" She was acting drunk, but it was early in the day, and Mother only drank an occasional glass of wine with dinner. She never overindulged.

"What?" Her voice rose an octave. "Of course not. That's absurd. I am the president of New Caelum. I do not need the help of any drugs."

I stood up and backed away a bit. "Okay. So what did Justin tell you about Christina?"

"Just that she called in on her PulsePoint, and that he was sending men out to get her. I just assumed she was somewhere inside the city—freshening up. I mean, can you *imagine* being out there all this time with such filth?" She squinched up her nose and shuddered.

Actually, yes, I could imagine it very well. "Well, Justin was mistaken," I said. He had to be. Cricket would never have admitted to her real identity. "I did bring a girl back to New Caelum. She was sent to us by Dr. Caine Quinton. It wasn't Christina, though."

Mom's shoulders rotated back at the sound of Caine's name. "Dr. Quinton? You saw him? How is he?" She smiled politely while picking a fallen hair off of her sweater.

I crossed the room to check the liquor cabinet. Not that that told me anything. Mother always had a well-stocked bar for entertaining the council. "He was fine, Mother," I said absentmindedly, then caught myself. "No, he *wasn't* fine." I faced her again. "He's trying to run a settlement and build a healthy community." I purposely left out the bit about our own Ryder and Key delivering Bad Sam to the people of that settlement.

"Well, of course he wasn't fine. What did he expect?" She waved her hand as if dismissing both Caine and me. "He chose his path. He chose to play the hero and devote his life to helping the poor souls who were unlucky enough to find themselves stuck on outside. Instead of..."

"Unlucky?" I'd never heard my mother speak about those on the outside in that way. "You act like the people on the outside were just victim of some lottery system. Like they had a glimmer of hope in the beginning and just drew the wrong straw."

"Oh, whatever." She stood and walked to me again. "I'm just so happy to have you back. And with Christina." She smiled. "Now, I'm going to have my bath before dinner. Justin will be here to eat with us."

I started to tell her again that Christina wasn't here, but I knew my breath would have been wasted. Not to mention that I'd have been lying.

~~~~~

"Get up, West." a man's voice barked, jolting me from my sleep. I grunted, my hand massaging the crick in my neck, and the voice sang, "I have a surprise for you."

I'd fallen asleep sitting up in this very uncomfortable chair, waiting for my mother to finish bathing. Waiting for anything to happen, really. I knew that once I'd reentered New Caelum, I'd be at the mercy of the city's rules. I'd been sequestered until I could be debriefed—and until it was proven that I didn't have Bad Sam. Now I stared into the dark, almost black, eyes of Justin Rhodes.

I stood and backed away from him, rubbing a hand over my face in attempt to shake the fog from my head. I knew I'd lost a lot of sleep during the nights I'd been away, but I couldn't believe I'd let myself fall asleep without knowing the fate of Cricket.

"What's wrong, West? You're acting a little nervous." Justin undid the buttons at his wrists and began to roll his sleeves up to his elbows.

"I just woke up to you in my face, Justin. What did you expect?" *Asshole.* "Why? Is there something I should be nervous about?"

"Well, let's see. You left the city without permission. For all we know, you've been exposed to Bad Sam multiple times. And then you ask to come back?"

Justin nodded toward two guards who stood just inside the door to our suite; they had masks over their faces and surgical gloves on their hands. At Justin's nod, they left their posts by the door and crossed over to me.

I instinctively held my hands up and backed away. "What's going on?"

"Just a precaution, my friend."

One guard held my arms behind my back while the other rubbed a device across my forehead. "It's normal," the guard said—referring to my temperature, I supposed. He then pushed my shirtsleeve to above my elbow, tied a band around my upper arm, and proceeded to extract blood from my vein. After he had placed a piece of gauze over the injection site, the other guard released me.

Justin clapped his hands together. "Great. As long as your blood test comes back negative, it would appear that you are virus free."

"It will." I concentrated on keeping my breathing even and saying nothing that would upset Justin. "I've been careful, and I've shown no signs." Not to mention, Dr. Quinton had determined that I was immune to Bad Sam.

"Also, I expect you to regularly submit your temperature through your PulsePoint now that you're back."

A door behind me opened. I turned to find my mother, dressed in a simple black dress. Her hair was pulled into a tight bun at the base of her neck.

"I thought I heard voices." She breezed over to Justin and gave him a peck on the cheek, then wiped the lipstick from his skin.

"Hello, Ginger, darling." Justin turned his head and spoke against her lips. When he faced me, he smiled. "I guess your mother told you?"

I gawked at their display of affection. "Actually, no, she must have left something out." I pulled down the sleeve of my shirt; anything to keep my hands busy.

"Your mother and I are getting married."

"Why?" It was all I could think to say.

"Westlin," Mom scolded. "Don't be rude."

Willow and I hated this guy. My *mother* hated him.

"It's okay, darling." Justin hugged Mother close. "We'll give West a minute to get used to it."

"Was that the surprise?" I asked, remembering Justin's irritating voice when he'd first entered. Mother didn't seem the least bit worried that a deadly virus was sweeping through her daughter's body, and I had to find a way to bring the conversation around to what we were going to do about discovering a cure.

"No. Actually, the surprise should be here any minute." Justin glanced down at the mini-PulsePoint on his wrist, then smiled at me. "You're going to love this."

He walked to the entrance of our suite and with the click of a few buttons, the door slid open. "Ah. Here she is now."

Cricket rounded the corner and approached the entrance to the suite, flanked by two guards. At the sight of her, I nearly lost my ability to breathe. She was dressed in a sapphire-colored satin dress. Her blond hair was pulled back and smoothly tucked into some sort of braid. Even the hair that usually hung against her cheek was braided along the right side of her head. She fidgeted like crazy with her hands, and her face tilted to the right.

She was beautiful, and my wildly beating heart was testament to that fact. However, that wasn't the surprise; it was the color she wore that was the surprise.

"Welcome, Cricket," Justin said. "This is my lovely fiancée, President Ginger Layne."

Cricket held out her hand to Mother. "Nice to meet you, ma'am." Her voice was even and seemed void of emotion.

"And of course you know our Westlin." Justin gestured my way.

She turned to me, and that was when I saw the spark of pure, unfiltered anger in her eyes. She held out her hand to me. "Nice to see you again, West. And so soon." The second sentence held an especially sharp edge.

I wrapped my fingers around her hand and squeezed, holding on to her palm long enough to feel a slight tremor in her handshake. When I looked up at her face, what I saw tore me apart. Though she was making eye contact, she was still leaning her head to the side, attempting to hide her scars. I could have punched Justin in that moment.

I swallowed hard. "Yes, it is very nice to see you again, Cricket." The coolness of her hand warmed under my touch, and I didn't want to let go.

"Uh-huh. Okay then." Justin rubbed his hands together. "Let's eat."

As if on cue, a door slid open. A couple of servers rolled in a formally decorated table, then set chairs around it. Justin led Mother over and guided her to sit.

I turned back to Cricket. Her eyes had widened a bit. I ducked my head to get her attention. "Are you okay? Did they do anything to hurt you?"

"No. They haven't physically harmed me. But West," she said through gritted teeth, "what's going on here?"

I brought a finger to my lips, warning her not to speak much. "We must eat first." I leaned closer to her ear and breathed in a scent of jasmine, a favorite of my sister's. Many of the city's soaps and shampoos were produced by the men and women who worked in New Caelum's greenhouses. "I'll find you later. I promise. Just as soon as I've earned back my privileges."

I pulled back, then offered her my arm. "Shall we?" As the gentleman I was raised to be, I led Cricket to a chair next to my mother, then sat as close as I could—but not close enough—on the other side of her.

The servers placed covered plates in front of each of us and poured wine in our glasses. Noting the look on Cricket's face, and knowing that I was very dehydrated after my time on the outside, I motioned for the server. "Can we please get some water?"

The server looked to Justin. Only after Justin nodded did the server leave and come back with water. Cricket gulped down the entire glass when it was placed in front of her.

"So, Justin... Mother... when is the big day?" I lifted my water glass and saluted them, trying not to puke in the process.

Mother looked from me to Justin. "I guess it sounds sudden to you?"

"Sudden for you to agree to marry this man while I'm off on the outside of New Caelum trying to find someone who can cure your only daughter of the disease that killed off most of our country? You think that would seem sudden to me?"

Justin spoke through clenched teeth. "Westlin, careful."

"Well," Mother said, "when your sister became ill, the people of New Caelum thought it best to put the election on hold. Justin... my partner..." she smiled and nodded toward the weasel beside her, "...suggested, and I agreed, that a merger of our relationship would make New Caelum even stronger than it already is."

Mother made marriage sound like a business transaction. And since I knew which party at the table needed strength in order to make it through another election, it was easy to see who was pushing for the arrangement. "So, this is for political gain?"

Justin stood suddenly, knocking over an entire glass of red wine. The wine streamed across the white tablecloth and almost into Cricket's lap. She instinctively stood and backed away, letting the wine roll off the table and puddle on the floor at her feet.

Justin's face reddened. His hands curled into fists against the tablecloth. "Westlin, I'm only going to remind you once: You will swallow this hostility and do what you can to help our cause, or the promise I made you when I allowed you back inside New Caelum will come true."

The muscles in my back tensed as I considered whether Justin could come up with any convincing "proof" to convince Cricket, or anyone else, that I was capable of reproducing Bad Sam and sending it out into the settlements.

The servers cleaned up the mess enough for us to eat. I took my seat again.

"My apologies, Cricket," Justin said across the table. "West and I promise to behave for the rest of dinner. Don't we, West?"

I nodded. "I'm sorry, too." I lifted my water glass to her. At that moment, I would have loved to have known what was going through her head about this city she'd run from.

Cricket sat back down without looking at either Justin or me. A server removed the cover from her food, and then did the same with mine, revealing plates of steamed vegetables, beans, and rice. Cooked broccoli and Brussels sprouts had never smelled so good.

"You may eat." Justin smiled at Cricket.

I dug my fisted knuckles into my knees just listening to the way he condescended her, like she was a helpless child. She must have looked pretty unrefined to him when she'd first arrived, and he'd wasted no time making sure she got cleaned up and dressed in the perfect color. I eyed Justin curiously. He'd dressed her this way on purpose. What was he planning?

I ate a few bites of vegetables and rice. Cricket barely looked up from her food. I couldn't decide if she was retreating into the shy, reserved girl that she once was, or if she was debating whether she could stab a fork in Justin's eye and make a run for it. Either way, she didn't come to New Caelum to be wined, dined, and patronized.

"Can we at least talk about my sister?" I asked, bursting the proverbial elephant-sized balloon in the room.

Mom stopped chewing for a minute, but after a quick glance toward Justin, continued to eat while Justin spoke.

"Your sister is doing okay," Justin said. "She's been sick for five days now. She's definitely reached a critical time in the illness, and we need to decide how to treat her in the next forty-eight to seventy-two hours, or she'll begin to hemorrhage from many different parts of her body, and her organs will begin to shut down."

"Justin," I replied in as level a tone as I could manage, "I mean this with the utmost respect for Mother, you, and our entire medical staff here inside New Caelum..." I wanted to hurl just hearing those words exit my mouth. "... but when can we expect Dr. Hempel to start working on the data Cricket brought in?"

"He already is."

Cricket's fork fell from her hand and clanked against her plate. She glanced from me to Justin. "Sorry. I just..." She swallowed. "Why am I not helping him?"

Justin touched the napkin to each corner of his mouth. "Because, Cricket, our doctors know exactly what they're doing, and I wouldn't be a very nice host if I didn't see to it that you were properly fed. Look at you. You're skin and bones. When you've both finished your meals, West will give you a tour of the grounds, and then escort you to the labs." His PulsePoint pinged, and he glanced down. "Well, good news. It appears you've both been cleared of the Samael Strain."

Cricket and I traded hard looks. That was much faster than Caine Quinton could test for the virus.

We immediately began stuffing food in our mouths while trying not to look like animals. When both of our plates had been cleared, I drank a little more water and stood. As I rounded the table and gave my mother a kiss on the cheek, Justin's cold stare followed my every step. Then I held out a hand to help Cricket to her feet.

Just when I thought Cricket and I were free to go, Justin pushed his chair back and stood, blocking my exit. "Cricket, you may wait just outside the door. I need to speak with West for a moment."

Cricket nodded, and two guards led her to the greeting area outside our suite.

Justin's expression was unreadable. The entire evening had been one cryptic moment after another. He moved in close to me. "Here's the deal, West. You have a week to convince Cricket to remain with us."

"Or what?"

"Or the council will force her to stay."

"She'll never agree to stay inside New Caelum."

"Why not? This is a wonderful home. It's safe and disease-free."

"Why is this so important to you?"

"Because I know Cricket is actually Christina Black, and we need her here."

I glanced toward Mother. She appeared oblivious to our conversation. Justin had her on some sort of massive muscle relaxant or something. I was sure of it.

"Why do you want Christina Black?" I didn't even bother wasting time denying Cricket's true identity.

"Because she's the sole survivor of a disease that took down our entire country. She's the key to making sure we have a permanent cure, maybe even a vaccine. And once we have that, there will never be any question who should run New Caelum." He threw back the rest of his wine. "I don't need to remind you that you're next in the line of succession, do I?"

"So?"

"Your mother and I won't be able to run New Caelum forever. Nor does the council wish it."

"The council loves my mother."

"The council is made up of people who want only the best for New Caelum. And they're noticing changes in the attitudes of our citizens."

"What are you talking about?"

"You will be next to take over."

This was not news, nor did it answer my question. "What if I don't want to govern this city? Besides, that's not going to happen for a while." I wasn't even close to ready.

"You don't have a choice. And it will happen sooner than you think." Justin smiled. "The council has asked that you begin your formal training for your role immediately. Will Ryder rejoin the city? You'll need him."

I cocked my head and studied Justin's face. Did he know that four of the scouts that had been sent out were now infected with Bad Sam? In case he didn't, I decided to hold on to that piece of information for now. "I hope so. I assume he's doing whatever it is you asked him to do."

Justin laughed. "Yes, I was aware of the scouts leaving the city."

"You gave orders against the president's knowledge."

"The council gave those orders. And your mother knew about the scouting mission before they left the city. Didn't you, darling?" He smiled down at my mother, who was still calmly eating her dinner.

"Yes, and I think it was a good idea to see what was going on outside our walls," she said. It sounded like a very rehearsed statement, and certainly not one she agreed with.

My mother was definitely not herself. On the day Willow became sick, she'd insisted that Willow had been purposely infected with Bad Sam as some ploy to get her out of the way.

I remembered thinking there had to be more to it.

As I glanced toward the door, I wondered about the council's plan to send scouts out to the settlements. How much of that had actually been about finding Christina?

"What do you want from me right now, Justin?" I asked.

"You will wine and dine Christina Black. You will entice her to stay inside the city with you. And when the people of this city discover that you have found your long lost childhood love—the person who will save us from Bad Sam forever... well, they will have no choice but to treat us—your mother, me, you, and Christina—as royalty."

"You've lost your mind."

Without warning, Justin grabbed the lapels of my jacket and held me forcefully in front of him. "Your sister is on her deathbed, West. You do want to cure her, don't you?"

I clenched my hands into fists at my side and breathed hard into Justin's face. "Is that some sort of threat?"

"I can see to it that the cure is not found in time..." He released me, patting my jacket back into place. "Or I can make sure that you and Christina have uninterrupted time to help Dr. Hempel find a treatment."

I glanced over at the guards—Justin's guards. "And all I have to do is—"

"Walk a straight line, do as you're told, and convince Christina to stay with us inside New Caelum."

....

chapter twenty-five

Cricket

West led me along another sleek hallway that was accented with colored lights. It reminded me of a children's hospital my parents had once taken me to. "I remember a hallway like this," I said.

"Maybe you remember being here."

"No, I remember my parents driving me to a place like this. They either worked there, or volunteered... or, no, I was a patient there." I gave my head a shake. "The memory is very fuzzy."

It didn't matter. That was a long time ago.

My mind reeled at how I'd been treated since I arrived inside New Caelum. On the one hand, I was like a princess to be pampered; yet it was also abundantly clear that I was a prisoner of this extravagant city.

I wasn't concerned about being held prisoner. The people of New Caelum had no clue just how resourceful those of us who'd lived outside the city truly were. When Justin, West, and President Layne figured out what the timing mechanism in my backpack really meant, they'd make sure I made it out of here safely. With the cure.

What did concern me was finding a cure for Bad Sam as quickly as possible. With every passing minute, my heart ached for those now suffering with the virus. I could only hope they remained mostly unconscious while their fever fought the infection. But I knew that every time they woke, they would be forced to endure a level of pain that would make them wish they were dead.

West wasn't saying much, but he seemed to be trying to walk as closely as he could to me without touching me. Maybe he was subconsciously trying to protect me.

We continued around a curve in the hallway. I had no idea where we were or where we were headed. We passed several men and women, all dressed in either white or powder blue, very different from the jeweled shade of blue I wore, and each one gave me a quick once-over before nodding at West.

I opened my mouth to ask West if there was any significance to the colors people wore in New Caelum, but suddenly he grabbed my upper arm and jerked me around a corner, down an adjoining hallway. Before I could object, he opened a door and shoved me inside, into the dark, and followed me in. Once the door was closed behind us, he flipped a switch. A dim light shone overhead. We were in some sort of supply closet.

He turned me and positioned me against the door. I breathed hard while taking in the severe look in his eyes. "West—"

He propped his hands against the door on both sides of my head, trapping me. "Why did you have to come here?"

"You know why I came here. You *knew* I was coming here." I spoke softly. I was tempted to place a hand on his cheek, to calm him, but instead I eased my hand up to his chest to keep distance between us.

He closed his eyes and sucked in a deep breath through his nose. "But you left me." When he looked at me again, his face had softened. He enclosed my hand in his and held it tightly against his chest. "Why did you shut me out of your plan? You were never going to be able to do this alone."

"I was fully prepared to do this by myself," I snapped. Then my voice softened. "Besides... I wanted you to have a chance at a life outside New Caelum. I thought since I was the one the doctors needed, I could—"

"What? You thought I would just let you enter New Caelum on your own? Risk your life?"

"I've survived far worse. I'll survive this."

"They know who you are. Justin knows you're Christina Black. And he has no intention of letting you leave here."

I stared back at West—through him, actually. Then I gave my head a shake. "It doesn't matter."

He pushed away from the door and walked a few steps away from me. The urge to follow him, to run my hands along his arms and back, to comfort him, was strong. The look on his face when he faced me again about did me in. I had to look away, ducking my face to the right.

He approached me again, slowly. Crooking a finger under my chin, he lifted it. Then he raised his other hand and reached behind my head. It took me a few seconds to realize that he was removing the pins from my hair, letting my hair fall to my shoulders. I immediately pulled several locks forward to cover my scarred cheek and neck.

"I'm sorry for the way Justin made you feel. But you never have to hide from me."

I swallowed hard. My heart sped up, beating out of control.

"You are beautiful."

I remembered the feelings I'd had when we were twelve and West kissed me. A lifetime ago. Those feelings had nothing on what was coursing through me now. Something had happened deep within my heart and in the pit of my stomach last night when we'd kissed in the sleeping bag. Our legs had rubbed together, and his hands had roamed my back while we were attempting to generate heat. And we had... generated heat. "West, we can't..."

"We can't what?" He leaned in closer, his lips hovering over mine. His breath feathered against my face and smelled faintly of red wine.

"We have to think about your sister and your friends."

"I haven't stopped thinking about them." West ran his fingers along my forehead, tracing them along the hair that now hung against my face. "But you are back in my life. That is no accident. And dammit, I'm not waiting for some 'other life,' like you said in that stupid goodbye note."

"West, we were kids," I breathed. Anxiety built in my chest. "I don't believe in fate or destiny or any of that crap." The timing just wasn't right for us. And never would be.

For the first time since I'd seen West inside New Caelum, his lips lifted slightly. "Well then, I guess it's a good thing I believe enough for both of us. Because I think fate, destiny, or some such crap is exactly the reason we're back together."

I wanted more than anything to trust West, but we were not *together*. Not the way he believed. I probably should have told him about the virus bomb that was now inside his city, but something stopped me. The bomb was my only insurance policy. "What now?"

"I'm supposed to give you a tour of the executive wing where you'll be staying, then take you to the labs where Dr. Hempel is already working on the stuff you brought with you."

"Then let's go. Skip the tour, though, and take me straight to the lab. The quicker we find a cure, the less your sister and your friends have to suffer."

West stepped back, but not before I saw a flicker of uncertainty flash across his face. He was worried about something more than just the virus.

He was also keeping something from me.

chapter twenty-six

West

When we arrived at the lab, Dr. Hempel was in a frantic state. He was dressed head-to-toe in a white hazmat suit, and his gloved hands shook as he squeezed a substance onto a glass slide, swapped it with another slide on a microscope, and peered into the eyepiece.

Cricket circled the tall lab table. She and I both wore matching charcoal hazmat suits. Her head was cocked as she studied the doctor's movements. "Dr. Hempel."

His body jerked backward so suddenly he fell against a metal stool, causing it to screech along the tile floor. His eyes narrowed as he took in Cricket, then me. "Mr. Layne, I didn't hear you come in."

"Dr. Hempel, this is Cricket. She's responsible for the new lead on a cure."

When he looked at Cricket again, I thought his eyes might pop out of his head. "You're..."

Cricket held out her gloved hand. "Dr. Caine Quinton said you'd know what to do with the samples he sent." When Dr. Hempel refused to shake Cricket's hand, she let it fall back to her side. Probably safer if they didn't touch.

"Dr. Hempel, are you okay?" I asked.

The doctor turned and walked over to a table that held Cricket's backpack. From beside it, he picked up a strange box I didn't recognize. A digital number glowed red on the front of the box and seemed to be counting down. "Did Caine send this?" he asked.

Cricket fidgeted with her fingers. "No, he didn't. I brought that."

"What is it?" I asked.

Dr. Hempel sat the small machine back on the table. The number continued to get smaller.

I squeezed Cricket's shoulder, guiding her to face me when she didn't respond right away. "What is that?"

Something very close to fear swam in her eyes. She didn't want to tell me what the box was.

"What does that number mean?" I insisted.

She didn't dare look away from me. "It's a countdown timer. Based on what you and your friends told Caine and me about the timing of your sister's symptoms, that's how long we have before your sister is at risk for death."

I stared at the number. 51 hours, 34 minutes, and 13 seconds.

"When that timer expires, your sister could die if no successful treatment has yet been administered. Your friends who left New Caelum with you—who are now in the care of Caine—are likely to follow soon after. And Dylan closely behind them. Not to mention anyone else who was infected after we left the settlement." Cricket's face revealed fear, along with another emotion that was more unreadable. She was leaving something out.

Just then, the door to the lab slid open, and in walked Justin dressed in a charcoal gray hazmat suit that matched ours. He stopped short when he saw us. "Well, you two are here sooner than I expected."

I glanced sideways at a fidgety Cricket. "Cricket was eager to see Dr. Hempel. We'll continue the tour when we leave here." Why was he so hell-bent on controlling our movements inside the city?

"See to it that you show Cricket the Presidential Suite soon." He turned to Cricket. "When you're not here in the lab, I'd like for you to stay in your quarters, and not venture out into the general public areas just yet. There will be plenty of time to introduce you to the citizens of New Caelum later."

The way Justin spoke had me cringing. Cricket had no interest in being introduced to the people of New Caelum. And I had no idea what he was up to. I had to get my mother alone, and soon. But I couldn't leave Cricket to fend for herself.

Justin turned to the doctor. "Well, Dr. Hempel, what do you think? Are we going to be able to cook up a cure to Bad Sam?" His tone was so casual, like we were trying to cure the common cold.

"As has always been the case, Mr. Rhodes, I'm not sure. We don't have much time. It would help if I could have fewer interruptions."

"Good point. We will have food brought to you, and you can sleep in the exam room when you absolutely must. What else do you need?"

"Well, it's very difficult to evaluate possible cures without something or someone to test them on. We don't have lab rats, and we had yet to perfect a simulation of the Samael Strain to test with."

Justin held up a hand. "Actually, I already thought of that." Justin's lips suddenly tugged downward, yet no hint of sadness touched his eyes. "Unfortunately, there are a couple of children who have contracted Bad Sam. They are in the quarantine units down the hallway. You may test your cures on them."

A look of horror passed over Dr. Hempel's face, and an audible gasp escaped Cricket's mouth. "More people inside New Caelum have caught the virus?" she asked. "Because of contact with Willow? How can you be sure you don't have a widespread outbreak on your hands?"

Justin turned to her. "Because we have traced every person and location within the city they've had contact with. It's under control. We know when and how these two individuals were infected."

Justin's explanation didn't lessen the horrified look on Cricket's face.

"Can you use what Caine sent?" Justin asked Dr. Hempel.

Dr. Hempel shrugged. "He was much closer to finding a cure than anyone here has gotten. I'll try." His voice shook slightly. "I have very few antibodies from the sole survivor, though. They won't last forever."

Justin's head turned slightly toward Cricket, but he stopped short of revealing her true identity to Dr. Hempel. "You do what you can with what you have. Let me know immediately if you run out of whatever it is you need. I'll leave these guards with you. They won't allow any distractions." Justin turned, but just before he exited the lab, he spoke to the guards. "See to it that Dr. Hempel is not bothered. He needs anything, call me."

As soon as he was gone, Cricket let out a huge breath.

Dr. Hempel turned back to his microscope and notes. Without looking up at us, he said, "Unless you have some knowledge that isn't included in these notes from Dr. Quinton—or unless you can produce the survivor of the virus—the two of you can see yourself out." This time when Dr. Hempel spoke, his voice was stronger. Anger had seeped into it and crowded out the fear he had shown when we first arrived.

"What do you need from the survivor of Bad Sam?" Cricket asked.

"Nothing yet, but I might at some point."

"I'll produce the survivor for you if and when you need something from her. Until then, I'm not leaving. I need to know the minute you have a breakthrough, and what that breakthrough is."

Dr. Hempel lifted both eyebrows. "You're an outsider. You don't have the immune system the people of New Caelum have, and that makes you a risk to everyone. Get out. And make sure you decontaminate thoroughly when you go." He redirected his stare to the guards by the door, who immediately stepped forward.

I touched Cricket's arm. "Let's go. We'll check back in later."

She jerked her arm out of my reach, then glared at Dr. Hempel. "Fine. I'll leave. But I *will* be back." She nodded toward the clock behind him. "And Dr. Hempel?" Her voice contained the warning of an approaching blizzard. "Do take that clock seriously. I need to have a cure in my hands and be long gone from New Caelum when that clock hits all zeroes."

....

chapter twenty-seven

Cricket

Claustrophobia was starting to set in as West and I walked the hallways of New Caelum. How did these people live like this—cut off from the outside world— all these years?

Add to that, I had given up control of everything Caine had sent me here with, everything that could lead us to finding a cure. But Caine had assured me that if there was anyone who could do something with his research, it was Dr. Hempel.

"West, I need to see your sister."

He stopped in the middle of the hallway and faced me. "First you tell me what that clock is really counting down to."

"No. You'll know when you need to know."

He stepped closer to me. "So it's not just counting down the incubation period of Bad Sam."

"No, it's not." I stared straight into his eyes. I wanted to trust him, but how could I? I knew he was keeping information from me. And he'd never once mentioned what he and Justin had talked about after I was asked to leave the room.

West cocked his head. "Why are you keeping this from me?"

HEATHER SUNSERI

"I think you and I have different agendas, West. We're inside your city now, and I don't know what you're up to. Meanwhile, I'm a prisoner, for all intents and purposes. Can you look me in the eye and tell me that's not so?"

His lips formed a thin line. "That's unfair. I've been honest with you."

"And I've been honest with you. But honesty and full disclosure are two entirely different things, are they not? You of all people, in your leadership position, should know that."

He squinted as he seemed to ponder the situation. "I will not let you become trapped inside New Caelum against your wishes. I promised you that already."

"Great. And I promise you that that timer—and everything it means—will leave with me when I go. So can I see your sister or not?"

His jaw took on a hard edge. "Fine." He grabbed my hand and pulled me behind him. "But prepare yourself. It's not pretty."

I knew it wouldn't be. I'd already seen many suffer and die from the virus. Too many.

When we arrived in the infectious isolation wing, two guards in light gray stood outside the entrance. As we approached, they moved to block the door. "Mr. Layne, you may not enter at this time."

"Why not?" West stood taller. His hand rested on the Taser he kept at his waist. He was a different man inside New Caelum than the one I'd met outside. Here, he was confident, decisive. In his element.

"We have orders. Only family can enter."

"I *am* family."

216

One of the guards nodded toward me. "She isn't."

West looked down at his feet, chuckled, and squared his shoulders as he stood directly in front of the guard. "I am second in line to rule over New Caelum. So unless your orders have come from President Layne herself, you will step aside, or you both will find yourselves wearing beige by the end of the day."

The guards traded uneasy glances. I played with the strands of hair that shielded my face and remembered fondly the beige sweater I'd been wearing when I'd arrived at New Caelum.

"Mr. Layne, you know our orders come from Mr. Rhodes. If he finds out we disobeyed his orders—"

"Then don't let him find out. Either way, it seems the two of you are in a tough position. Disobey my order, and you face the consequences with me. Disobey Justin's order, and again you face punishment—but only if you're caught. Choose quickly, now. Time is limited."

The guards looked at each other, then stepped aside.

As we passed, I couldn't help but notice how they each gave me the once-over. And when their gazes landed on my cheek, their own faces scrunched up in disgust. West apparently noticed, too, because just as he was about to enter the isolation wing, he stopped, backed up, and then shoved an elbow into one of the guards' necks.

"You both will remember your places, and I will consider allowing you to keep your jobs on the executive level."

West released the guard, and the man's hand flew to his neck as he coughed. "Our apologies, Mr. Layne. It won't happen again," he sputtered.

West threatened the other guard with his Taser. "And what about you?"

"I'm sorry, sir. We were out of line."

West and I passed through the open doorway. When it closed, I grabbed his arm, prompting him to look at me. "Was that really necessary?"

"Yes. And not only for the reason you think." His clenched jaw softened, and he breathed a heavy sigh. He glanced over my shoulder. Two nurses stood far enough away that they wouldn't hear our hushed voices. "There's a shifting of power happening inside New Caelum, and not just since Willow's illness, I've felt this building for a while now. I don't know what's going on, but I know I can't let the guards think they can walk all over me."

I analyzed the determination on his face, and I hoped he had enough resolve in his heart to be the leader the people of New Caelum were going to need. Especially if they were facing an epidemic.

We walked up to what looked like a nurses' station. A lady and a man, both dressed in pale blue, stood at a computer. They had been staring our way when we entered, but had quickly turned away when we finally crossed the room.

"Good evening," West said.

"Good evening, Mr. Layne." The man gestured with his hand out. "Your sister is right this way."

The two nurses must have witnessed what had transpired at the door, because neither of them even looked my way.

"You know the rules. You may stand out here, but you may not enter the isolation chamber. If you do enter the isolation chamber, you will stay in there until you die."

Harsh. I guessed the nurses wouldn't believe me if I told them that neither of us could contract the virus.

"That's fine," West conceded. "We just want to see her. How is she doing?" West tried to continue to sound official, but his voice cracked just slightly when asking about his sister's well-being.

"I'm sorry, Mr. Layne, but she's not doing well at all. In the last twenty-four hours, she has suffered multiple seizures and her kidneys have nearly shut down. She is in severe pain, and she is starting to display lesions on her torso."

My eyes closed involuntarily as I fought back tears. No one knew the severity of pain Willow was in like I did.

"What are you doing to help her?"

"Unfortunately, we can't do much. She's receiving fluids, antibiotics, and the highest dose of pain medicine we can give her. We're monitoring her blood pressure and oxygen levels. As she loses blood, we replenish it."

We reached the window to Willow's chamber, and the nurse left us alone with a nod.

West leaned against the railing and peered inside. Willow appeared to be sleeping peacefully. Two more nurses were with her; one stood by the door while another looked to be jotting down readings onto a chart.

I slid my hand over West's, letting my fingers slide between his. "I'm sorry," I whispered.

"How did she contract Bad Sam in the first place?" West asked without turning away from his sister. He lifted his hand, adjusting his grip on mine, and squeezed tighter. "No one was more aware of the risks than she was."

"What do you mean?" I asked.

"Even though I'm the one who's next in line to run New Caelum, Willow has always taken it upon herself to learn everything there is to know about preventing future outbreaks—of Bad Sam, or of any other infectious disease. She likes to think up horrible scenarios and then come up with reaction plans for the city. I think it makes her feel more in control, knowing that whatever happens, she has a plan for it. She even has a plan for if we ever decide to allow citizens to venture out of the city."

I wondered what would happen to this city if they opened up their walls and allowed people to pass freely in and out. Worse, I wondered what would happen to my own community. I couldn't imagine people on the outside being accepting of such a scenario.

"How, after six years of complete eradication, did Bad Sam manage to return? In a city that was specifically designed, from the ground up, to *prevent* its return? And how, of all people, did my sister become the first one to contract this—this death sentence?" His voice cracked again.

"You know how," I said. And I didn't bother to remind him that Willow wasn't the first—just the first he'd heard about.

Slowly, he met my gaze. "They gave this to her." He knew this already. His mother had suggested it; I had suggested it. But perhaps now was the first time he really believed it.

I nodded. "Most likely." But who was "they"? And was that the only possible scenario?

"Who?"

"I don't know enough about what's going on inside the city, but New Caelum doesn't seem to be the utopia Justin and President Layne want everyone to believe it is. When the people in the lower sectors learn that the virus is back, this place is going to implode."

"No it won't," West argued. "The people of New Caelum have been kept healthy and safe by my mother and the rest of the government. They would never rise up against us."

He said "us" with warning in his voice, as if he were already one of the higher-ups. I pulled my hand from his and backed away a step. "And yet, someone with access to the virus—which was undoubtedly stored somewhere in your medical laboratories for the last six years—has now exposed several people to the disease. Do I need to remind you that your best friends are also lying in *my* hospital right now? Or that two other New Caelum residents who left your city the same night you did also appeared to have contracted the virus? Not that we'll ever know for sure, seeing as your guards gunned them down inside your own walls."

I didn't bother bringing up the fact that two other trucks had also left that night, and that we still had no idea what had happened to them. "Something is going on inside your city, West. If you're truly in line to govern, you probably ought to find out who had access to samples of Bad Sam."

~~~~~

It was near midnight when West and I returned to the Presidential Suite. He led me down a short hallway, opened one of the doors, and gestured for me to enter. "This is our guest room. You'll find everything you need in here."

The room was lavishly appointed, with way more than I needed or was used to. After taking it in, I turned back to West. His eyes were bloodshot and a V had formed between his eyes, telling me he was analyzing something. "What are you thinking?"

He shook his head and peered beyond me, refusing to make eye contact. "I don't know. I just can't help but think how well everything was going just last week. My friends were doing well in their new positions. Ryder and Key had been matched..." West's voice dropped off with the last word, and he squeezed the bridge of his nose. Maybe he hadn't meant to reveal something.

"Matched?"

West did look at me then. His face drooped even further. "They've been in love forever. But Ryder had been assigned to serve on the leadership staff—to serve me—which meant his future wife had to be approved."

"But they're so young to be getting... matched."

"The people of New Caelum decided a long time ago that they would see to it that the human race would thrive and grow. Because Bad Sam wiped out so much of the population, many believe we'll be stronger by reproducing more quickly. So they match us as soon as we have a career path, which typically happens around seventeen or eighteen."

I squeezed the pressure point on my wrist. I could feel my own pulse racing beneath my fingers. New Caelum was attempting to control every aspect of their people's lives, down to whom they procreated with. "Matched," I repeated as if I was testing the concept.

West was staring at me like he was trying to figure something out. I narrowed my gaze as I asked the question that hung between us like a dark curtain.

"Have you been matched?"

As soon as the words left my mouth, I backed up a step and threw my hand up. "No. Please don't answer that. Forget I even asked."

What good could possibly have come from me knowing that information? I was not a resident of New Caelum, and never would be. And West always would be.

And I didn't think I could possibly handle knowing that West was promised to someone else.

"Cricket." He followed me further into the room, closing the door behind him. Everything was eerily quiet. "I need you to understand something."

I raised my hand as he got nearer. "Don't."

His chest met my palm, but he continued forward until very little space was between us. He wrapped his fingers around mine and squeezed. "Don't what?" With his other hand, he traced the line of my hair down my cheek, grazing the skin all the way to my neck.

My heart beat wildly, and everything I had been thinking about my mission while inside New Caelum vanished. "I don't need to understand the rules and assignments... or the matchings... that go on inside your world."

He leaned his forehead against mine while sliding his hand to the back of my neck and massaging the tired muscles there. As much as I knew I should pull away, I didn't. "You're wrong," he whispered. "But we don't need to discuss it now."

He tilted his head, and when his lips found mine, it was as if the entire world fell away. I knew with every part of my being that I should put a stop to what was happening between us, but I couldn't. He was what had been missing from my life.

After a brief but passionate kiss, he released me and backed away a step. "Try to get some sleep."

He turned and left me standing there wondering what had just happened—what kept happening. I touched my lips, where the tingling lingered, as I willed the fog in my head to dissipate.

I gave West a few seconds' head start before I cracked the door from my guest room to see where he went. I barely caught a glimpse of his back as he exited the suite. I tried to follow him, but when I opened the door to leave, the guards turned and informed me that it was not safe for me to be outside of my assigned quarters, and that West would return shortly.

I glanced around at the immaculate and orderly living quarters of the most powerful leader left in the country—the only leader who'd had enough foresight to construct an enclosed city to contain and protect the richest and most elite people in the world. New Caelum had been pitched as a sort of Noah's Ark—but instead of protecting its inhabitants from a flood, it protected them from a deadly virus that swept the nation.

But the world's most powerful leader—President Layne— did not appear to be the same woman I remembered from when I was a child. The woman I had known was a figure to be reckoned with, in control of everything around her. She didn't accept "no" when she needed a "yes." Those who worked for her never crossed her if they wanted to keep their jobs. But she was also kind enough that in the rare instances when someone did defy her, they almost always regretted it afterward and sought forgiveness.

The woman who had eaten dinner with us tonight was not the same woman who had put herself in charge of saving humankind. And by the look on West's face during dinner, he, too, knew she wasn't herself. Which meant the change was recent. Had something happened to change her while West was on the outside?

And then there was Justin Rhodes, vice president to President Layne. He was clearly the real power in New Caelum. What was his story? And what was going on between him and West? On several occasions already, West had looked like he could have gone a couple of rounds with Justin—although so far he'd succeeded in showing restraint.

I returned to the guest room. The queen-sized bed was piled high with six pillows and a down comforter. Under different circumstances, I would have loved to have crawled into that luxurious bed and not have come out for days, but right now, sleep was the last thing on my mind.

I checked out the closets and dresser, and found them packed to the gills with clothing, mostly in the same shade of rich blue that I'd worn to dinner. In the back of one closet— there were three altogether—was a dress, in sapphire blue, that glittered with sequins and jewels. It was the loveliest dress I'd ever seen. And everything was in exactly my size.

Wait. Everything was in my size?

A sudden sensation of nausea had me grabbing at my stomach. I swallowed hard against a watering mouth. How could they have been ready with so many clothes that would fit me? I looked down at the shoes. They, too, fit me perfectly— and I had unusually small feet. It was as if they had *expected* me.

And the color, everything in this same royal blue... what did that mean?

I left the guest room behind and decided to explore the rest of the suite. Out in the hallway, all the doors were closed. I assumed that one of these was President Layne's bedroom— and West had said that she had already turned in for the night, so I tried to be as quiet as I could as I turned the knob of the door closest to mine.

Behind the door was what had to be West's room. His walls and bed were covered in dark paint and fabric, and his open closet was filled with nothing but charcoal and black clothing.

Colors definitely meant something here inside New Caelum. The dark gray and black clothing seemed to be the color of choice for the top-level executives, including West.

I hadn't seen anyone else wearing sapphire blue yet.

I didn't want to poke around in West's room, so I continued down to the very end of the hallway and again opened the door cautiously and quietly. It was a good thing I did, too—this was the door to President Layne's bedroom, and she was inside, sleeping with her back to the door.

I softly closed the door and moved on to the only other door in the hall—which led me to Willow's room. And this room was a dream. A four-poster bed was covered in all-white fabric, with curtains draped along its corners. Large white tree branches were painted on pale gray walls. For a splash of color, hot pink pillows sat in the middle of the bed, and larger hot pink pillows had been arranged in one corner to form some kind of reading nook. Willow's name was painted in a large scrolling font above her headboard.

Unlike the guest room, which had only necessary clothes and toiletries (though still far more than I could ever imagine needing), this room looked lived in. Willow had an extensive collection of books, a computer, and a jewelry box of necklaces, earrings, and bracelets. It was a room filled with both memories and... well, *things*. The kinds of things those of us on the outside hadn't bothered with for the past six years. When I opened her closet, I was only mildly surprised to find all charcoal and black clothes, just like in West's closet.

Unlike me and West, Willow had a window, and I crossed the room to take in her view. The suite was higher up than I had thought, and as I looked out at the mountains surrounding New Caelum, I was able to pick out the faint outline of *my* forest of trees in the darkness.

I reached up and ran my fingers along the cold glass. I couldn't help but wonder what my life would have been like if I had never left New Caelum—had never gotten to know the freedom of exploring that forest. Would I, too, have a closet full of dark clothes instead of royal blue? Would I still live here with the Laynes, or would I have been demoted to a lower class—as an orphan? After all, my parents apparently demanded even less respect than the lowest of the classes inside New Caelum, seeing as how they were sentenced to live out their lives in exile in another country—and probably died there.

I didn't get to wonder about a life inside New Caelum for long, because a shrill-sounding alarm broke the silence and caused my heart to leap into my throat. I turned and stared at Willow's closed door. Was the alarm because of me—because I wasn't in my room?

I took a step toward the door, intending to hurry back to the guest room, but as I did, I noticed the corner of a box sticking out from under the bed, and my curiosity got the better of me. Bending down, I slid the box out from under the bed and lifted the lid, revealing a quilt. A keepsake, maybe? Or just an extra bedcover for when Willow got cold. I didn't know why, but I found myself lifting the quilt and rubbing the soft fabric against my face. It reminded me of a blanket I'd had as a baby—one Mom had made for me.

Underneath the quilt were some old clothes. And unlike every other set of clothes in this place, they actually came in varying colors: white, pale blue, green, red, and the color of oatmeal. I was going to investigate these as well, but voices in the suite outside stopped me. I quickly patted the clothes down and stuffed the quilt inside the box, then pushed the box back under the bed, further this time, so the corner didn't stick out.

I hurried to the door and opened it slowly. The alarm was even more obnoxious in the hallway. I now recognized the voices as Justin's and West's; they sounded like they were in the living room, where we'd had dinner earlier.

I slipped out of Willow's room quietly. My door was just down the hall, but unlike Willow's door, mine was within view of the living room, so I doubted I could slip in without being noticed.

Then again, what was I even afraid of? Snooping was wrong, I supposed, but it wasn't like I'd left the suite, and no one had told me the other rooms were off-limits.

I closed Willow's door softly behind me and walked down the hallway. Sure enough, Justin and West were in the living room, and now they were screaming at each other—though maybe they were just trying to be heard over the alarm.

"I don't know why he's here, Justin." West held his hands out to the side, making himself appear bigger. "But my advice? Take him seriously. If you hurt him, Christina will never cooperate with you."

My pulse sped up, and I took a few more steps into the room. "Who's here?"

They hadn't even heard my approach. Both of their heads rotated toward me.

The alarm stopped—mercifully—and a guard appeared. "We've shut off the alarm in the executive wing of the building, Mr. Rhodes. As soon as we've confirmed that no other outsiders have infiltrated the space around New Caelum, we'll turn off the alarm everywhere."

"Very good. And the young man has been properly restrained?"

"Yes, sir."

West stared at me, his lips tugged downward. I cocked my head, studying his pleading eyes. He wanted to tell me something.

"Who's here?" I asked.

I spoke directly to West, but it was Justin who answered. "Apparently you have a knight in shining armor."

I kept my face completely emotionless. "Since I know for a fact that no such thing exists, why don't you tell me what you're talking about?"

"A boy who calls himself Dax made a ruckus outside our gates tonight."

I couldn't stop the gasp that escaped my lips. Dax was alive. And that meant he wasn't sick like his brother. But why would he come here?

"Did you hurt him?"

Justin's lips twitched upward. "Of course not. The boy started screaming about having some information regarding the virus, and said that killing him would result in dire consequences for the people of New Caelum. What does he mean by that, Christina? Is this boy threatening us?"

I shrugged. "I have no idea."

"Well, he's asking for you. Made a pretty strong argument for getting what he wants. Says that 'the mechanism you ordered from Zara' is in place."

My breathing sped up. By "mechanism," Dax meant bomb. I was partly relieved, but also terrified. I felt confident I could get myself out of this prison, but now I would have to save Dax as well.

"Justin," West said finally, his eyes glued to mine. "You gave me a directive earlier this evening, and I aim to fulfill it. Cricket is my responsibility. Right now, I'd like to take her to Dax. That's the only way we'll find out what he wants to tell us."

Justin glanced sideways at West. "Fine. But it's late. It can wait until morning. We'll have tested Dax for Bad Sam and decontaminated him by then. I'll be back first thing to have breakfast with you and your mother."

At that, Justin left. And West simply stood there staring at me.

I let out a breath I'd been holding. I had to believe that Dax would be okay.

"Did you mean what you said in your note?" West asked. His brown hair was disheveled; this had been a very long, tiring day for him as well.

"What?" My voice was barely above a whisper as I thought back to every single word I'd written to him. Of course I had meant it.

"Did you mean what you wrote to me? That in another life you would have loved that I had found you?"

"Why are you asking this?" I averted my gaze, looking toward the windows on the far side of the room—looking for an escape. I couldn't tell him what I was feeling. That I craved the feeling of his arms around me. That I had actually slept more soundly that one frigid night in the forest than I had in years.

I took a deep breath and turned my eyes back to his. Hazel in color, his irises were outlined in black. His clothes, dark with significance, brought out the brilliance of his eyes. And right now, those eyes were pleading with me.

"In another life... we would have had a chance," I said.

"We have a chance now."

I narrowed my eyes. "What are you talking about?"

West grabbed my elbow and pulled me down the hallway with a sense of urgency, but not in a scary way. He passed the guest room and led me through the door to his bedroom. After closing the door, he walked quickly to his bedside table and picked up what looked like some sort of remote control. He pushed a few buttons, and music poured out of speakers in two high corners of the room.

Then he walked toward me and leaned in close to my ear, his breath hot across my cheek. "They're listening to our every word, but the music will drown out our voices if we whisper."

I glanced up at him as his fingers circled around my wrist. "Is Dax okay?"

"He'll be fine. Justin is scared about something, but I don't know what. I found him having a serious conversation with Dr. Pooley earlier. You haven't met him, yet. He represents the medical sector on the council, and is Willow's doctor. They were examining the box you brought. The one with the clock on it."

I tried to pull back, but West held on tight. His other hand slid to the small of my back, pressing firmly and bringing my body closer, if that was possible. "I need you to be honest with me," he whispered. "What is that box? And does it have anything to do with what Dax was talking about?"

I decided it was time to play my hand, to find out just who West really was and what I truly meant to him. One way or the other, my insurance policy was in place. I'd either have West's help, or I wouldn't.

I tilted my head back so that I could see his eyes. Though I knew eyes could lie, it was unlikely that I would misread the initial reaction on his face. "The mechanism that Dax is reporting as 'in place'... It's a bomb. The timer is the countdown."

West's face remained stoic at first. His eyes widened just slightly, then his cheeks dropped a bit. "What do you mean? It's obviously too small to do too much damage."

"It's not that kind of bomb."

....

chapter twenty-eight

West

"What kind of bomb is it, then?" I studied Cricket's face, looking for any clue as to what she was plotting. But as her eyes remained fixed on mine, unchanging, I suspected that I—and even more so, Justin—had underestimated the people surviving outside of New Caelum. I knew for certain that I had underestimated Cricket's ability to take care of herself once she got inside my city.

"If I'm not released from New Caelum before that clock hits zero, your computerized air purification system will be disabled, and several vials of the virus will be released into your ventilation system—into the air your people breathe." Cricket looked down at my hand on her arm, then back at me, her gaze severe.

I didn't realize until that moment that I had a monstrous grip around her elbow. I let my fingers slip away, but kept my hand pressed to the small of her back, not wanting to let her go. "How could you possibly have built a bomb that would do that?"

Cricket explained the sophisticated bomb and computer virus that was designed to cripple New Caelum, and how she and Zara had used our own state-of-the-art system to do it. I wasn't sure if I was angry or turned on by her tenacious self-preservation strategy, but the heat building beneath my palm on her back didn't do anything to calm the blood flowing through my veins. She was threatening to kill the very people my mom aimed to protect—people I was meant to protect.

"Say something," she said. Her voice echoed through what seemed like a long underground tunnel.

My mind raced around the many scenarios. Was she insane? "Are you so angry about being forced to live outside of New Caelum that you want everyone inside New Caelum to suffer the way you did?"

"What? No." She tried to pull away again, but I wouldn't let her. "Let me go, West."

"No." We had to have this talk or I would never know the truth. I didn't want to spend another minute the way I had spent the last six years—not knowing about the fate of my first love. "I need to know. Why did you come here? What did you hope to accomplish? Do you and the other outsiders not even care about what happens to us inside?"

Her back tensed and her eyes widened. A laugh escaped her lips. "Ha! Pot, meet kettle."

"Okay, I deserved that. But Cricket, what is this? Some sort of revenge mission?"

"Please understand." Her gaze remained intense.

"I'm trying to," I said quickly.

"I was entering a city virtually unknown to me without any way to defend myself. And I'd already experienced what you and your people do to people like me when you don't get your way."

I squeezed my eyes, remembering how I'd tasered her to the point that she fell unconscious.

"And I have no intention of being held prisoner inside New Caelum," she continued. "That bomb is simply leverage—the only thing I could think of to ensure I have a way back out. If things go badly, I need Justin to believe I would sabotage your perfect little utopia. You people already think we're savages, so I'm sure he won't doubt me. But West, I want you to believe me: the last thing I want is for anyone to get this terrible virus. As long as Justin and President Layne cooperate, I'll make sure the mechanism to scramble your air filtration system is deactivated, and that the virus bomb is destroyed."

When I opened my eyes, her eyes were still locked on mine. "So you didn't come here to destroy New Caelum." I said.

"You know I didn't. I came to find a cure for Bad Sam, to stop it before it spreads again. I want your sister to see another birthday. I don't want your friends Ryder and Key to suffer and die. I want to save Dylan. I came for you."

My heart constricted. I was accusing her of so many things, yet I was discovering that I was very wrong about her heart. "And you'd risk your entire future to come inside New Caelum so that you could save them."

Cricket stopped fighting me. The muscles in her back relaxed. She lifted her hand and touched my cheek. "No one deserves to suffer the way I did. I risked my future to make sure your sister would have one."

"If that bomb should detonate and Bad Sam breaks out among my people..."

"It won't. And besides, this is an opportunity for your city to prove they can work with those of us on the outside."

She had a point. Wasn't that what I wanted eventually? To merge the citizens of New Caelum with those on the outside? Wouldn't it be easier to do that if key people on both sides found a way to work together?

I covered her hand with my palm and leaned my face into her touch. As I stared into her eyes, I couldn't imagine letting her walk away from New Caelum again. From me.

"I think I'm falling in love with you."

The words were out of my mouth before I could stop them. Instead of locking her up with Dax, like I should have after hearing about this bomb, I was confessing my true feelings for her.

Her entire body stiffened beneath my touch. "Don't say that."

"Why?" I whispered.

The muscles moved in her throat as she swallowed hard. "I would rather die than go through the pain of that disease again. But I'd also rather die than be confined inside the suffocating walls of this city. That's not going to change." She looked away, hiding her eyes from me.

"You not wanting to live inside this city with me doesn't change how I feel. Or how I know you feel."

"I can't, West."

"You don't have to admit your feelings to me. Not yet. But you will... eventually. For now, we'll play it your way."

She looked up at me through a veil of dark lashes, evidence of her once-dark brown hair. "I will not stay in this city, West. No matter what I'm feeling."

My lips twitched knowingly. I hated that she felt like my city was a prison, but given how she had been treated since she'd arrived, I couldn't blame her. "I will help you," I said.

She lifted a brow.

"Under one condition," I added.

"What is that?"

I leaned in close to her ear again, attempting to keep our conversation private and taking in her sweet scent. "Justin wants me to convince you to stay inside New Caelum. You have to give me the chance to at least try. Or at least look like you're giving me a chance."

She pulled back with a raised brow. "What do I have to do?"

"I need you to act like my charm is working when we're in front of Justin and my mother, or anytime we're in public. I can't stop this feeling that Justin, Mother, and the council are planning my future but haven't bothered to tell me about it."

Not to mention that one of them was behind the Bad Sam outbreak. And I was going to figure out who.

~~~~~

Cricket was dressed in a different sapphire dress the next morning. Picking at a plate of eggs and bacon, she sat with Justin and Mother at the dining room table. When I entered, she set her fork down and placed her napkin beside her plate. I gave my head a little shake, warning her not to get up. She sighed silently in response.

She was ready to see Dax and was not going to be very patient about it.

But after our talk last night, she'd have to practice a little self-restraint. We had to make Justin and the others believe

237

that Cricket was considering a life inside New Caelum—force them to let their guard down where that was concerned.

"Good morning." I leaned over and kissed Mother on her cheek.

"Morning, Westlin," she responded, her voice curt. "You will meet with me later this morning to discuss how to handle food distribution on the south side of New Caelum." Mother sounded more like her old self, the person she was before Willow had come down with Bad Sam. Justin didn't even look up from the news screen on his PulsePoint. He was rapidly swiping through the morning's headlines.

I walked the length of the table, grazing Cricket's shoulder as I passed her. Anything to touch her. When I glanced back at Mother, I saw her staring at Cricket. Something was definitely different about Mother compared to the previous night. She seemed more... normal, maybe.

I grabbed a piece of toast and some bacon. Premium meat, like bacon, was only available to the highest class of citizens within New Caelum. There simply wasn't enough to spread throughout the city.

"Cricket, how did you sleep last night?" Mother asked.

"Fine, President Layne."

"Mother, how is Willow this morning?" I asked, drawing her attention away from Cricket.

She looked across the table at me, her eyes ice cold. "She's in critical condition and in need of a cure." She turned back to Cricket. "Cricket, how close was Caine to a cure to the virus?"

Cricket cleared her throat. "Well, we *thought* he was close."

"What do you mean?"

"He treated some infected rats, and it was going well. They seemed to be getting better, but just before I came here, the last of the rats that we thought had a chance at survival died." Cricket's face fell, and I knew it was not only because they'd failed to find a cure, but because she hated that they were forced to experiment on the rats.

Mother's lips pressed into a thin line. "I see."

"I'm truly sorry about Willow, ma'am. I would like the opportunity to help Dr. Hempel in the lab. I'll do anything I can to make sure your daughter finds relief."

Mother set her coffee cup back on the matching saucer, letting the ceramic pieces clank together. "Why have you pretended to be someone other than Christina Black?"

I moved to the edge of my seat and almost stood to defend Cricket, but she swallowed hard, rotated her shoulders back, and faced Mother. "President Layne, I have not meant to offend you or the memory I have of you helping me when I was twelve. I only meant to protect myself."

Cricket was nicer about it than I would have been. I didn't understand what had gotten into my mother. I was glad she wasn't the person she'd been last night, but—had she always been this direct and cold?

I guessed that maybe she had. Perhaps I had just never thought about what her tough exterior might look like to the outside world. The people on the inside knew of the sacrifices she'd made to keep them safe.

"Well, I thank you for coming to my daughter's aid," Mother said. "And I know that West was more than pleased to hear that you were alive."

I couldn't believe Mother could say that so plainly, without even acknowledging that she was the one who'd led me to believe that Cricket was dead in the first place. "What the hell, Mother? Of course I was pleased—you'd led me to believe that my best friend had died of the most painful disease ever known to man!"

I stood, letting my napkin fall to the ground. Mother simply stared at me, her mouth agape. I moved closer to Cricket.

"We're going now. Cricket and I have a lot to do today, including checking in on Dr. Hempel." How I could possibly make finding a cure to history's most deadly disease sound like such a mundane item on our to-do list was beyond me.

Cricket pushed away from the table, and I grabbed her hand and pulled her toward the door. The guards stepped aside when we approached, letting us pass without incident, but two of them followed us as we headed in the direction of the detention center, where the city detained lawbreakers.

Fifteen minutes later, after passing through several aboveground tunnels, we arrived at a complex south of the government officials' quarters and stopped in front of a nondescript door. I noticed Cricket taking several deep breaths.

"You okay?" I asked.

She pulled her hand from my grasp. "Yes." She looked up at me, pleading with eyes that matched her deep blue dress. "Would it be too much to ask to let me talk to Dax alone?"

My heart sank a little. There was something between Dax and Cricket. He wasn't just protective of her—there was more. And she, too, seemed to have feelings beyond simple friendship for him.

"The guards aren't going to allow you to speak to Dax by yourself, Cricket. That's not within my control." And if it were, I wouldn't have allowed it anyway.

She stared at the door. "It's fine. Let's just go in."

....

chapter twenty-nine

Cricket

I entered the holding room ahead of West and stopped abruptly when I saw Dax. "Oh my gosh, Dax!" His face looked like it had been used as a punching bag.

He was seated at a plain table, and stood when he saw me. His metal chair scraped against the floor. He nervously wiped his hands on his pants as he circled the table to meet me. For a moment his face brightened, and he opened his arms like he was about to embrace me, but then he saw West behind me and his expression faltered, his arms returning to his side.

I ran the few steps to him anyway. He slipped an arm around my back and hugged me briefly. I pulled back, letting my hand hover over his bruised cheek and busted bottom lip. Clearly, Dax had not received the same treatment I had. His left eye was swollen and circled in dark red, which mixed with the beginnings of a deep bruise running from his nose and across his cheekbone. Dried blood decorated his split lip. However, he was clean. I was sure he had been forced to take a decontamination shower and had been subjected to a complete physical and blood tests.

I glared at West. "Is this how New Caelum treats their guests?"

West shrugged. "New Caelum doesn't receive guests. No one from the outside has ever entered the walls of New Caelum since they were closed off. Until now."

Dax had yet to say anything. I hugged him again, laying my head against his chest. "I'm sorry I pushed you away. I hated to hurt you. I just wanted you to be safe."

He smoothed my hair. "Are you okay? They haven't hurt you, have they?"

I shook my head, looking up at him. "Dylan?"

That's when he backed away. His lips tugged downward. "He's really sick, Crick. I don't think he's going to make it." He redirected his gaze to West and scowled. "And your two friends..." His voice lowered, harsh and gruff. "They're even worse. They're bleeding from open sores and from their eyes."

Dax's voice lacked compassion, and he curved his fingers into fists at his side. "New Caelum did this to my brother. They used two of their own people as weapons. And now they've sentenced them, and my brother, to die."

Dax tried to step around me, but I threw my body in front of him. "Look at me," I said, grabbing his face and directing it toward mine. I knew West wasn't responsible for the virus spreading. "The doctor here, the one Caine sent me to see, is working on a treatment. Caine says this doctor is the best."

Dax's face fell even further, if that was possible. "I've got a message from Caine. He told me not to tell anyone but you." He stared around me to West.

"The guards won't allow it," West said behind me.

Dax nodded, though he looked disappointed. "Fine. The guards can be in the room, but West goes."

I turned to West. He squared his shoulders, preparing for an argument.

"Give me two minutes," I pleaded. "That's all I need."

Anger flashed across his face, but he relented. "Fine. But if he hurts you in any way, the guards will—"

"What? Kill me?" Dax said in a whisper, purposely keeping his voice out of earshot of the guards. "I got that message loud and clear when your people shot at Zara and me a couple of days ago." He put an arm around me and pulled me in closer, in a somewhat possessive hold. "I'm the last person who's going to hurt her."

West held up two fingers. His jaw was set in rigid lines. "Two minutes."

I nodded.

When West was gone, I led Dax over to the only two chairs in the room. We sat, and Dax held both of my hands while he stared straight into my eyes. "Caine said to tell you that there's a problem with some of the antibody samples. The earlier samples had higher concentrations of antibodies than the ones he took more recently. He said you'd know what that meant."

I stared blankly at Dax while I digested the information, processing it for the truth it revealed. If what he was saying was true, my blood was becoming less and less useful as a treatment for the virus. "Did he say which samples I have with me?"

"He said that some of the samples you've delivered to New Caelum should do the job."

But future samples might not. In other words, I might no longer be protected against Bad Sam.

"What does all this mean, Cricket? I'm so scared for my brother. And for you."

I leaned in and wrapped my arms around Dax while fighting back tears. I couldn't let him see how much this news upset me. "It's going to be okay. I'm not sure what it means, exactly," I lied. As tears threatened to burn my eyes, I hugged him tighter. "I'm sorry they hurt you."

He pulled back. "How do we get you out of here?"

"I can't leave yet—not until we find the cure Dylan needs. Dr. Hempel has better equipment than Caine. He might be our only hope."

"What can I do to help?"

"I'm not sure." I touched his cheek, but he grabbed my hand and began rubbing it between his palms. "Is Zara okay?" I asked.

"Yeah, she's fine. The New Caelum goons shot at us as we fled the outer gate. One bullet went through her coat, but it only grazed her arm. She's pretty pissed though."

"At the New Caelum goons or at me?"

"Both."

I chuckled. Though Zara and I hardly ever got along, she knew I didn't mean her harm. "I'll make it up to her."

West cleared his throat behind us, letting us know he was back.

I squeezed Dax's hands. "I'll come back soon. We only have two more days before Dr. Hempel is out of time. The executives here don't know what the time clock means yet. I was trying not to cause a panic. But if the people of New Caelum know what's good for them, you and I will walk out of this place before that clock hits zero. And we simply have to have faith that we'll have enough time left to save Dylan."

I stood and was about to walk away when Dax grabbed my forearm. "Be straight with me. Who is West to you? Are you *with* him?" He nodded toward West, who could clearly hear him.

I wished Dax could take those questions back, but I knew he couldn't. How could I explain just how complicated my relationship with West was?

"We have to go," West said behind me.

My silence was all the answer Dax needed.

~~~~~

The guards who had trailed us here followed us again. I couldn't breathe. I stopped and placed my hands on a wall, keeping my back to West.

Dax's words echoed inside my head. The antibodies to Bad Sam that flowed through my blood were weakening. Maybe surviving Bad Sam didn't guarantee immunity forever. It wasn't like we knew everything about this virus, and we certainly didn't have any long-term studies on survivors, seeing as I was the only one.

West placed a hand on my shoulder. "What did he tell you?"

I took in a deep breath, willing my pulse to slow. When I thought I'd be able to speak with a calm voice, I turned and faced West. "You either let him go, or you put him somewhere more comfortable and instruct your goons not to touch him again."

West opened his mouth to say something, stopped himself, then started again. "I'll talk to Justin."

"Do you want to know why I left New Caelum when I was twelve? The real reason?"

"I've been wondering about that ever since I found you again."

"I didn't want to live in a city where a person is protected and cared for based on how much money they have, or the importance of the knowledge they hold."

West cocked his head. "What are you talking about? That's not true."

"It *is* true. The people of New Caelum were only allowed inside because they had enough money to buy their way in—or because they had power, or some special skill needed to sustain a city of people that may never venture back outside. Oh, and of course they included a handful of peasants to cook, clean, and serve them."

"That's not fair. It all happened so fast. Our country was dying. Makeshift hospitals were popping up everywhere, trying to save people. No, not save—they could only make the sick comfortable as they died. There was nowhere to hide, and humanity was dying off. My mother and the other leaders of this country made hard decisions, but they did it in order to save humankind. They had the foresight and wisdom to create a place where they could shut out the deadly virus. They couldn't let just anyone in."

A hysterical laugh escaped my lips. "Do you *hear* yourself? 'Couldn't let just anyone in?' Our country was dying, and the smartest medical professionals, scientists, and engineers in the world, along with the most powerful politicians in our country, turned their backs on the world, right when their skills were needed the most. Sure, New Caelum saved a chosen few, but they abandoned the rest—just closed their doors and let them die. They turned their backs on the brave people who were actually trying to *do* something, actually out there trying to *help*. People like my parents."

"I'm sorry about your parents. Mother was always sorry about your parents."

"I left because I couldn't bear to see your mother every day for the rest of my life. And Caine gave me a way out."

"What do you mean?"

"Caine and your mother were friends. They knew each other from back when they worked together at the Raleigh Medical Center. Your mother was on some sort of presidential cabinet out of Washington, but she traveled to Raleigh. Caine was on the original governing board to form New Caelum as soon as the Centers for Disease Control predicted that Bad Sam would be near one hundred percent fatal. But something made him decide not to be a part of New Caelum. And when he found out I was sick, he offered to take me with him. Your mother allowed it."

West was silent, gazing into the distance.

"What is it?" I asked.

"Nothing... I don't know... There was something my mom said when she told me you were gone. I can't remember..." He gave his head a little shake. "We need to go. We need to check in on Dr. Hempel. And then later, you and I have plans."

I cocked my head.

"I've been ordered to convince you to stay within New Caelum. You promised to let me try."

I groaned. There was no way I was staying inside this cold, sterile place. On the other hand, I really wanted to learn how the city operated. "You'll make sure Dax is well taken care of?"

"Yes."

"Fine. I'd like you to show me around New Caelum. After we see Dr. Hempel."

chapter thirty

....

West

I dropped Cricket at the labs and made sure she was suited up securely inside the best hazmat gear New Caelum had to offer. She'd seemed more jittery than usual ever since she'd had her two-minute talk with Dax. Considering she was immune to the deadly disease we all feared, she seemed awfully nervous about entering the laboratory wing.

I held her shoulders, urging her to look at me. "You okay?"

She nodded. "Just hoping he's made progress."

We both looked toward the clock on the other side of the lab. Though I now knew what the countdown was really for, I also knew that it was a conservative estimate of the time left before the virus took my sister's life.

Less than two days.

"I'll be back as soon as I can," I said. "I promised I would meet with Justin and Mother this morning."

Cricket nodded, then entered the labs, where she joined a growing number of doctors and medical staff. Dr. Pooley, my sister's doctor, stood beside Dr. Hempel. Was it a good sign that Dr. Hempel seemed to be bringing in reinforcements?

My PulsePoint pinged at my side—a message from Mother: "West, get back to the suite immediately."

Cricket was watching over the doctors' shoulders as they talked. I wanted to stay; I hated to leave her here without me. But Mother was a force not to be ignored.

I left the medical center and headed back toward home, taking the long way. I'd always enjoyed detouring through New Caelum's indoor gardens, where our vegetables and fruit were manufactured with incredible greenhouse and chemical technologies.

As I walked through the greens section—spinach, lettuce of all kinds, kale, mustard greens—on the lower level, I heard my name. I turned to find Mrs. Canary running toward me. She was dressed in bright yellows and greens, the colors of the earth and the sun, in keeping with her job in Agriculture and Food Production. She was one of the city's highest-ranking workers in that sector, in charge of monitoring all activity within our gardens, and until recently, she had represented the Agriculture sector on the council.

She was also Ryder's mother.

My heart fell to my stomach at the sight of her excitedly waving me down. "West, I'm glad I ran into you. I'm so sorry to hear your sister hasn't felt well. They're saying it was just the flu though, right?" The question was harmless, but she seemed to watch me closely. When I nodded, she smiled, but her hand on my forearm trembled. She was nervous about something. "What a relief. I'm praying for her quick recovery."

"Thank you, ma'am." Hearing my PulsePoint ping again, I started to turn, knowing it was Mother wondering where I was.

"West, before you go... Have you heard anything from Ryder? I haven't seen him in over a week. And since I'm no longer on the council..." Her face fell. I had never heard the full story of why Mrs. Canary had been removed from the council.

How was I supposed to tell this kind woman that her son was dying? That he, my sister, and Ryder's girlfriend all had Bad Sam, the deadly virus that had killed millions? And of course there was no way I could tell someone outside the leadership branch that New Caelum had sent representatives to scout the outside. Ryder wasn't even supposed to have been one of those scouts; it was Mother who had seen to it that he be added, after she'd learned of the mission.

"I'm so sorry, Mrs. Canary. I haven't seen him in a few days. You know Ryder, though—he's probably wrapped up in some high-security project. I'll find out for you."

"Thank you, dear." She squeezed my arm.

I eyed this woman who had been like a second mother to me, and curiosity got the best of me. "Mrs. Canary, why are you no longer on the council?"

Mrs. Canary turned rigid. She glanced right and left, looking to see if anyone was within earshot. "I can't talk council business with you, West. You know that."

"You're right. I'm sorry I made you uncomfortable," I said. Yet keeping my voice low, I continued, "Did you know that the council wanted to send scouts out into the settlements outside our city?"

She narrowed her gaze, letting her lips press into a thin line.

"I know," I said. "You can't talk about it. It's just, the council is putting pressure on me to become more involved, and I would have liked to have had a friendly face on the council. Someone I trusted."

Mrs. Canary looked around again. Workers were tending nearby crops and watering the plants. No one seemed to pay us any attention. "I can't tell you things that are talked about within the council, West. But since you *are* a member of the higher government, you should know that I've heard rumors recently."

I leaned in closer. "Mrs. Canary, I know you wouldn't repeat idle gossip."

Her eyes told me she was confirming that what others were spreading as gossip was in fact the truth. "I've heard that the council is desperate to produce a vaccine for Bad Sam. Most believe that the council would never allow their citizens to reenter the city after they've ventured into the outside world without being absolutely sure that they would not be bringing the virus back inside."

I nodded while processing what she was telling me. "And the only way to be absolutely sure is to vaccinate their citizens *before* they leave. How desperate is the council?"

She grabbed on to my arm. "I don't know. Like I said, that's only what I've heard on the outside. Hypothetically speaking though, I could never be a part of a council that would test possible vaccines on human subjects, then expose them to the virus to see if the vaccine worked."

I backed up a step and stared into the eyes of my best friend's mother. There was no deception there; just sorrow and anger.

I stared at her a few more seconds trying to reconcile what she was telling me.

My PulsePoint pinged again, startling me. "It's nice to see you." I tried to smile. Nothing I could do or say was going to reassure either of us that any of this was okay. "I'll let Ryder know to call you as soon as I see him."

"Okay, hon." She patted my hand. "And tell your mother hello for me. And that I would love to have tea with her again soon. Maybe she and I can finally talk about the big news she said she had for me." She gave me a warm smile, then turned and strolled away in the opposite direction.

My PulsePoint pinged a third time, and I turned and made my way to the elevators, heading straight up to see Mother.

When I entered the suite, she was alone, staring out the large window on the opposite side of the room.

"Why did the council send scouts out into the settlements against your wishes?" I asked. "And I know you didn't agree to that mission, like Justin wants me to believe."

"Don't start with me, West." She turned with one arm across her chest; the other held a glass of red wine. It wasn't even noon. "How are you doing with Christina?"

I wanted to talk to her about what I'd just learned from Mrs. Canary; but confronting her with that now was probably not the best way to go about things. Especially since I was fairly sure Justin was listening in on everything we said inside the suite. "I'm doing fine with Cricket, Mother. How are *you* doing with her?"

"I don't know what you mean."

"I think you do. You want her to join us here inside New Caelum, yet you know that *you're* the very reason she has no desire to do so."

"It's not my fault those parents of hers wouldn't listen. They had some wild theory about how to stop Bad Sam from killing its victims, but it apparently required them to return to *Africa*, of all places, to get more of... I don't know what. I honestly think they were insane by that point. We all nearly were. I wanted them to be here with us in New Caelum, West, I really did. But we simply couldn't wait for them. We had to shut down all international transportation. They knew, West. They knew we were shutting the doors. It was *their* decision not to be here. Not mine."

"Maybe you should tell this to Cricket."

"To what end? If I had thought it would help her, I would have told her long ago. But the way I see it, she's better off believing I'm at fault. This way she gets to hate me—instead of hating her own parents for deserting her."

Mother had a point. But she was also changing the subject.

"Fine. I didn't come here to talk about Cricket. I want to know why you're marrying Justin. What changed while I was out looking for Christina? I came back and you were a completely different person."

"Yes, I do apologize for that." She took another sip of wine. "Dr. Pooley gave me a sedative. I didn't react well to it."

"Okay, that explains why you were acting weird, but... Mother! Marrying *Justin*?"

She glanced nervously behind me, toward the door, then turned again toward the windows. "Sometimes, West, we must fulfill obligations for the greater good."

"What about Willow?"

"Willow is my motivation for everything I'm doing. With Christina's antibodies, Dr. Hempel will figure out a treatment."

"I ran into Ryder's mom. She said she'd like to have tea with you again soon."

Mother wordlessly walked to the liquor cabinet and poured herself another glass of wine.

"Are you even going to talk to her? She has no idea her son is dying."

"Ryder's mother will heal. In time, we'll make sure she knows that her son was a hero."

A knot formed in my stomach. I wasn't even sure I understood what our conversation was about anymore. "And Key? I suppose since she had no family, no one will miss her?" Could she even hear herself?

"Of course she'll be missed. She was on her way to becoming a wonderful doctor. She wasn't supposed to go with you. That must have been Ryder's doing. How were Ryder and Key even exposed to the virus?"

"You're asking *me*? How was *Willow* exposed?" I practically screamed it.

Mother swallowed a sip of wine and gave me a cold stare. "You will watch yourself, Westlin Layne. You are the hope for the next generation of New Caelum. You will be forced to make hard decisions in the future. A city of people will depend on you. That is why—"

She was interrupted by the sound of the door opening behind me. Justin entered. "Did you tell him yet?"

"I was just about to."

"Well, don't let me stop you." Justin waved a hand and proceeded to pour himself a drink. What was with these two drinking before we'd even had lunch?

"Westlin, I've decided to step down as president of New Caelum after Justin and I are married."

"What? Why?" I tried to put emotion behind my words, to pretend that the presidency mattered to me.

Mother hooked her hand around Justin's arm. "I've decided to be First Lady of New Caelum instead."

I couldn't possibly keep my mouth from hanging open. "Are you telling me that you're handing your presidency over to Justin? And the council has agreed to this?"

"That's right. And yes, they have," Justin declared. "And you will be my vice president."

At that, I choked on my own spit. "Are you crazy?"

"The people of New Caelum love you, West. And with Cricket by your side?"

"This is too much." I was beginning to understand their need for mind-altering substances from the liquor cabinet. I, however, vowed to do whatever I had to do to keep my wits about me. "I'm going to need time to consider this."

"Of course." Mother waved her hand, but somehow, I was pretty sure that in allowing me "time," she had in mind minutes—not the days, weeks, or even months I would need.

Cricket was going to flip out. She might accelerate her little bomb of viruses when she heard everything I'd learned in the past thirty minutes.

....

chapter thirty-one

Cricket

My hand trembled as I set a slide into the microscope for Dr. Hempel. "Have you slept?" My hand was shaking, and I was concerned about *his* lack of rest.

The strange doctor wouldn't look at me. "Three hours in the last forty-eight."

Through his mask, I could see that his eyes were watering. Beads of sweat pooled along his forehead. "Are you feeling okay?" I asked.

"Yes, fine. Why?"

"No reason." I glanced around the lab. Half a dozen people in hazmat suits—pale blue, unlike the white worn by Dr. Hempel and Dr. Pooley—were at work on various tasks. "Are all of these people working on a cure for the virus?"

"That, or at least a treatment. If we can help a person fight the secondary infections, keep vital organs from cannibalizing, we believe we can help some patients to survive. And that will provide us with even more antibodies to help us fight the disease more effectively in the future."

"What about the antibodies I brought with me?"

Dr. Hempel removed the slide he was studying and replaced it with another. "Here. Look at this one." He glanced nervously across the room in Dr. Pooley's direction.

I peered through the lens at what looked like a long, skinny piece of string smushed between two pieces of glass. "Those are the antibodies?" I'd seen those in the past with Caine.

"Yes." He changed out the slides again. "Now, look at this one."

When I viewed the next slide, the "string" appeared broken, and there was less of it.

"Based on the dates written on the vials, the healthy antibody sample is from three years ago. The other is from last week. Whoever's been providing these samples... well, it appears that their ability to form healthy antibodies is diminishing."

Even though Dr. Hempel was only confirming the message that Dax had already delivered from Caine, a queasy feeling erupted in my stomach. How long had I been walking around with reduced immunity? Had I been careful enough last week when I was around Key and Ryder?

"But," Dr. Hempel lifted a finger. "I have discovered a way to work around this." He placed a third slide on the stage. "In this slide"—he gestured for me to look—"I have added a protein compound to the antibodies. It's something I've been working on for the last couple of years."

"The antibodies have reformed," I said. "But they look... different."

"They're even stronger. This is the treatment I hope will work. And it might get us closer to a vaccine—it could be a way to trick our immune systems into producing manufactured antibodies."

"Why do I feel like there's a 'but' coming next?"

"Dr. Pooley and I still feel like we're missing something. The person with these antibodies had some sort of medical help."

"What do you mean? What kind of help?"

"Well, the protein compound we came up with complements a patient's existing immune system, helping a patient fight the infections caused by the virus, but it's still a manufactured chemical. Whereas the original survivor had some sort of substance in their blood that promoted the antibodies you see on this slide. As a result, that person was able to fight through the failure of vital organs that most Bad Sam patients eventually die from." He gestured again to the first slide he had shown me. "Something else, something inside the original survivor's blood, helped them fight the Samael Strain and produce the antibodies you see on that slide."

Something inside my blood...

His explanation triggered something in my memory that I couldn't quite put my finger on. "But do you think you've found an answer? Do you think what you've come up with will help Willow?"

He held up a hand. "First we try it on one of our patients in the next room."

"What? But we're running out of time." The clock across the room told us we had less than thirty-six hours. "By the time you figure out if this is working, Willow could be dead." Or could soon be past the point of saving. "Those children didn't come down with the virus until several days after Willow. Why would you treat them first?"

Dr. Pooley, who had been doing his own thing and charting numbers across from us, turned our way. "I've been monitoring Willow and treating her symptoms. She's hanging in there. We've got time to make sure this treatment works before taking any risks with Willow."

Bile rose to my throat as I realized what Dr. Pooley meant by that statement. "By 'make sure it works,' you mean test it first on the 'less important' patients?" The children were being used as lab rats! I slammed my gloved fist on the counter. "Because they didn't come from as much money and power as Willow, they're disposable?"

I realized a little too late that I had raised my voice. Two guards standing at the door pulled Tasers from their waistbands.

"I'm sorry." I held out my hands in defense. "I'll calm down." I took a deep cleansing breath and whispered to the doctors, "Those two children... How did they contract the virus?"

Dr. Pooley stepped closer. "With all due respect, an outsider does not get to come into our lab and start asking questions about how we run things."

I reared back like I'd been slapped. I wanted to say to them, "With all due respect, those are my antibodies you're using for your experiments," but I stopped myself.

Then it dawned on me why they were ignoring my question. Thoughts of the countless nights when the incinerators had run flashed in my mind. I was willing to bet that those children had been given the virus specifically so that they could *become* human lab rats. They hadn't contracted the disease by accident; they were just two more guinea pigs, part of a long line of experiments designed to find a cure or vaccine for Bad Sam.

I stared at the two doctors, knowing I couldn't voice my suspicions. What would they do to me if I accused them of this?

Bile rose in my throat, and I pressed a hand to my stomach. Dr. Pooley and Dr. Hempel traded glances with each other and shifted uncomfortably.

My mind turned to Ryder, Key, and Dylan. They weren't getting the same treatment as Willow. They couldn't be, because Caine didn't have the same high-tech medicines and machines available to him, nor did he have the manpower of caregivers. The clock sitting on the counter behind Dr. Hempel was more for them than it was for Willow. Unfortunately, these doctors were confident that they had longer than that clock indicated—which meant I would have to show my hand sooner rather than later.

"So, how sure are you that this treatment will work?" I asked, trying to pretend that I hadn't just realized how twisted the people of New Caelum truly were.

"As soon as Justin gives the go-ahead, we will give the patients the treatment. I'm very hopeful," Dr. Hempel said, trying to reassure me.

I continued to cling to the fact that Caine trusted Dr. Hempel.

Dr. Pooley went back to work, so I took the opportunity to ask Dr. Hempel one additional question. "What happens to the person who supplied the antibody samples? What does it mean that their antibodies are diminishing?"

"These samples came from someone who somehow survived the virus. As a result, they developed antibodies that made them immune to contracting it again. I think you knew this already." He raised his eyes from the microscope viewer to peer at me.

I bit my lower lip, but made no motion with my head or eyes that would confirm or deny the truth of his supposition.

"But now, she is losing her immunity. Wherever she is—and I presume she is close to Dr. Caine Quinton—I hope she has learned the proper protocol for dealing with infectious diseases. She should no longer rely on her own immunity to keep herself safe from the Samael Strain."

~~~~~

In the decontamination chamber, I pulled down on the lever and drenched myself in the sterilization substance for twice the recommended length of time. A knock on the window made me look up. West was on the other side of the glass, motioning for me to hurry.

I continued into the next room, where a woman as suited up as I was helped me strip out of the hazmat suit and threw each piece of equipment into a biohazard waste container. I stripped down to my bra and panties—thankful there were no windows in this room—then hurriedly dressed in my sapphire-colored pants and satin top.

The clothes still baffled me, yet I felt prettier in them than I'd ever felt in my life.

When I finally exited the decontamination chambers, West waited for me with an unreadable expression. An alarm and a voice message were sounding overhead, one I hadn't heard inside the lab. "What is that?"

"That's the public announcement system."

"What's it saying?"

Worry was etched in the V that formed between his eyes. "Mother has called a city-wide meeting."

....

chapter thirty-two

West

Though my heart raced like a hummingbird as I wondered what would prompt my mother to call a public assembly, I could hardly take my eyes off of Cricket. The blue satin that draped across her shoulders made the sapphire of her eyes stand out even more. Even amidst the devastating conditions that had reunited us, I constantly pondered ways I could make our very different lives join together.

As we entered the common area, I also couldn't help but wonder if today would be the day she discovered why very few people wore the royal blue that Mother and Justin had insisted she wear since she'd entered New Caelum. Would she believe me when I told her that I'd had nothing to do with the decision?

Though I didn't fight them over it.

We entered the vast multi-leveled atrium from an entrance near the top of the structure. Cricket looked up to the expansive glass roof, and then down at the thousands of people who had gathered below. Thank goodness she was too busy taking in her surroundings to notice that scores of people were staring at her—at us. I knew the reasons for their stares were complimentary—a result of the color she wore and of course, her beauty—but stares like that would make even the most confident person feel self-conscious.

I grabbed Cricket's hand and pulled her behind me to a balcony where we could watch Mother's speech alone—a benefit of being born of privilege. Cricket walked immediately to the edge and leaned over.

I instinctively reached out a hand and held on to her waist. She looked back at me, and I explained, "I'm sure the railing is secure, but I don't want to test it. It's a long way down."

She smiled. It was a beautiful sight. She didn't show it often. She hadn't had a lot to smile about lately, I supposed.

She turned, and I looked out over the atrium. The color of dress on each level of the tall space tended to be fairly uniform. The lowest level was mostly green; the next level up was mostly purple food preparers, and so on. It was like a vertical rainbow. The top level, where Cricket and I stood, consisted mostly of white and black, with a very few sapphire blue mixed in.

"What do all the colors mean?" She was seeing colors she'd already seen—black, white, pale blue—but I suspected this was the first time she had seen green, yellow, red, or the light beige worn by the lowest of the classes.

It was also the first time she had asked about the colors' meaning.

"They all have different meanings," I told her. "Most reflect what type of job you hold: white is for doctors, powder blue is for nurses and other healthcare workers, green is for our gardeners and food growers, and black and dark gray are for the top level officials and their family members, including council members."

"Do people ever get to wear more than one color?"

"Only if they hold more than one job, but that's highly unusual. The colors hold a lot of meaning, and people are usually very proud of the colors they wear." I sat in a chair behind her. "Any news from Dr. Hempel?" I changed the subject before she asked about her own color. I wasn't ready yet to explain her sapphire blue.

She turned to me, and almost immediately, lines formed along her forehead. "What do you mean?"

"Is he any closer to a treatment?" How would I tell her that she was right when she suspected my city was infecting innocent people with a horrific disease?

"Oh. Yes. He has a treatment he wants to try on one of the other sick residents tonight." Worry was etched in the lines around her squinted eyes. "As soon as he gets approval from Justin."

I tugged on her hand, leading her to sit beside me. "What's wrong? You look worried. Did something happen in the lab?"

Her brows furrowed and she shook her head. She seemed to be holding something back.

"Hey." I rubbed my thumb across her hand. "Tell me."

"I want to believe that there are good people inside your city, but West, I'm afraid they're testing the treatment on random patients they injected with the virus."

I pulled her forward and wrapped my arms around her in a hug. "I promise you, Cricket, I'm going to find out what's going on here. And if anything like that is happening, I'll do everything I can to stop it." I kissed the side of her head before releasing her.

Although what she'd just said was certainly enough reason to put a worried look on Cricket's face, I was sure there was more to it. She was holding something else back.

And how could I blame her? Wasn't I holding back my own share of information?

She continued to take in the atmosphere outside of our little balcony, refusing to make eye contact with me. "This is all just very overwhelming."

Suddenly, she lifted her arm and pointed. "Hey, look! There's Dax." She stood.

I suppressed a growl of frustration. Sure enough, Dax stood in a balcony directly across from us, flanked by a couple of representatives from leadership staff. Why was he here?

"Who is he with?" she asked.

"Those are some of Justin's staff members." I searched for Justin, but didn't find him. Had Justin made sure that Dax was here? Did he specifically want him to witness this public assembly, whatever it was about?

"He's dressed in a dark brown. What does that mean?"

"It means he's a guest of New Caelum's leader," I lied. There was no color for guests, because New Caelum didn't receive any. I examined Dax more closely. He wore a GPS tracker-bracelet on his wrist, and the people I'd identified as Justin's staff were actually a couple of city guards dressed in off-duty attire.

Dark brown was actually the prisoners' color. We didn't have many, but when we did, we had to dress them in something that set them apart.

She turned and narrowed her gaze. "What does *my* color mean?"

"Well, it uh..."

A crackling over the loudspeaker saved me from answering. Mother had appeared at the podium. "Hello, New Caelum."

She spoke into a microphone, and loudspeakers carried her voice to every level of the atrium. I leaned in to Cricket and whispered, "Every citizen of New Caelum can hear Mother's broadcast, even those a mile away in different buildings. The city was designed from the very beginning so that announcements could be heard throughout the city. Open communication has always been a fundamental principle of New Caelum. Mother never wanted to hide the truth from the citizens. What happened this past week has been the first time she's kept a major secret from our people."

"You mean the news that Bad Sam is back."

I nodded.

Mother continued. "Welcome. I come to you today with grave news."

Cricket glanced over at me, concern in her eyes, before facing forward again. Mother moved her head slowly, making eye contact with representatives in each direction and on every level of the atrium. Was she going to be honest with her people and tell them about Willow?

She leaned in close to the microphone again. "Representatives from outside of our city have come to us."

A low roar of astonished chatter broke out. Cricket scooted forward on her seat. Her head turned toward Dax, who looked over at Cricket, then back to Mother. Cricket's hands began to rub back and forth against the fabric over her knee.

Mother raised her hand to silence the crowd. "It's all right. The visitors have been quarantined and sufficiently examined and tested for any and all infectious diseases. They are not a threat. They bring information to us—valuable information.

"I know that you want to know what's happening in the outside world. I have wanted to know, as well. Now we do. The outside world fought hard against Bad Sam, but our sources tell us that the deadly virus is back."

Screams erupted. Many people cried out, "No!" There was so much shouting all at once that I couldn't even understand most of it.

Cricket stood abruptly, knocking her chair over backward. She turned to me, "Get Dax in here with us, now! The mob will kill him out there."

"Cricket, I can't—"

"Make it happen, West!"

chapter thirty-three

....

Cricket

West ventured to the other side of the atrium.

The crowd was cheering. Dax was standing in front of two of Justin's staff members, but I could see the stun guns on their belts. And given how close they stood to Dax, they were clearly guards. I had known West was lying to me when he'd said brown was the color guests wore. He'd told us earlier that day that New Caelum had never received guests inside the city walls.

West appeared behind Dax, spoke to the guards, and gestured in my direction. He also conversed with Dax, who glanced briefly toward me and then nodded to West. I was relieved when West, Dax, and the guards all began walking in my direction.

By this time, the crowd was settling down. President Layne approached the microphone again. "We here..." She spoke slowly, giving her people time to quiet further. "We here inside New Caelum are strong." She emphasized the word strong with a fist pump. "Our walls are secure and our air is clean." Citizens of her city were hanging on her every word at this point, looking to her for—what? Hope? "These people only got inside our walls because we allowed them inside."

My fingers curled into fists; my fingernails dug into my palms, nearly drawing blood. How dare this woman tell these people that the outside was infected with a deadly virus? She had to know that the only reason outsiders had contracted Bad Sam was because the citizens from within New Caelum had taken the virus to them.

She was a different person yesterday—weak, feeble, submissive in front of Justin. But now? She was a model of the strength and hope this city needed.

All based on lies she spoon-fed the people before her.

"It was planned," I whispered to myself. West had said that some people inside the city had been grumbling to get out. They were ready to explore the outside again. To own land. To live on their own. To run their own lives and make their own decisions. Apparently, someone inside New Caelum didn't want that to happen. Someone with power—someone who would lose control if the people discovered that the outside was inhabitable and ready to be rebuilt.

"Hey." Dax's voice behind me made me jump.

I turned and threw my arms around his neck. "You're okay," I breathed.

"What is this, Cricket?" he asked against my neck.

"I don't know." I released him and looked at West. The guards stood at the door. They didn't take their eyes off of Dax.

President Layne continued to speak. "To show you just how strong we are, I'm here to announce changes being made within leadership. Changes that will prove we are ready for anything. Our ability to lead this city and to sustain our way of life will last for as long as we need it to."

I turned to West. "Do you know what she's doing?"

He only shook his head, his eyes glued to his mother.

Justin suddenly appeared and stood beside President Layne. The smile and confidence on his face, just minutes after the city had been told that the world outside of New Caelum was still plagued with disease, reeked of arrogance. Yet the people all around us cheered when they saw him. They whooped and hollered like he was a rock star.

My mouth fell open, and I stepped even closer to the edge. West stepped directly beside me to my left. Dax was just to my right and slightly behind me. I could feel the heat of anger radiating from his body as he hovered there.

"There's going to be a wedding," Layne said. She nodded as the people exploded in cheers again. She and Justin traded glances that could only be described as loving—a stark contrast to what I'd witnessed between them since I arrived. These people were very different people when standing in front of their citizens than they were in private. "That's right. Your vice president and I are going to marry. And you all are invited." A huge smile lit up her face as she scanned each section of the atrium, one by one.

I narrowed my gaze at President Layne. The people around her gawked at her openly, hanging on her every word. Ecstatic grins spread across their faces upon hearing the news of a wedding, even amid the turmoil of the virus's resurgence outside.

Dax's brief touch to my forearm steadied me slightly, but that changed when President Layne lifted her head and looked directly up at us. Justin joined her, making eye contact only with me. Goose bumps formed along my arms, and a chill skipped down my body. I wanted to retreat into myself.

"Oh, no," West said beside me. He grabbed my hand and squeezed. The contact made me uncomfortable, with Dax standing on the other side of me.

President Layne smiled. "If you're excited about that, the next thing I have to tell you is *really* going to blow your minds." She and Justin joined hands, and with their free hands they gestured toward the balcony where West, Dax, and I stood. "There will be *two* weddings."

Everyone turned, and when they saw us, there was a collective gasp in the room.

"What is she talking about?" I asked through gritted teeth. West had told me that President Layne and Justin had some ludicrous plan for me to stay—but marriage?

West's mouth hung open. "I can't believe she just did that." He stood motionless, like he was terrified to move.

The people staring up looked on with equal parts excitement and shock. While some were clearly overjoyed by the news, many whispered behind cupped hands.

"They don't even know me," I said.

"Friends, we will formally introduce you to my son's lovely bride in the coming days. For now..." I didn't even hear what President Layne said next. Her voice sounded like it was coming from some faraway tunnel.

Why was someone on the inside so hell-bent on keeping me inside New Caelum? This was far bigger than just the personal wishes of President Layne and Vice President Rhodes. I glanced at West, who looked as perplexed as me.

"I'm an outsider," I said. "They should have a thousand questions."

"I know I do," Dax said.

My spine stiffened. I had forgotten he was even there. Turning slowly, I faced him. "Dax, I have no idea why she's doing this." And part of me didn't care. I had no intention of staying inside New Caelum, no matter what their plans.

"What is going on here, Cricket?" Dax said angrily. "You don't even know this guy, let alone these crazy people who shut themselves off from the world and turned their backs on humanity."

"Dax, there's so much you don't know. I just need you to trust me for now." What was I saying? Apparently, there was a lot I didn't know either.

Dax's lips parted as he stared at me in disbelief. "Trust you about what? You're not thinking about staying here inside New Caelum, are you?"

"She *does* know me," West interrupted, sliding an arm around my back and gripping my waist. "And it's none of your business if she stays here."

I closed my eyes tight, wishing this could happen so differently. But I'd promised West I would pretend—that I would be who they wanted me to be in public while West figured out what was going on.

"The *hell* it's not my business." Dax grabbed my arm and tugged me toward him, though I resisted and stumbled backward against West, who steadied me.

The guards moved closer, hands on their Tasers. I threw myself in front of them. "Dax, please."

"Please *what*, Cricket?" He stepped to me and grabbed my arms. "You're not thinking straight."

"Let her go." West now had his own Taser in his left hand, while motioning for the guards to stand down.

Dax searched my eyes. "What the hell? You know you only have one more day, and you better be long gone from here."

"I know. And I'm going to need for you to give me that time in order to figure a few things out." I placed my hand on Dax's cheek.

"You're looking at me the same way you did at the hospital. Right before you asked me to run away so I wouldn't contract Bad Sam."

"But you didn't." I rubbed a thumb across his cheek. I wished I could explain everything to my friend, but there wasn't time. "You're so stubborn."

Dax scowled. "What is it about this place that has you all twisted up?"

There was so much I had never confided in Dax. I had never thought I would have to. But my past had fully caught up with my present. "I promise I'll tell you everything soon. I wish I could say nothing will change between us, but... I'm not who you think I am." I turned to West. "I'm trusting you. No harm comes to him."

I let West stare deep into my eyes—to let him see that I was keeping my promise to give him a chance to teach me all that he could in the next twenty-four hours. The specks of gold in his hazel green eyes practically glowed in appreciation of the silent vow I was making.

He turned to his guards. "Return Dax to his quarters," he ordered.

278

I sent a silent apology to Dax. He glared back, helpless and confused, before being led away.

President Layne's words grew louder again, prompting me to turn back to West. "To my son and his future bride. May they be the future of New Caelum."

The crowd erupted in applause. I didn't know what to do. I had so many questions, and the only way I was going to get answers was if I played along with the charade launched by President Layne and Vice President Rhodes.

Looking up at West, I wondered how much acting I would really have to do to feign a romantic connection to West. His fingers drifted along my face, sliding around it until his palm rested at the nape of my neck between my hair and my skin. He applied pressure, directing my face up to his, then whispered so that only I could hear him. "I'm going to kiss you now, Christina Black. And don't think for a second that this has anything to do with anyone else around us. Let them have their show—but this is between you and me."

I wasn't prepared for his words, or for the way his touch tingled on my neck and down my spine. He leaned in, tilting his head to the right then the left, until he closed the remaining space separating us and touched his lips to mine.

The low roar of the crowd sounded like nothing more than the distant rumble of a train as I forgot all the reasons I shouldn't let my long-lost childhood friend kiss me.

When he released me, we turned to face the crowd, who cheered approval. But just as I felt a smile touch my lips, I caught a glimpse of Dax out of the corner of my eye. The guards were holding him in place across from us—so he could watch the show. Then the guards pushed him through the door, but not before I saw anguish cross his face.

chapter thirty-four

....

West

Cricket disappeared into the lab with Dr. Pooley and Dr. Hempel immediately after Mother's dramatic performance. Though she hadn't fought the spectacle my mother had made of us, putting us on display like circus animals, she'd barely spoken to me afterward, just asked to be taken to the lab, not even returning to the suite for dinner.

And yet... I had not imagined that kiss. She felt something for me. A person can't fake that.

But our circumstances were working against us.

My life was here, inside New Caelum. Hers was outside. How would I ever convince her to see the bigger picture—a future that merged our two worlds, that concentrated on the rebuilding of humanity?

My mother and the council were going about it all wrong. They were trying to force Cricket to join New Caelum, and you don't force Cricket to do anything.

I decided it was time for me and Cricket to talk—whether she wanted to or not. I made my way to the lab, and with a nurse's assistance, I suited up and entered. Cricket stood across the room, her back to me. Several nurses and lab techs worked at stations around the room.

As I approached, I realized she was staring at the countdown timer, which now had little more than twenty-four hours left. By midnight tomorrow, she would need to have disarmed the computer virus and the bomb inside New Caelum, or the people in the city would have far bigger problems than worrying about the safety of the outside world.

"Hi," I said behind her, making her jump and turn to me. "Sorry. I didn't mean to scare you."

I realized she was crying behind the mask covering her face. "What's wrong? What's happened?" I rushed to her and started to wrap my arms around her, but she backed up, and I remembered the protocol—no touching each other inside the infectious disease lab.

I dropped my arms to my side. "Sorry. I wasn't thinking."

With no way of wiping her nose or eyes, her face was wet with tears and snot, and her eyes were bloodshot. She was a mess.

"Tell me what's going on." I stretched my fingers and curled them into fists.

"She's dead. She was just a child," Cricket sobbed. "Justin approved the treatments, but something went wrong when Dr. Pooley injected the little girl with the serum. I didn't even know her name."

I bent my neck forward and stared at the floor in front of me. I wanted to throw something. This little girl's death weighed heavily on my chest. "Alexa."

Cricket cocked her head. "Alexa?"

"That was her name." I swallowed hard against the emotion of losing another citizen of New Caelum—an innocent child. A fiery anger spread across my neck and down my spine—and then I realized that not only was a sweet girl dead, but we still didn't have a cure for my sister. Why weren't Cricket's antibodies working? Or was it something else that wasn't working?

"Come on. Let's get out of here." I had to stop myself again from reaching out and touching her.

"I can't. There's not enough time. I have to stay here and see if I can help Dr. Hempel."

"You need a break. You've provided the tools the doctors need. Let Dr. Hempel and Dr. Pooley have some space. We'll come back later."

"But I've listened to Caine talk for years about what worked and what didn't. And before that, I listened to my parents talk about the disease."

"Caine experimented on rats. And you were just a child when you heard your parents. You couldn't possibly be expected to remember what they said." Not to mention, Mother thought they had been going a little crazy before they took that last trip. Of course, I wouldn't tell Cricket that. "Come on. Let's get out of here," I said again. "Time away will do you some good."

After a few seconds of staring at me silently, she gave in with a sigh.

I let her pass through the decontamination chamber first. When I found her on the other side, she had cleaned up her face and was standing by the window of one of the iso units, looking in at the little boy still fighting for his life. Dr. Pooley was in the room with him.

"Hey," I whispered. "Where's Dr. Hempel?"

Cricket shrugged. "He was so angry when the little girl died, he stormed out. I assumed to cool off."

Cricket sniffed. Her eyes were a little swollen. "I'd give anything to be back on top of my mountain tonight. I just feel completely claustrophobic and helpless."

I knew Cricket didn't mean for her words to hurt me, but they stabbed at my heart. Would she ever feel at home inside New Caelum? Could I expect her to find happiness beside me?

I reached down and linked my fingers with hers. "Come on. I've got an idea."

~~~~~

"Keep your eyes closed."

"West," Cricket whined. "This is wrong. Thank you for getting me out of the lab for a while, but we can't run away from everything like we could when we were twelve."

"Just keep them closed." Keeping my hands on her arms, I guided her through the door. She was so skinny beneath my touch. "Two more steps."

Once we were completely through the door, Cricket stopped. I was at her back. She leaned into me as her head tilted backward, and she took in a deep cleansing breath. "We're outside." I could hear the smile in her voice. For the first time in days, her voice was upbeat, hopeful.

I whispered close to her ear. "Open your eyes."

She did. Her body remained still as her head turned and surveyed this tiny spot in the sky—the best I could do—a spot where memories were formed.

Slowly, she stepped away from me and farther out onto the roof. "It's so much smaller than I remember."

"*We* were much smaller the last time we were out here."

Cricket rubbed her arms. It was even colder now than it had been on the night we spent together on the mountain.

"Oh, right. Just a sec." I ducked back inside the building and grabbed a couple of large down comforters I had stashed earlier.

When I returned, Cricket was staring up at the sky, taking in deep breaths. "It smells like snow."

"How can it *smell* like snow?" I laughed.

"I don't know. The air, when it's this cold, has a clean, refreshing smell to it."

I smiled. "I think you're just slightly nuts."

The hint of a giggle escaped her lips, and I would have given anything to have recorded that beautiful sound—the sound of all the bad melting away, even if only for a split second.

"Maybe I am. Maybe we're all a little nuts at this point."

While holding one blanket between my legs, I draped the other around her shoulders and brought the fabric together in front, then pulled her closer to me. The whites of her eyes glistened in the cold air, while the electricity of her blue irises drew me even nearer to her.

She stared up at me, and her brows pulled inward. She narrowed her eyes as a blend of pain, confusion, and fear crossed her face. "West... I... We really need to talk."

I closed my eyes briefly. "I know."

"I don't want to hurt you, but I'm afraid you think something is happening between us that simply can't—and never will."

"No!"

Cricket flinched as I spoke louder than I had intended. I readjusted my grip on the blanket that was holding her near to me.

"I'm fully aware of what our situation is and is not, but I will not let you deny what is happening between us," I said. I touched my forehead to hers. "Please don't leave me."

She lifted her hand and pried the blanket from my hands. She pulled away and walked a few steps, her back to me. "Did you see how the people of your city looked at me today?"

"Yes. They saw a beautiful, strong woman at my side. New Caelum celebrates any and all unions."

She turned and smiled at me. "They saw an outsider. One with scars on her face. Like everyone I meet, they wonder what horrific event caused these scars. I represent their worst fears."

"You represent hope."

"You're kidding yourself."

"Don't you get it?" I pushed away the hair hanging across her right cheek and tucked it behind her ear. "I don't care what others think. Forget about my mother, the council, or the people of New Caelum. The people who matter will love you. I'm next in line to run this city, and I want you by my side. You hold the future of our civilization. You will be the one who will link my world with the outside—your world."

Cricket burst into laughter. "Now I know you've lost it. Did you hear your mother today?"

"Yes. That was not my mother. The things she said were not her views. My mother is a reasonable woman. And though she hasn't been ready to venture outside our walls, she wasn't fully against exploring the idea either." I wasn't sure where Mother's message had come from today.

"No. She and Justin have no intention of taking the people of New Caelum back out into the world," Cricket said. "And that's a good thing, because the people on the outside will never roll out red carpets to welcome you. Not to mention..." She stopped talking and looked away.

"What?" I asked. "Don't hold back now."

"Nothing. I shouldn't have—"

"Cricket. I am not my mother, and I'm nothing like Justin. I *will* take over running this city eventually." Possibly sooner rather than later. "I already have a team of supporters who will help me make the changes we need in order for us to emerge from this cocoon. Tell me what you were about to say."

Squaring her shoulders, Cricket took in a deep breath. "I don't believe the people who contracted this virus did so as a result of an accident. I think everything that is happening has been meticulously planned, including the fact that I'm here. And your mother knows more than she's telling you."

"My mother protected you when you got sick. She said you wanted to leave the city, so she found a way for that to happen, and then she kept your secret. She only brought you back to save her daughter. She wants nothing but the best for you, Cricket. Something else is going on here. I don't know what yet, but don't write my mother off just yet."

"Fine. Let me ask you this then: why do you think Justin, or the council, or whoever, wants you to convince me to stay inside New Caelum?" She pulled the blanket tightly around her.

I studied her face. Was I seeing compassion there? Pity? "Why do *you* think?" I asked warily.

Instead of answering, she asked me a question. "What's the one thing that's special about me, West? Do you think they want me here for my beautiful looks? My charming personality?"

I wanted her here for all of those things, but I knew she wasn't really asking me.

"No. They want me here for my *antibodies*. They want to own a Bad Sam survivor. And West... it means they don't expect to have one of their own."

She was talking about Willow.

"No. You're wrong." She had to be, right? I walked over to the edge of the roof and looked out over the wall toward the west.

Cricket slid her hands under my arms from behind and wrapped her blanket across my chest in a hug. "I'm sorry." She buried her face into my back, kissing me through my jacket. "I don't want you to give up hope, but I want you to consider everything that's going on here."

I nodded. She wanted me to consider just how corrupt my government actually was. I turned in her arms, placing my own arms around her and staring down at her. "This is why I need you here with me. We would make a great team. I *am* going to stop the people on the council, and anyone else who has harmed our people."

"I believe you. And I'll do what I can to help you. But I can't make any promises right now. You've got a huge battle ahead of you. For now, I just want to concentrate on getting your sister treated, and on leaving here tomorrow night—hopefully with a way to treat our friends on the outside as well."

I turned back around, leading Cricket to stand in front of me with her back to my chest. With the second blanket wrapped around me, I enfolded Cricket in my embrace as we both stared off into the distance. We stayed like that for a while.

As I imagined what life was like for people living in the west, I was suddenly hit by a glaring realization. "There were four trucks that went out the night I left New Caelum in search of you."

"I know."

"Only two are accounted for."

"I know."

"If what we're saying is true—that everyone who went out was infected—then there are still four other sick people on the outside. And if they entered any of the settlements to the west..."

"Then the outside could be plagued with Bad Sam again, just like your mother told her people today."

And just like someone had wanted.

And I was pretty sure I knew who.

....

chapter thirty-five

Cricket

The view from the roof was nice, but the sky looked completely different here compared to the way it looked in the mountains, or even Boone Blackston. The city lights prevented me from seeing the millions of stars I knew were out there.

Looking to the east, I saw the outline of the forest trees against a moonlit sky. My friends from the settlement—the only family I'd known since I'd lost my parents—were out there. Surviving, I hoped.

I tried not to worry too much about them. We had initiated quarantine procedures quickly, so they were at low risk for contracting the virus. And they had always remained prepared for the return of Bad Sam. They knew how to isolate themselves.

Plus, the people of Boone Blackston trusted each other. A code of honor existed among residents of the settlement. If someone developed a fever, he would quarantine himself. Dylan, like every other outsider, would rather die than spread death.

However, we still didn't have a cure. And if people in the other settlements had been less careful—or less fortunate—the virus would be devastating.

Is that what New Caelum wanted? Why would *anyone* want such a thing? Or was that not the ultimate motive? Maybe what the leadership of New Caelum wanted was a way to keep their citizens safely tucked inside a bubble of fear. And by inflicting Bad Sam on the people on the outside, people inside would stop talking about exploring the outside world.

This possibility made me feel less guilty about my little insurance policy ticking away. Besides, I wasn't here to solve the woes of New Caelum's corrupt government; I just wanted to find a treatment for Bad Sam.

I shivered as a chill skipped down my body. West and I lay beside each other on one down blanket, and we were covered by another. His head was propped up on an elbow, and his other arm lay across my stomach. When I trembled, he pulled me closer, tucking me into his chest.

"I brought you something." He pulled my necklace out and held it up, dangling it from his fingers. "I forgot I even had it. I found it the first night I ventured out into the outside."

Sitting up, I took the necklace from him, examining the beads.

"It was a gift from my parents, you know." Tears sprang to my eyes. "They gave it to me the last time I saw them. They said it would keep me safe while they were gone."

"I remember that day," West said while feathering his fingers along my arm. "My mother spoke of some wild idea your parents had to stop Bad Sam at its source. They thought they already had the proof, but they needed to travel to Africa to gather additional resources. This was before people realized Bad Sam would completely destroy our country as we knew it."

I stared at the beads. They were dark green with specks of crimson red—blood red. Bloodstones, they were called.

Legend had it—or so my parents told me when they gave me the necklace—that bloodstones had medicinal value. That when worn next to the skin, the stones boosted the strength of a person's immune system, creating an unwelcome environment for toxins and infection. I remembered telling my parents that I thought it was stupid to think that simply wearing a necklace would ward off disease.

I never forgot what they said next. "It's what's inside that counts," I whispered to myself. "You have everything you need to keep yourself safe. One day you will be asked to do something benevolent for someone who doesn't deserve it. Hold these close to you. They'll protect your heart."

"What?" West asked, sitting up beside me.

I shook my head and turned to him. "Oh, nothing. My parents always had these little sayings—words of wisdom they hoped I would live by. I think... I think maybe they knew they wouldn't be seeing me again."

West nodded. "I'm sorry." He squeezed me a little closer.

I stared at the beads again, repeating my parents' words in my head: It's what's inside that counts.

West watched me closely. "It's a beautiful necklace."

I smiled. "My parents collected these beads. I have a bunch more of them in a box back at the settlement, and my parents left a ton of them back at our old house. They must have really liked them."

It was curious, now that I thought about it. Why had my parents collected so many of these beads? "They'll protect your heart," I whispered again. Memories flashed before me of heated late night discussions, of my parents taking me to a hospital after one of their trips.

"I think I know what's missing from Dr. Hempel's treatment."

"What? How?"

"I've had it all along." I jumped up. "Remember when I told you the hallway leading to the lab looked familiar to me?"

I nodded.

"My parents took me somewhere after they came home from one of their last trips. The memories are still a little fuzzy, but they're becoming clearer. It was a hospital. A children's hospital, maybe. I remember sitting in a conference room around this large table while they showed some doctors the bloodstones. I also have these vague memories of getting a shot. I stayed there for a couple of days... or a week... I don't know."

I rubbed my eyes, willing for the memories to be less fuzzy. "No, it wasn't a shot. It was an IV. And the doctors took blood from me, I think, and I remember... and this memory is vivid." I turned to West. "I remember the doctors shaking their heads outside my room and my parents looking sad."

"Why do you remember that so well?"

"Because I thought I was dying. Why else would I have been admitted to a hospital? Why else would my parents keep so many secrets? It was like they were trying to protect me from the truth."

"Did you ask them?"

"Yeah, as soon as they reentered my room. They hugged me and smiled, and they assured me I was healthier than anyone in the world." I looked down at West, the pieces slowly clicking into place. "I think I know how to help your sister."

....

chapter thirty-six

West

"Dr. Hempel will know what to do," Cricket said for the fifth time on the short walk to the lab and medical wing. "He has to." The last three words came out in a panicked whisper.

Then we turned the corner to the main entrance to the medical wing, and came face to face with four armed guards dressed in red hazmat suits.

I stopped abruptly, and Cricket ran into my back. The red suits could only mean one thing—someone else had contracted the Samael Strain.

"Who is it?" I asked. "What's happened?"

The guards shifted. One of them pointed his Taser at me. "You will both stay back."

I squared my shoulders. "You will stand down and not point that weapon at me."

"We have our orders, Mr. Layne. And right now, we don't answer to you."

"Answer to me or not, I am not a threat to you. Point the Taser elsewhere."

Through the hazmat mask, I could see confusion and conflict pass over the guard's face. He adjusted the aim of his weapon slightly. "Sorry, sir. We only aim to keep you and Miss Black safe."

Cricket stepped around me, fearless. "Someone else is sick, aren't they?"

"I'm afraid so."

"Who?" She grabbed my arm in a death grip.

"Dr. Hempel."

My eyes slammed shut. Cricket rolled into me, burying her face into my chest, and her body shook. I raised my hand and smoothed her hair, then wrapped her in a hug. Her body was rigid against mine.

Then she pulled away, all emotion stripped from her face. She looked up at me with determination in her eyes. "I need to get in there," she said through gritted teeth. "I need to talk to Dr. Hempel right now."

"I'm sorry, Miss Black, but you may not enter. It's not safe."

Her face hardened even further. She ignored the directive, and instead turned and ran full speed toward the doors. But one of the guards caught her before she even got close to the entrance.

"I have to see him!" she shouted. "Right! Now!"

"Mr. Layne. You must restrain her, or we will be forced to shock her."

I wrapped my arms around Cricket and pulled her backward. She weighed barely more than a hundred pounds. "Cricket. You have to calm down."

She crumbled to the ground, and I knelt with her. "You don't understand," she cried. "I have to see him before he succumbs to the fever. We might not have much time before he can't help us at all. Caine said Dr. Hempel was the only one who could help us. And if he falls unconscious before I've talked to him..."

I brushed her hair out of her face. "Look at me. It's going to be okay."

I wished there was more conviction behind my words. Instead, a heavy feeling of dread and devastation weighed on my chest, like we could very well be witnessing the beginning of the end for New Caelum. The Samael Strain was spreading. It was one thing to have three citizens with the virus, but now Dr. Hempel, our best hope for finding a cure, would be taken from us as well.

Cricket stilled in my arms. She looked up at me, her eyes wide as she sucked in and blew out air with concentrated effort. "Call Justin. I need to see him immediately."

"No need. I'm right here." Justin stood behind us, dressed in casual clothes. His hair was disheveled, like he'd just gotten of bed. "My guards had already alerted me to the fact that the two of you were headed toward the lab."

Cricket scrambled to her feet to face him. I stood behind her, my hand on her back to steady her.

"What exactly do you two think you're doing?" Justin asked. "It's the middle of the night."

"I need to get inside the lab." Cricket's hands shook at her sides.

"There's no need for that. Dr. Pooley has taken over Dr. Hempel's efforts. He's confident that he can tweak the treatment to work better than it did on the girl."

299

"You mean the girl who *died*?" Cricket's voice was somehow devoid of emotion. "Willow doesn't have much time, Justin. By Caine's calculations, her organs could already be starting to shut down."

"And we're doing everything we can to save her. Now, you should get some sleep." Justin started to turn away from us.

Cricket rotated her shoulders. "I have the final ingredient we need."

Careful, Cricket, I wanted to warn. *Don't tell him too much.* Something about Justin had always rubbed me the wrong way. I'd always thought it was because he was after my mother's presidency, but now I suspected it went much deeper than that.

Justin turned back. "What do you mean? How?"

"Dr. Hempel and Caine are both close to a treatment—a cocktail of substances, including antibodies from my blood— but I think they're missing a key ingredient that may have helped me survive Bad Sam. Something my parents discovered."

"What are you talking about?" Justin walked closer. "Your parents did absolutely nothing to help us with the pandemic that destroyed our nation."

"Only because you didn't give them a chance! They had found the one thing that would help us survive, but you and President Layne shut them out. Their hypothesis was right, but thanks to you, they never got to see it. They didn't get to see that I survived! And even though no one would listen to them, they risked their lives—and mine, actually—when they left here. But they did it anyway, because they wanted to save our nation."

"I'm listening. What is this key ingredient?"

"Let me see Dr. Hempel."

Good girl. Don't tell him what the ingredient is.

"No. I cannot risk you being around Dr. Hempel."

"You can't risk *not* letting me in," Cricket quickly snapped.

Justin's face reddened. He stepped closer, towering over Cricket. "Do not threaten me." The guards shifted. They all had Tasers in their hands.

I placed a steady hand on my own weapon, for what good it would do. We were completely surrounded and outnumbered.

"I've been a threat since the minute you let me enter New Caelum," Cricket said. "But you knew that, didn't you?"

Justin cocked his head. A grin played at the corners of his lips. "The council has wanted to locate you for a while now, but Ginger wouldn't give you up. Said you could be anywhere. But you weren't just 'anywhere.' You were right where she knew you would be. She'd kept your survival a secret."

"But then Willow contracted Bad Sam."

"That's right. She did." Justin's jaw hardened. "And the council hijacked my scouting mission."

I inhaled sharply. "What do you mean by that?" If the council was responsible for infecting citizens of Bad Sam on the inside, had they also infected the scouts they sent out into the settlements? That didn't make sense.

"We were just supposed to be checking out what was going on with the outside settlements. But then Willow got sick, and Ginger sent West out, too, against the council's wishes."

"Why did the council care if I left?" I asked.

If I hadn't been watching Justin closely, I would have missed the faltering of his expression, although he forced a grin. "You'll have to ask the council that. But my guess? You're just too precious. They didn't want to risk sending you out among the weak and diseased."

Justin was full of crap. I didn't think the council cared that I had left. But he *was* right about one thing. I needed to confront the members of the council. I was starting to believe there might be several versions of truth among the council members. I had a hard time believing that Mrs. Canary was the only council member, former or present, to have disagreed with the council's recent tactics.

Cricket shifted beside me. "Are you two done? None of this accomplishes anything. I still need to see Dr. Hempel, and I need to see him right now."

"Like I told you before," Justin said, "Dr. Pooley has taken over. He doesn't need anything from you at this time. We'll let you know after we've tested another version of the treatment on our other patient."

Cricket reared back. "Did you not hear me? I have an ingredient that you need."

"The only ingredient we ever needed from *you* was your blood. And now we have that." Justin pulled his PulsePoint from his waistband. "Now, we have another matter to discuss."

My fingers twitched at my side. Justin was purposely keeping Cricket from entering the lab, and I had no idea why.

"West, I'm assuming you had no idea that Cricket entered our city with a computer virus attached to her PulsePoint."

"What? A virus?" I feigned disbelief. An uneasy feeling erupted in my stomach, but I needed to do whatever necessary to get Cricket inside that lab. And right now, I was going to have to play along. "What kind of virus?"

"A virus that appears to be scheduled to take down our air filtration system as of midnight tomorrow."

I turned to Cricket. "Is this true?" I pleaded with my eyes that she would see through my act.

"Yes, it's true." She stared blankly at me before turning to Justin. "It's also true that a bomb has been placed inside your city that is scheduled to detonate at the same time that the computer virus takes down your air filtration system."

Justin met Cricket's stare, but said nothing.

"That's right," she continued. "This bomb is filled with six vials of the Samael Strain. It will seep into your air ducts." The guards shifted behind us; a gasp escaped from two of them. Cricket continued without missing a beat. "All of this can be avoided, though, if you'll just let me inside that lab to see Dr. Hempel." Cricket grabbed my arm and willed me to focus. "Willow will die if I don't get inside that lab and talk to Dr. Hempel before he gets too sick to help us."

"That won't be happening," Justin said. He nodded to his guards. They approached Cricket and took her by the arms. "Lock her in a room next to her knight."

"What? You can't do that." Panic registered in Cricket's wide eyes.

"I can. You made a mistake by threatening me." Justin stepped closer to Cricket.

"I came here to help Willow. That's it. But as of tomorrow evening, I will walk out of here with Dax and my PulsePoint, and you will have everything you need to destroy the bomb that is hidden somewhere inside this city. *Or*, this entire city will be infected with the virus. It's your choice."

Justin smiled. "You don't have the nerve. That would be murder."

"Tomato, Tomahto. I see it as self-defense. Not to mention payback. You infected innocent people, so I infect you. *I* choose what I do in this life. Not you."

And that was it, wasn't it? Cricket believed in free will above all else. She needed to believe that everything that occurred in her life was of her own choosing. And New Caelum, my mother, and the council believed the exact opposite. The powers of New Caelum made decisions so that their people didn't have to.

The fact remained, however, that Cricket's choices would be extremely limited once Justin explained to the council that she'd arrived inside New Caelum with a weapon of mass destruction.

I took a deep breath, letting it out slowly as I stepped away from Cricket. With my back to her, I said to Justin, "I had no idea she had done this. Can IT stop it?"

"They're working on it."

"Have the guards lock her up beside the other outsider." I swallowed the desire to cringe at my words. Locking her up took us that much further away from finding a cure. But if I didn't pretend to take Justin's side in this, we'd both be locked up—and that would be the end for us. For everyone. At least this way, I had the chance to do something.

And I already had a plan to get her back inside the lab.

"West," Cricket cried behind me. "You can't do this. You have to let me inside the lab."

I couldn't look at her. If I did, Justin would see the evidence of my feelings all over my face. He'd know that I already knew about the bomb, and I would be locked up right along with her. I squeezed my eyes tight, hesitating only a moment before I began walking again. "It's late. We'll deal with this in the morning."

"West! Think about Willow!" Cricket pleaded. Then, just before I turned the corner and left her in the hands of guards loyal to Justin, she said in the calmest of voices, "You're a coward. I won't forgive you for this."

Cricket

Hearing West give the order to lock me up was like being tasered by him all over again—except this time, it was a direct shock to the heart.

Justin's guards didn't hesitate to manhandle me as they shoved me through the city's tunnels. At this time of night, the halls were dimly lit in soft shades of green and blue against light gray walls and white tiled floors. West was right. New Caelum was very much like a hospital—sterile and cold, and not somewhere I wanted to live.

We entered an unfamiliar area of the city, which wasn't surprising since I'd still seen so little of New Caelum. There just hadn't been enough time. I found myself thinking, *Maybe next time*, but immediately squashed the thought. I would not be returning to New Caelum.

If I ever made it out of here to begin with.

What was West thinking? He wouldn't even look at me when he gave the order. How had I misread him so greatly? Or was it just an act? I thought he *knew* me. Did he finally decide I had gone too far by bringing Bad Sam into his city?

307

I stretched my fingers wide, then slowly curled them into tight fists, letting my nails cut into my palms. Suddenly I was consumed with the thought that if Westlin Layne truly believed I wouldn't keep my word and tell his guards the location of the bomb, then he could stew in his anger. Because after all, I wasn't the one who had brought the Samael Strain back to the people of this country.

After several more hallways, I was completely lost. Even if I'd had the strength to escape three guards armed with Tasers, I'd be caught immediately in this maze of hallways and tunnels.

At last we stopped in front of a glass door, and the guards pushed me through. Inside was what could only be described as a reception area of some sort, and a lady sat at a small desk balancing a pencil on the tip of her finger. The only light in the entire room came from a library lamp on her desk.

The lady stood when we approached, but said nothing. She was dressed head to toe in red, pencil-thin pants and a red blouse that showed just a hint of cleavage. Her jet-black hair was cut in a short bob. Bangs lay flat against her forehead and just about covered her eyebrows. She couldn't have been more than nineteen or twenty, if that.

"We've been ordered to place this girl beside the other one."

The woman assessed me closely. "Fine. For how long?" She gnawed on a cuticle.

"Mr. Layne or Vice President Rhodes will be by to deal with her tomorrow."

"Whatever." No one said anything for several seconds after that. Finally, the lady in red raised an eyebrow and gestured with an exaggerated hand motion to her left. "Well? What are you waiting for? An invitation?"

With a hard jerk, the guards pulled me in the direction of an open door and shoved me in. A light flickered on above me, and the door slammed behind me.

I was officially imprisoned.

....

chapter thirty-eight

West

It was nearly three a.m., and I hadn't heard a sound outside my bedroom in over an hour. I couldn't wait much longer. I stared at my PulsePoint, which told me that Justin was officially offline. Hopefully that meant he would be asleep for the next several hours.

Unfortunately, he had taken the wedding announcement as an invitation to begin sleeping in my mother's bedroom. However, I *did* know exactly where he was.

I quickly typed a message and pressed send. Ten seconds later I got the response I needed.

Your guards are in place and ready.

Good. See you in five.

I replaced my PulsePoint on my belt next to my Taser, then as quietly as possible slipped out of my room and toward the door to exit the suite.

"West."

The tiny hairs on the back of my neck stood at attention at the sound of my mother's voice. I turned slowly. She was wrapped in a long black silk robe. Her eyes were puffy and filled with emotion.

"Mother. What are you doing out of bed?" I glanced nervously toward her bedroom.

"Don't worry about Justin," she said in answer to my silent question. "I found the drugs he's been giving me." Her lips quirked slightly before turning serious.

My shoulders fell forward in relief. "Still, Mother, you should be sleeping."

"Willow was never meant to survive. You know that, right?" A tear slid down her cheek.

I'd never seen her look so frightened. "Don't say that. You have to keep hoping. I'm still fighting for her."

"I know you are. That's why I need you to know that the council is behind everything. I don't know if it's the entire council, or just *some* members, but it's definitely them. They found out that I knew the whereabouts of Christina Black, and they knew she would be the key to developing the vaccine our city needed."

"But why did that matter? Why did we need a vaccine for a virus that was gone from our city?"

"Because the council knows that the city is getting restless. More and more citizens are wanting to venture back outside."

"So Cricket was right from the very beginning." And Mrs. Canary confirmed it for me. "They've been intentionally infecting people with the virus in the hope that they might save one of them. Because without a survivor, they don't have the antibodies." Not to mention that would have meant they'd found a treatment.

More tears slid down my mother's face. "I didn't know about it until recently, I swear. Not until they infected your sister. They used Willow to force my hand. So that I would tell them where Christina was."

"Why didn't you just tell them where she was in the first place?" I cringed at the thought, but I needed to hear Mother's version of this—to verify she wasn't part of the council's plan. "You had the resources. You could have simply sent guards for her."

"If I had left it up to the council, Christina would have been locked in a room in the medical sector, never to be heard from again, while they harvested antibodies from her. Christina was like a daughter to me, West. I promised her parents I would treat her like one of my own. I was trying to protect her. But when Willow got sick... I couldn't just let Willow die."

"So you sent *me* for Christina. Because you wanted her to be able to choose whether she returned or not. Our guards wouldn't have given her that choice."

Mother shrugged. "She was your first love. But she was my responsibility, and I failed her years ago."

"And where does Justin fit into this? Is he working with the council?"

"Somehow, Justin convinced the council that he was on board with the scouting mission; he cast himself as being more agreeable than I was about the idea of reentering the outside. At the same time, he was making a play for the presidency."

"So he infected Willow with the virus?"

Mother remained expressionless. "No. Some members of the council, desperate for a vaccine for Bad Sam, infected Willow. And I've almost narrowed it down to exactly which members. Justin had nothing to do with it—but it played directly into what he needed."

"To slow down the election." I grabbed the chair next to her. "So why send Bad Sam out into the settlements?"

"Why go after a presidency of a city that might not exist at some point? By putting Bad Sam back out in the outside world, it scares our citizens to stay right where they are."

"Continuing to give him a city to preside over."

"That's right."

"And what does he have over you, Mom? Why did you agree to give him the presidency? And to *marry* him? Why would you do that?"

She looked me directly in the eye. "I would do anything for my son."

"*Me*? What does any of this have to do with me?"

Mother didn't answer straight away. "You know," she said, "after you left to find Christina, Justin got great joy out of cutting your ties to the city."

"Shutting off my PulsePoint."

"That's right. He would have been delighted if you had never returned. And then, when the two scouts entered our walls infected with Bad Sam, he got his wish. With Bad Sam running rampant on the outside, it was decided that none of the scouts would be allowed to return to the city. It was too great a risk."

"That's... that's heartless."

Mother was silent.

"But, the council still wanted to bring in Christina."

"Yes. The council wanted Christina. And I wanted you. And Justin... Justin has surprising influence with certain council members. He assured me that he could convince the council to bring both of you in together. A 'package deal,' he called it."

"But only after you agreed to marry him and hand over the presidency."

She nodded. "The marriage is just for show, West. For all his faults, Justin is a clever manipulator. He knew that our people would never believe the council had simply handed the presidency to him. But a marriage would increase his legitimacy in the eyes of the people. As would his relationship with you."

"He claimed that the council was ready to groom me to take over."

Mother stood and placed a cool hand on my face. "That part is true. You have two things that neither I nor Justin can give them: Christina, and the hearts of the people."

I cocked my head, not understanding.

"The younger people—the up-and-coming generation of leaders—love you. They will follow you to the ends of the earth. If you tell them the outside is too dangerous, they'll believe you. If you tell them it's time to establish homes around the country again, they'll ask you to lead them there. The council knows this."

I stared deeply into my mother's eyes. "But I don't have Christina." I bowed my head. "I don't even deserve Christina. She's so good and brave and unselfish."

"So are you, my son. Or you wouldn't have developed your own team of guards and supporters that are ready and waiting for you tonight."

"How did you—"

"Know?" She smiled. "Please. I'm president of this big city. I have eyes in every sector. And my supporters will join your supporters."

315

As if on cue, my PulsePoint pinged at my waist: *Where are you?*

I quickly typed a reply: *Start without me. I have something I need to take care of first.*

I leaned in and gave my mother a kiss on the cheek. "Cricket is still going to get a chance to save Willow. But I'm going to need your help."

"Anything."

....

chapter thirty-nine

Cricket

I lay on the bed and stared at the ceiling of a room very similar to the one I was taken to on my first day back inside New Caelum. A clock hanging over the door ticked loudly with each passing second. Hope slipped away as the hour hand moved closer to the five.

My stomach growled loudly, reminding me that I had skipped dinner the night before, yet the thought of food repulsed me as I thought of the people who were fighting for their life.

Instinctively, my hand went to my neck. As I fingered the bloodstone beads my parents had given me, and the small charm hand-carved by West, I went over Caine's notes in my head—notes I had helped him take as he tried over and over again to develop a medicine to treat Bad Sam.

Caine's treatment *had* worked. The rats had been getting better. It was just that their hearts and other organs had given out anyway. "That's what the bloodstones did for me," I said to myself.

But I had figured this out while I was on the roof with West. The problem now was how to get the bloodstones into the patients' bloodstreams. I lay an arm across my forehead and closed my eyes. "Nothing's that simple."

Then I remembered something my dad used to tell people when he was preparing a team for a trip to Africa—something he learned from his time in the Navy. He would tell his team to never expect to have enough medical supplies to treat every injury or illness. Be prepared to work with the bare minimum and to do it effectively. And he would tell them of another principle coined by the Navy: "Keep it Simple, Stupid." I whispered the phrase to myself over and over while listening to the ticking of the clock.

At the sound of the door rattling, I rose and jumped to my feet.

It was the girl from the reception desk. "Well, well. So, this is what all the fuss is about. The famous Christina Black." She crossed her arms and leaned against the doorjamb.

I gave her a once-over. I probably could defend myself against her, but based on the fact that she wore red—meaning she was a member of military or emergency personnel, according to West—I assumed she was fully capable of handling anything I could throw at her.

"Don't you talk? West assured me you were very nice."

I raised a brow. "Oh yeah? And what else did West say about me?" Even I could hear the contempt in my voice as I spat out his name.

She grinned. "Don't get your panties in a bundle. He asked me to help. I'm Shiloh. Come on."

She motioned me forward and out into the reception area. Then she lifted her arm, punched a few buttons on her wrist PulsePoint, and flashed it against a sensor beside the door next to mine. That door clicked and opened to a dark room, but instead of entering, she backed away from it.

"Dax, I've brought you a surprise, so if you're planning on wrestling me to the ground again, please know that someone is here to see you, and she is entering first." Shiloh smiled at me. "Dax and I like to play this little game."

I eyed Shiloh with extreme curiosity. I would have liked to have seen this woman, barely bigger than I, wrestle Dax, a man twice my size.

I entered the dark room with slow steps, not sure if I trusted this Shiloh quite yet. "Dax? It's me, Cricket."

He stepped out of the shadows, his blond hair catching the light of the lamp just outside the door. When he saw me, he scooped me into his arms.

Shiloh flipped on a bright overhead light, revealing a white room identical to my own, and then she turned and disappeared.

Dax squinted his eyes against the light, and placed his hands on my cheeks. "Are you okay?"

"I'm fine."

Shiloh returned with a small duffel bag. "We don't have much time." She set the duffel on the small bed and began rummaging through it.

"We don't have much time for what?" I asked.

"Here." She thrust a bundle of white at my chest. "Put these on. And Dax, these are for you." She handed him light gray clothes, the color guards wore.

I looked down at the white clothing she'd given me. "Can you get me in to see Dr. Hempel?"

"That's the plan." She pulled a brown wig and some eye-glasses from the bag.

Dax looked from me to Shiloh and back. "Will someone tell *me* the plan?"

Understanding, I began to shed my royal blue clothes, turning when I removed my top so that Dax would only see my back. "This is our disguise, Dax. Do as she says. Because she's right. We're running out of time." I quickly slipped into a pair of scrubs and a white lab coat.

Shiloh helped me with the wig, adjusting the straight brown hair and bangs so they framed my face and hid the blond strands underneath. When she was done, she backed up a step. "You *are* pretty. He wasn't wrong about that."

I assumed she meant West. "West had me locked up," I said.

"Yes, and now he's letting you cure his sister."

So that's what this was about.

Shiloh set some other things on the bed: a couple of belts, Tasers, small flashlights, and a PulsePoint. I reached out and snatched the PulsePoint, turning it over to verify that it was, in fact, my own.

"West thought you might need that."

I eyed Shiloh. "Where is he?"

"I wouldn't know." She looked away from me and down at the PulsePoint on her wrist. Something close to irritation flitted across her face. "We need to go."

"Wait." Dax ran a hand through his hair, his eyes locked on mine. He held a Taser loosely in his hand. "Look, I'm more than thrilled to use this on someone. West, even." A fleeting grin played with the corner of his lips. "But the last time I saw you, the president of this stupid city told her flock of sheep that you were marrying their stupid prince."

"Prince," Shiloh laughed. "He'd like that." When Dax furrowed his brows at her, she held her hands up. "Sorry. I'm just trying to help." She backed up toward the door. "I'll give you two a minute, but don't take long. Our window is closing quickly."

Dax placed the Taser and one of the flashlights on his belt. "Can you at least give me the thirty-second version of what you're planning?"

I took in a deep breath. "The doctor that Caine said could give us a cure for Bad Sam is now sick."

"What? How did that happen?"

"I can only guess that he mishandled the virus."

"Or whoever gave Ryder and Key the virus also infected the doc."

"That's also possible. I think the government is somehow behind the reappearance of Bad Sam, but I have no proof yet."

"You think they sent the virus out into our settlements on purpose?" His brows tilted inward, and deep lines of shock formed across his forehead.

"It looks that way, but I don't know why."

"And who is West to you?"

Good question. I was starting to believe that West was a figment of my imagination—my past catching up to me to play tricks on my heart.

Reaching down and grabbing Dax's hands, I let a heavy sigh pass through my lips before looking up at him, my eyes holding his gaze. "I want to tell you everything. I do. And I will. But right now, we need to get to the labs, get a treatment for Dylan, and get out of here so that we can let New Caelum destroy the bomb, or the innocent people of this city are going to have another deadly virus outbreak on their hands. And if the virus spreads inside..."

"The people will flee to the outside."

"Yes. Or a large part of the city's population will die. Or both."

"You promised me we would run away from another outbreak," Dax said.

It was true. Dax and I had spent hours and hours in the past talking about human nature and our need to survive. We'd always promised each other that if there was another outbreak, we would flee the heavily populated areas and ride out the illness together. We would not look to anyone else for help. We wouldn't risk infecting another.

I blinked away any emotion from my eyes. "Yes, but that was before our friends—and your brother—got sick."

"So... you're not staying and marrying this West-person?" Dax smiled like he was joking, but I think a part of him was scared I would do exactly that.

"No," I said, and my heart constricted. "Let's get to the lab and get what we need so that we can get away from this crazy city."

"Lead the way."

~~~~~

According to Shiloh, it wasn't out of the ordinary for representatives of red, gray, and white to walk together in the middle of the night through the halls of New Caelum, and she assured me that I looked nothing like myself under this brown wig that perfectly hid my scars. "However," she warned, "it could get a little tricky once we get inside the medical sector. Dr. Hempel is in an isolation unit within the main research lab, so that he can be close to Dr. Pooley while he works."

"How do you know so much?" I asked, glancing out into the darkness as we passed through one of the tunnels leading us between buildings. "What's your role inside this city of hierarchy? Besides being a part of the emergency sector, that is." I couldn't hide the disdain in my voice. I was starting to believe every person inside the city was given a specified role, not for their own individual good or even for the good of the city as a whole, but for the good of the government who ran things.

"I am a supporter of a growing movement to overthrow the council and turn the city into a full-fledged democracy. We believe that the people should have the right to decide for themselves what happens to them. And we support doing away with the dictatorship we seem to have now, and cherishing all of our differences and the gifts we provide to New Caelum."

Interesting. "And does this growing movement support the marriage of President Layne and Vice President Rhodes?"

"We don't care who they marry," she deadpanned. "We just don't want them running our lives."

I traded glances with Dax. He looked confused, but was probably liking this Shiloh and her sense of rebellion.

"And who do you and your fellow minions support as your leader?" he asked. "Or are you a bunch of free spirits who want to do away with all government?"

She evil-eyed Dax. "Every large group needs leadership. We simply believe that the leader we need is one who will endorse equal rights among the citizens."

"And who does your group hope will lead you?" I knew the answer before I even asked it.

At the end of the pedway, she stopped to open a door for us. She allowed Dax to enter first, then stood directly in front of me. "West is the future of this city. He will be our next president."

"But West is already being groomed to take over. What does your group hope to accomplish that the council isn't already doing?"

"The president, although popular, doesn't really hold that much power. The council is truly running this city, and most people know that the council is corrupt. The council will never lead us forward; in fact, they deliberately hold us back. Only West is ready to lead us into the next era."

"Why was I so important?"

She tilted her head, and a grin lifted the corners of her lips. "Because while many of us are ready to reenter the outside, the council understands the importance of a vaccine to prevent future outbreaks of Bad Sam."

I studied her eyes. She was being quite forthcoming. "Sounds to me like there's enough support behind West already without adding me to the mix." They had my antibodies now. "Why do you need me inside the city?"

"You guys coming?" Dax asked from inside.

Shiloh leaned closer. "Why do we need you? We don't. But West *wants* you." She turned and walked through the door, joining Dax and leaving me trailing behind them.

~~~~~

We were approaching the main medical laboratories. My pulse sped up with each step we took. There was no guarantee that my theory would work—that the beads my parents had left me would be the missing ingredient in Caine's or Dr. Hempel's already tried and failed drug cocktail. What if what I was remembering about that mysterious hospital visit was something else entirely? What if it wasn't so simple?

We turned the next corner to find an army of red hazmat suits at the end of the hallway. Shiloh stopped, and Dax and I collided with her back. We quickly retreated out of sight. Shiloh darted for the first door we saw, and we followed her through it, into a stairwell.

Shiloh pressed something on her PulsePoint, then spoke into it. "We're in the north stairwell of the hospital." Her voice echoed around us.

West's voice came across the PulsePoint. "The fifth floor is packed with red."

"We saw that. What now?"

"Go back out the door you just entered. Proceed away from the lab, to Room 517. I left red hazmat gear for Christina and Dax there."

My eyes widened as West said my given name. Dax's head jerked up. His eyes found mine, but I looked away. I had promised I would tell him everything. But now was not the time.

"Did you give Christina her PulsePoint?" West asked Shiloh.

"Yes."

"Point yours toward her."

Shiloh tilted her wrist in my direction, and I immediately saw West's face. Though the screen was small, I was amazed at how in control he looked. When he saw me, his face softened. "I'm sorry. In order to get Justin out of the hospital wing and away from you, I had to convince him that I believed you were a threat to our city."

"I *am* a threat to your city," I said curtly.

He smiled. "No you're not. I know you'll make sure the bomb is destroyed. After you find a cure and save my sister. I can't say I don't believe in miracles; you're evidence that miracles do exist. But my sister is barely hanging on."

A knot formed over my heart. West was losing hope. I could see it in his eyes. "I'll do what I can. I just need to get into the lab."

He nodded. "Once you're suited up, you should be able to get in. The others won't recognize you with that dark hair under the hazmat mask, and your face will be mostly covered. And Dr. Pooley knows you're coming. But you won't have much time once you're inside. The others will figure it out eventually. I'll jam the locking system for as long as possible, but when the alarm sounds on your PulsePoint, you'll need to get out of there. I'll send a map for your exit through your device."

"What happens after that?" I was asking so many things with that simple question, more than he could possibly answer across the tiny screen or in the small amount of time we had. Ever since West had found me again, I knew our timing wasn't right, and might never be right.

He paused a moment. His hazel eyes appeared bright green in the small screen. "I'll be in touch," he said, but I could hear the desire to say more. "Good luck."

Shiloh's screen went dark. She lowered her wrist. "Okay then. Let's go."

We looked both ways as we exited the stairwell. Shiloh darted right. We followed her to the room at West's instructions. When we reached Room 517, Dax and I entered first. The room was dark. As I felt around for a light switch, I heard a male voice from behind us, in the hallway.

"You there."

I froze. Dax plastered himself against the wall behind the door, pulling me with him.

Shiloh didn't enter. Instead, she let the door close. "Hello, Mr. Rhodes."

I turned my frantic gaze on Dax. He wrapped his hand around mine and squeezed.

"Shiloh, what are you doing over here in the hospital sector?"

"I was ordered here by my superior, but I was told to dress in protective clothing. I forgot where they keep the gear that I need."

A moment of silence passed. "Follow me," Justin ordered.

Their footsteps retreated from the door, and Dax and I let out a collective sigh.

Dax clicked on the small flashlight Shiloh had given us.

I looked around the small room—a large medical supply closet of some sort. In the corner was a metal rod where several white lab coats hung beside two complete red hazmat suits. I scrambled over to them and started to slip one of them on over my clothes.

But Dax stepped closer to me and reached a hand to cup my cheek. "You're the infamous Christina Black, aren't you? The one person who survived. The one person who's immune to Bad Sam. And the person West came looking for."

"Yes." I squeezed my eyes shut, knowing I was only answering "yes" to a portion of his question. Yes, I was Christina Black, but I no longer knew if I was immune to Bad Sam. "I'm sorry I didn't tell you. I so badly wanted to forget that part of my life. But it seems my past has caught up with me."

"I understand. I can't help but want to save you now, though. To get you out of here. To learn why West didn't even recognize the Cricket I've come to know." Deep lines formed across his forehead. "But... Dylan."

"I know." I touched a finger to Dax's lips. "I have to do what I can. I can't promise anything, but if there's a chance that I'm able to help anyone with this disease, I have to try."

"I'm with you all the way."

I started to argue with him, to convince him to stay behind, but I realized that if we didn't stick together, I didn't know how I'd get him out of New Caelum.

"Listen to me," I said. "When we're in the lab, you touch nothing. And you don't remove any part of this protective gear until I say. You understand?"

Dax nodded.

We suited up. When I was satisfied that both of our sets of gear were on properly and completely, and that my necklace was safely tucked in a pocket on the belt beside my PulsePoint, I led us from the closet and turned toward the lab. This time when we rounded the corner, we came face to face with ten or so guards in black protective gear and at least that many emergency personnel in red. Dax and I squeezed through the crowd, making our way to the main doors to the laboratory. No one even noticed us.

"Listen up," a voice boomed behind us. The people around us shifted and turned toward the voice. I didn't want to turn, but felt we should. When we did, I realized the voice belonged to Justin.

"There are two outsiders inside our city. Their pictures have been sent to your PulsePoints. If you see them, bring them directly to me. But do nothing to harm them. I need them alive and conscious. Now, all of you in red, follow me. I need you to—"

I didn't wait for Justin to finish his sentence before lifting my PulsePoint to the scanner beside the door. As soon as the lock clicked, I pulled Dax with me into the lab. No one tried to stop us.

As soon as we entered the lab, a doctor in protective gear approached. "We no longer need any emergency personnel. Weren't you told?"

I swallowed hard. "I'm under orders to speak to Dr. Pooley immediately."

"That's not possible. Dr. Pooley is not to be disturbed. No one is to enter his lab until Mr. Rhodes gives the okay."

"It's okay, Maria." A voice sounded through a speaker over-head. We turned toward the lab, where Dr. Pooley spoke through an intercom from inside. "And could you be a doll and get me some food? Something with plenty of protein? And maybe some fruit?"

"Some fruit," Maria said, irritation in her voice. "I'll have to decontaminate if I leave."

"Yes, I know. I'm sorry to trouble you. Thank you."

Maria left in a huff, and Dr. Pooley pointed us toward the entrance to the main lab. Dax and I had not been inside an area sensitive to Bad Sam yet, so we entered without changing gear.

"This lab is way bigger than Caine's." Dax's voice came through the speaker in his mask.

"Yes. They take every precaution to prevent the spread of disease."

"Yeah, well, they've done a *terrific* job of it. With all this, how did it manage to spread?"

I shrugged at the question that had haunted me the entire time I'd been inside New Caelum, though I new the answer lay within the deception of a group of people that swore to protect this city. Inside the lab, we joined Dr. Pooley. Behind him the timer continued to count down. 14 hours, 34 minutes, and 32 seconds.

"West says you might have figured out what our treatment is missing," Dr. Pooley said, without looking up from his microscope.

I lifted my hand and revealed my necklace. "I believe my parents injected me with the substance found inside a bloodstone."

Dr. Pooley's eyes widened briefly. He lifted his hand, cupping his chin and massaging his whiskers as he considered what I had said. Then he leaned his head back and belted out a loud laugh. I traded a puzzled glance with Dax.

"You mean to tell me that we've hung our last hope on some silly bead from a child's necklace?"

I lowered my hand back to my side. The necklace dangled against my thigh. "This isn't just any necklace. This is a medicinal mineral. It's very rare in our country, but it's worn widely in the countries of Africa. My parents believed that this stone was the reason why people in those countries were better at fighting many diseases—not just Bad Sam. The people in those countries used the medicinal properties from this stone in many ways. I think that's why they returned to Africa—to obtain additional bloodstones."

"But we don't know if anyone is alive in any of those countries, do we?"

No, we don't, I wanted to scream. *Because President Layne stopped all travel and cut off all communication with the rest of the world.*

Panic mounted inside me like magma inside a volcano. I glanced backward toward the isolation unit, where I was sure Dr. Hempel must be. "Can't we at least try? West said you were going to help me."

My PulsePoint vibrated at my side. I glanced down at it and found a text message from West: *You will see guards in red and black enter the outer chambers any second. They won't be able to access the room yet because of the scrambled lock codes, but when the alarm sounds, know that you have about ten minutes before they unscramble the codes.*

I glanced toward Dax, helpless. "We don't have time for this," I said, no longer caring that Dr. Pooley could hear us. I pulled the PulsePoint from my belt and began typing: *Dr. Pooley is not cooperating.*

Can you come up with a treatment yourself?

What? No. I shook my head, though West clearly couldn't see me.

"What is it?" Dax asked.

I handed him the PulsePoint.

"You can. You've helped Caine for years."

"I've *watched* Caine for years. I've never really *done* anything."

Movement out of the corner of my eye distracted me. Dax and I turned toward the outer chamber, where guards dressed in red and black had gathered, all armed with Tasers. The last one to enter was Justin. I could see the stern look in his eye.

"We're out of time."

"You were out of time before you even started," Dr. Pooley said behind me.

"Cricket, look out!" Dax screamed.

I whipped around just as Dr. Pooley came at me with a syringe and needle. I grabbed his arm, falling backward to the ground. He straddled me and was about to jab the needle into my arm when Dax kicked the syringe out of Dr. Pooley's hand, then landed a boot into Dr. Pooley's head, knocking him off of me and unconscious.

I sat up, panting and holding a hand over my heart, and met Dax's gaze. "Thank you."

He let out a relieved breath. "My pleasure." And I was sure he meant it. I think he'd been wanting to hit something or someone ever since he'd arrived inside New Caelum.

So, it looked like it was up to me to test my theory and develop a cure for Bad Sam. I pushed myself up and surveyed the lab. Could I do this? Behind Dr. Pooley's unconscious body was the row of refrigerators where Dr. Hempel and Dr. Pooley had been storing the substances they'd been using and creating, including the refrigerator the virus was stored in.

I opened the refrigerators and removed trays of vials. I could quickly see the difference in Dr. Pooley's handwriting as compared to Dr. Hempel's and Caine's. I sorted through vial after vial, all tagged with dates and names and other cryptic indicators. As I looked over the many trays, all marked by different doctors, a slow burn developed in my chest.

"I can't do this," I whispered. "I don't even know where to begin." I closed my eyes. What had I been thinking? I couldn't do this alone. I needed Dr. Hempel. Or Caine.

Suddenly, the alarm West had warned me about sounded from my PulsePoint. My eyes flew open. "We have ten minutes."

"Cricket, can you do it?" Dax asked, his voice surprisingly calm. "If not, no one will blame you, but if you can't, let's get the hell out of here."

I looked back at him. "Keep it simple, stupid," I said softly. "I can do this."

I glanced at the timer and marked the minute. "Watch the timer."

Keeping it simple and sticking to what I knew, I searched through the trays of vials until I finally found the ones I had brought with me. The tray that Caine had been using on the rats.

"The earlier dates will have stronger antibodies," I said to myself. "I'll use those." I turned in all directions looking for the tool I needed. "Quick, over there." I pointed across the lab. "Grab that mortar and pestle." Every scientist needed one.

Dax handed me the tool, and I quickly pulled one of my beads off of my necklace and placed it in the small bowl. I crushed and ground the bead until it made a fine powder, trying not to wonder what I was doing or if it would even work. I couldn't afford doubts. It had to work.

The guards in hazmats banged on the windows.

"Christina, let me in so we can talk." It was Justin, speaking over the intercom from the other side of the window. "I think you've somehow gotten the impression that we don't want your help in obtaining a cure for Willow and Dr. Hempel. We just didn't take kindly to you threatening us with your computer virus and your Bad Sam bomb."

I looked up, distracted and angered. "If you had simply allowed me to work with Dr. Hempel, I and my weapons would have been gone from here by now. And you would have your treatment." I poured the bloodstone powder into a beaker. I had no idea how much of it would be needed for each person.

Keep it simple, stupid, I repeated to myself.

"Christina, West would really like you to stay with him. And I know you'd like that, too."

Dax's jaw hardened. "Can we shut him up?"

"We can work something out. Open the door, Christina," Justin continued. "The council and our city want you to join us here."

"Feel free to crush the intercom over there."

Dax walked over to the windows. He grabbed a metal stool and slammed it repeatedly into the intercom until the vice president's voice crackled into incoherent static. "There. That's better."

I smiled, but continued to separate the vials in front of me into two trays.

"Why are you separating these?"

I cringed inwardly and looked up into Dax's brown eyes—eyes I'd studied so often since we'd met. He was my friend. Aside from Nina, he was my *best* friend. I had kept too many secrets from him. He deserved to know this one.

"This set"—I pointed to the vials on my left—"is filled with a medicine that Caine developed from antibodies he took from me a few years ago. The others"—I gestured to my right— "used antibodies taken from me more recently."

"Why does it matter? Are the fresher antibodies more effective?"

I shook my head, and he read the expression on my face.

"What are you saying?"

"You know now that I'm not immune to Bad Sam the same way Caine and Nina are. My immunity came from developing antibodies after I survived the virus. Well..."

"Has your immunity to Bad Sam weakened?" he asked, his voice cracking slightly. "That's what Caine meant with the message he sent me here with, isn't it?"

"Yes."

Dax only stared at me. His Adam's apple moved as he swallowed.

"Now tell me the time," I said.

He gave his head a shake, then glanced toward the timer. "You have four minutes."

Four minutes, and I hadn't heard from West in over ten. How was I going to get out of this lab without West giving us an escape route?

Remembering to keep it simple, I mixed plain saline solution with the powder from the bloodstone. Now I was ready to add the last ingredient to the vials. I carefully removed the lids from each of the six vials with the older antibodies.

"I hope this works." Using a dropper, I added equal amounts of the bloodstone mixture to all six vials.

Then I quickly replaced the lids, and I packed up everything I wanted to take with me in the same dry ice containers I'd brought from Boone Blackston's hospital. I also snatched a couple of vials from Dr. Hempel's collection—the ones containing the chemical he'd shown me yesterday. He'd said that that chemical might repair the antibodies running through my blood; maybe Caine could learn something from it.

"How are we going to get out of here?" Dax asked. "Do you plan on West coming to our rescue?"

I hadn't really been planning on West's help since the minute he'd allowed Justin to lock me up. "No. But I do have a plan."

I used my PulsePoint to scan and unlock the refrigerator marked with the biohazard symbol—where live viruses were stored. I grabbed the vials of Bad Sam I had brought with me and placed them in their proper cases. After pouring dry ice over the vials, I closed them up. But I kept one vial out, enclosing it safely in my hand.

Then I led Dax through the decontamination chambers. After we had sufficiently rid ourselves of any virus we may have been exposed to inside the lab, we quickly suited back up in dark gray hazmat suits.

When we faced the exit, I cast a worried look at Dax.

"I'm not one to usually panic," he said. "But we're trapped in here."

"Stay close to me."

He raised an eyebrow. "You expected me to stray?" He glanced down at my hand. "What are you holding, anyway?"

I started to answer when the outer doors clicked. They had broken through the lock codes. "Here we go."

I shoved through the door and came face to face with several men and one girl—Shiloh—in red. Was she there to help? It didn't matter.

I stepped in front of Dax and held out my hand. "Don't come any closer. This vial contains live Samael Strain."

Shiloh's eyes widened, and her hands went out to her side. They all started to back up.

Everyone except for Justin. "You are resourceful, aren't you?"

"You left me no choice. Do your people even know what you and your government have done?"

"You couldn't possibly know anything about our government."

"I know plenty. Now back up." I shook the vial for effect, and they did as I ordered, including Justin. "Your people should know that you deliberately infected members of your own community with Bad Sam and then sent them out into the settlements. That's the only reason the outside is plagued with illness. Is anyone here missing their friend Garrett?"

Everything in the lab went deathly quiet. Then the rustling of a hazmat suit got my attention. A girl who had to be about my age stepped forward. "My brother has been missing for seven days."

"Your brother is Garrett?"

She nodded, fear etched into the lines around her eyes.

"I'm so very sorry, but guards in red hazmat gear killed your brother and his friend when they returned from a scouting mission infected with Bad Sam." I studied the faces of each of the people in front of me through their masks. I then raised my voice to drive the point home. "Scouts from your city were deliberately infected with Bad Sam while *still inside this city.*"

"Why should we believe you?" someone yelled.

"You don't have to believe me. But eventually, more evidence of what I'm telling you will come to light. For now, all I need is for you to back away, because I will have no problem whatsoever dropping this vial of virus against the floor. And when I do, Bad Sam will be inside your city, and there will be no stopping its spread."

Shiloh typed something on her PulsePoint. Justin's face reddened. His hands hung to his sides, helpless.

Dax and I reached the outer door and pushed through it. When a guard appeared, I held the vial out in front of me. "Step back and let us pass."

"Do as she says," Justin ordered in frustration. "I never should have let you and West back inside this city."

Several of the guards' heads whipped around in Justin's direction. That's when I knew I had them. Though they weren't quite ready to believe their government was corrupt, they *were* West's supporters.

"West is the one person in leadership right now who is thinking clearly," I said. "West has the people of New Caelum's best interests at heart and on his mind. He has been willing to sacrifice his own needs to lead you." I glanced at Shiloh. A smile played at the corners of her lips. I was pretty sure she was here to help me, but I didn't need her. There was no sense risking her life with what I had to do next. "If anyone follows us, I will throw this vial like a grenade."

And with that, we reach the staircase door. We darted inside and disappeared.

....

chapter forty

West

I'd always wondered if a person actually saw stars when he took a hit to the head. I could now definitely say "yes"—as I saw plenty of them after one of Justin's guards landed a solid left hook to my jaw.

"How did she get into the lab, West? Who helped Christina and her friend escape the holding room?"

I remained silent. My hands were tied behind my back behind a wooden chair. Where the hell were my reinforcements? They should have been here already. And where was Mother?

The door slid open, and another guard entered. "They should be inside the lab in less than two minutes," he said. "Justin said to just hold West here until he could get up here."

"You both realize what Christina Black is doing, right?" I asked.

The second guard—who was even larger than the one that clocked me—leaned in close to my face. I held my breath when the rotten egg smell of his breath hit me. "We don't care. Our orders are to keep you busy and use whatever force we deem necessary."

The other asshole joined in. "And no one needed to tell us twice. We're delighted to have the opportunity to take the prince of New Caelum down a notch."

I smiled. "You're making a big mistake."

"Oh yeah?" the first guard asked. "Why do you say that?"

"You're fighting on the wrong team."

They both laughed.

"I'm not kidding. The council is dead. Soon there will be a new vice president, maybe even a new president, and you, my friends, will find yourselves on the losing team."

The first guard marched over and lifted me to my feet by my hair. Then he slammed a fist into my gut. I fell to my knees and came close to falling on my face. Instead I lowered my forehead slowly to the ground while coughing.

"Marc, man, be careful. Justin said not to hurt him."

The door slid open, and in walked my mother. It was about freaking time. After a quick glance at me, she faced the two guards, who stood at attention. "What have you discovered?" she asked them.

"Nothing, ma'am." The guards exchanged a sideways glance.

"Justin will not be pleased." She turned to me, reached down, squeezed my jaw with her hand, and forced me to look at her—all a part of the act she and I had discussed. "Who is working with you to help Christina?"

I smiled, knowing full well my mouth was bleeding. She cringed. "No one," I said. "Christina has always been a rebellious one. She has a mind of her own."

"That much is true. Well, we'll have to tame her soon enough." She sighed and turned back to the guards. "Jacob, Marcus, you will report back to your superiors at once. There will be a city-wide meeting this afternoon, and we need every guard and emergency worker to be prepared."

"What about Mr. Layne, ma'am?"

"My own guards will place my son into custody. Now go."

The guards turned and left without another word. When they were gone, I quickly turned. As soon as Mother had my hands untied, I scrambled over to my PulsePoint. "Took you long enough," I said, while typing a message to Shiloh.

"Sorry. Wasn't easy to round up enough of my trusted guards to change the course of command on a moment's notice."

"But no problems? Who's guarding Willow?"

"If Christina comes up with a treatment and can make it to the floor where Willow is quarantined without getting caught, she'll have no problem getting into the iso unit." I heard the doubt in Mother's voice.

My own PulsePoint pinged: *The guards are in. Cricket and Dax will be caught, but I'll be close.*

"What's the status of the computer virus?" Mother asked.

"IT is still working on it. Right now I have to find Councilman Gatewood." Mr. Gatewood was the one councilman Mother insisted we could trust.

"We better get going then. It won't take long before Justin starts putting things together and locks us both up."

My PulsePoint pinged with another message from Shiloh: *There's a problem.*

What? I asked.

Cricket and Dax have disappeared. They're in dark gray hazmats, so they could be anywhere.

······································

chapter forty-one

Cricket

"D o you know where we're going?"

"Kind of. Just try to blend in and act like you're somebody." My hand with the virus shook. I was holding a hugely lethal weapon, and I couldn't take the time to stop and secure it inside my pack.

The halls were busy with people in red and charcoal-colored hazmat suits. But no one was even looking our way, which felt slightly eerie. One floor up and a long, colorful curve of a hallway later, we approached a double set of doors with leadership guards standing outside. I slowed. Dax was on my heels.

The guards didn't even ask us any questions; they simply held the doors open for us. "Has to be West," I said. "He must be here."

Dax and I darted by the guards.

Just like the last time I'd been inside the isolation suite, we found several nurses monitoring Willow. I walked up to the glass to stare at her. She looked terrible. One nurse blotted Willow's neck with white gauze.

"She's bleeding from her pores," I said, mostly to myself.

"Hello, Christina."

I spun around. It was West's mother, wearing black protective gear. "Hi, President Layne."

"Please, call me Ginger. You did once upon a time."

"That was a long time ago."

Dax remained motionless beside me.

"It wasn't that long ago. I remember it like it was yesterday."

"President Layne, I have a treatment. I don't know if it will help Willow, but I'm afraid it's our last chance. I think it's as good of a chance as we've had."

If I hadn't been watching her closely, I would have missed the glimmer of hope that flashed in the president's eye. But she crossed her arms across her stomach and looked away, as if she was trying to hide her emotions. "I'm afraid it might be too late for Willow."

I turned my head toward Willow. Nothing but the blinking lights on the machines beside her showed any sign of life. When I turned back, I caught President Layne blinking back tears. She was losing her daughter.

I reached out a hand, but stopped short of touching President Layne. "Ginger, if everyone thinks it's too late, what do we have to lose by trying?"

A doctor and a nurse hovered nearby, awaiting some command from their president—the mother of their patient. She turned her head and gave them a slight nod. "Let the girl administer her treatment."

The doctor gestured for me to head down the short hallway and into the room that would lead through the decontamination chambers. Just before I entered the room, I looked back at Dax. "Wait out here for me, okay?"

He didn't respond, but his face tightened, and deep trenches formed across his forehead.

"Miss Black, would you mind decontaminating, then changing into another set of protective gear before you enter Willow's room?"

I did as the doctor asked. After decontamination, I placed the vial of the Samael Strain into the container with the other vials. After I'd re-suited up in a charcoal hazmat, I pulled out a vial of my cure. Or what I hoped might be a successful treatment.

Inside Willow's room, my heart constricted into a tight ball when I heard the labored sound of her breathing. Every time she inhaled, it was like she had been held underwater and was just coming up for that first breath of air.

I held the vial out to the doctor. "Here's the treatment that I hope will help Willow. The dosing instructions are written on the side of the vials." Thank goodness Caine had been so meticulous with his written instructions.

He stared at the vial for a few seconds before taking it from me. "Don't get your hopes up. Her heart is weak. Her kidneys have shut down."

"Try it, please."

He took the vial from me and handed it to the nurse. I watched as she extracted the liquid from the vial into a syringe and then pushed the liquid directly into the IV line already in place.

It would take a miracle for this drug to work, and though I thought I didn't believe in miracles, West was right: I was somewhat of a living miracle myself. And who was to say that my parents hadn't left me with those beads so that we would one day discover their use?

"Do you have any idea how quickly this medicine might work?" the doctor asked me.

I hadn't thought about that. With the rats, it had taken... "A day or two?"

The doctor looked solemn. "I hope she has that long."

The nurses in the room continued to monitor fluid levels, Willow's heart rate and blood pressure, and all the other machines. I wanted to wait with Willow, to see if she showed improvement, but I couldn't afford to stay. The clock was ticking.

I stood up to leave, but before I did, I walked over and touched Willow's hand. "I've missed you, my friend."

As I stared at her—studying her pale face, the beads of sweat that formed along her hairline, and the open sores along her neck—I remembered clearly the pain and discomfort I had felt six years ago, when I was fighting for my life. I thought about how many times I had begged for God to just take my life, to rid me of the suffering, like he had done for so many before me.

On the other side of the decontamination chamber, I began to strip out of the protective gear. As I removed it, I noticed a small slice in the back of my suit and an area of wetness on my clothes where the disinfectant substance had seeped through. Had the slice been there all along? I hadn't really had a chance to look at the suit when I put it on, because the doctor had helped me suit up.

I lifted my head, and right in front of me was the doctor, still protected inside a hazmat suit.

"That suit was left here especially for you by Justin," the doctor said. "He said to tell you that he was sorry to hear about the waning immunity of your blood against the Samael Strain. Apparently Dr. Pooley overheard Dr. Hempel telling you this."

Then the doctor turned and walked out of the room, and I stared open-mouthed at his retreating back. My hand shook as I just stood there. I couldn't move. I was scared to.

A knock at the window alerted me to Dax standing just outside the room where I was changing. I swallowed hard and scrambled to slip into another charcoal hazmat, the only color in that room besides white and pale blue.

From inside my pack, I removed a second vial of the treatment. I opened the small refrigerator in the room and tucked the vial in a corner in the back.

When I exited the room, President Layne was waiting with Dax. "Thank you, Christina. You have shown my daughter great compassion. I only wish you two could have spent more time together."

"She was my friend."

"Cricket, we really need to get out of here." Dax touched my arm, and I flinched, making him draw his fingers back. "You've got what you came for, and the president has promised us safe passage out."

I turned to the president. "You have?"

"I was trying to think of a way to repay your kindness, and I've decided the best thing I could do for you at this moment is to show you a way out of New Caelum."

"Thank you." I had been wanting to leave New Caelum since the moment I'd arrived. But was I really going to leave without seeing West again?

"Cricket, come on. Let's go."

Just before leaving the isolation suite, I quickly sent West a note:

I left something for Dr. Hempel and the other sick child in the back of a refrigerator in the chamber outside of Willow's room. Please tell Dr. Hempel thank you. Though I didn't use his work, he did teach me what our medications had been missing. And West, I'm sorry our timing was so bad. I will miss you. I'm glad you found me, even if it was only for a brief time.

Love, C

The president and two of her guards personally led us down a back stairwell of the leadership wing to the ground floor. With each step I took, it became more difficult to breathe. I massaged what felt like a huge weight on my chest, trying to calm the panic I knew I was feeling both because I was leaving West...

... And because I'd just been exposed to the Samael Strain.

"Christina," President Layne said when we reached the door that would take Dax and me back out into our world. "I am sorry for how our city has treated you."

She had no idea just how badly her city—in the form of Justin Rhodes—had treated me.

"I so badly want to encourage you to stay here with us, but I promised West I would carry out your wishes."

I drew back as if I'd been slapped. "West asked you to send me away?"

"No, sweetie. He asked me to see to it that he kept his promise to you. He would have been here to say goodbye, but our city is in a state of unrest and needs him. He's going to be a wonderful leader."

"He already is."

President Layne smiled, and the warmth of it told me that West was going to be just fine in his city.

"You know that Justin and your council are corrupt, right?" I said.

She nodded. "I know. Fortunately for me, West already had a plan."

"Cricket?" Dax had a hand on the door. He was more than ready to leave.

"President Layne, I have one last request."

"Anything, dear."

"Please don't encourage West to find me again."

I simply couldn't bear it if he had to watch me die.

....

chapter forty-two

West

"Thank you for coming." I stood at the front of a long conference table, the sleeves of my black shirt rolled to the elbows. The faces of each council member stared back at me with emotions ranging from curiosity to contempt. "We don't have much time."

"Westlin, what is this about?" the council member from the education sector asked.

"I called you here to—"

I was cut off by the sound of the door opening. Justin and three of his guards stood in the doorway. "Looks like I'm late."

I smiled. "Actually, Justin, you're right on time. We even saved you a seat beside Dr. Pooley. Your guards can wait outside."

Justin turned and nodded to his guards, then walked to his seat, his narrowed gaze on me the entire time. He no longer wore protective gear—none of us did—as we were in a leadership room, far away from the medical sector.

"As I was saying, I called you all here today to talk about the condition of our city." I gave Shiloh a quick nod, and she ducked out of the room as I continued. "Because I am short on time, I'm not going to tell you how I know the things I do, only that I have enough proof to support every claim that I will make from here on out—and I have shared that proof with key council members around the table." A few of those members, who Mother was positive we could trust, nodded in support.

Shiloh appeared at the door. "Everyone is in place." Mrs. Canary, Ryder's mom, slipped into the room beside her.

"Wait just a minute," Dr. Pooley stood. "She can't be in here. She's no longer a member of council."

"Just what is going on?" Justin joined in. "Why are we allowing West to run any kind of meeting at all? Where is our president?"

Mr. Gatewood, the council member from the emergency sector, spoke up from his position on the other side of Dr. Pooley. "We're letting him lead this meeting because I've already heard and seen enough of what he's here to talk to us about to know that we need to hear him out."

"And Mrs. Canary is here because I've asked her to rejoin the council," I said.

"You don't have the authority to do that," Justin replied.

Shiloh moved to stand behind Justin. Her Taser was out, and Justin shifted uncomfortably.

"Justin, you no longer hold an office in this city. My mother has asked me to step in as her vice president. That gives me all the authority I need for now."

Justin pushed away from the table; his chair slammed against the back wall. Shiloh smiled at the outburst while still holding her Taser, just waiting for a nod from me to take Justin to the ground.

"You can't remove me from office."

"No, but I can," Mr. Gatewood said, "with a majority vote from the rest of the council. That vote was taken just before you arrived. You will sit down and hear what Vice President Layne has to say."

After Justin had grudgingly retaken his seat, I leaned in toward the table. "I have assembled an entire team of staff, investigators, and my own guards to carry out the decisions we're about to implement. And I assure you that my guards, along with my mother's, far outnumber any guards who might resist us. I can also assure you that my mother is fully aware of everything I'm telling you.

"I know that members of this council infected my sister, along with at least eight other citizens of this city, with the Samael Strain. I know also that Dr. Pooley was partly responsible for this atrocity.

"Wait just a minute!" Dr. Pooley screamed. "You have no proof of that."

I glanced over my shoulder at Councilwoman Canary. She stepped up to the table. "I assure you we have all the evidence we need. If you'd like to make a case for your life when this matter goes to trial, I would sit down and say nothing more."

Guards moved to stand on either side of Dr. Pooley, convincing him to sit back down.

"I also know that Justin Rhodes and some members of this council approved the release of scouts into the outside—scouts who were deliberately infected with the Samael Strain." I glanced around the table at each of the faces in an effort to determine which members had prior knowledge of these events. By the sincere look of shock on the faces of most council members, my guess was that the conspirators were limited to a handful.

"Since I don't know exactly who was responsible, each of you will be investigated and questioned. Those of you who are proven to have taken part in the infection of another human being with Bad Sam will be tried for murder, and if you are found guilty, you will be punished to the full extent of the law."

"Why are we listening to this boy?" Justin interjected. "He brought a girl in from the outside and allowed her to plant a bomb loaded with the Samael Strain within our city walls! A bomb, I'll remind you, that is *still there*, waiting to infect every single one of our citizens with this deadly disease!"

"Our guests brought that bomb here strictly as insurance, to prevent us from holding them here against their will," I said calmly. "They never intended to cause harm to any citizen of New Caelum. And that bomb has now been destroyed. Cricket and her friend exited through our city gates ten minutes ago, and immediately after, I witnessed, by video, the bomb being thrown into our incinerators."

"What about the computer virus set to take down our entire air purification system?" the council member from our technology sector asked.

"We appreciate your team's hard work on that problem. But that virus has now been deactivated." The virus, too, had been deactivated immediately after Cricket left the city, just as she had promised it would be.

Justin banged a fist on the table. "None of this changes the fact that Christina is a threat to our city."

I faced Justin and kept my voice even. "Christina Black entered our city, unselfishly and heroically, to give us medical information that she felt would help us to develop a cure for the Samael Strain. She worked with our medical team to save my sister and to prevent others from suffering from the same horrible disease she once suffered from. But let me be clear on this point—*you* invited her here when you released Bad Sam on the world. You forced my mother to find her. And we rewarded Christina by treating her cruelly. This is not the kind of city I want to live in.

"Your lower sectors are in a state of uprising as we speak. The higher sectors will follow in the next few hours as word continues to spread of how you gunned down two of our scouts inside our walls and left the other scouts to die on the outside. Our citizens are demanding change. My team of supporters is already in place to calm the situation. Not by force, but with promises of the very change they seek."

Shiloh smiled at me from across the table. She'd been preparing for this moment.

"What do you need from us?" the council member from the emergency personnel sector asked.

"I need all available guards who still support the president to be ready to contain the situation. There is no need for this to get out of control. I'm hopeful that words of truth and promise of change from President Layne and myself will calm the city and give us time to rectify the situation we find ourselves in."

I nodded to the various guards around the room. "Guards, you will take Mr. Rhodes and Dr. Pooley into custody, along with anyone else Mr. Gatewood orders."

The door opened, and in walked Mother. Tears streamed down her face.

"Mother." I took two quick steps to her. "What's wrong? Is it Willow?"

She wiped her nose with a tissue, then looked up at me, laughing through a sob. "She's improving. Her vitals are improving, West."

"What? Are you sure?"

"She's still very sick, and she has a long road. And Christina warned me that she could improve and still not make it, but—"

"She's given us hope." I pulled my mother into a tight hug. Hopefully, Ryder, Key, and Dylan had a chance as well. And since the disease hadn't progressed as far in Dr. Hempel, or in the boy in the iso unit, they'd have an even a greater chance of surviving.

Mrs. Canary entered the room behind Mother. I hadn't even seen her leave. "Ms. President, Mr. Vice President, the citizens of New Caelum have gathered in the atrium. They're ready for you."

~~~~~

My mother and I both spoke to the citizens of New Caelum that day. We told them the truth about the status of Bad Sam. We were careful not to make promises we couldn't keep, but we promised them they would have a say and a choice in every huge decision made in the future, starting with whether we would reenter the outside.

Our holding rooms were now filled with people who had sympathized with Justin, who had refused to follow order. Not to mention Justin, Dr. Pooley, and the other council members against whom Mrs. Canary had provided evidence of corruption.

After our speeches were over, Mother and I walked the hallways together to visit Willow. But when we entered the isolation suite, we were met with quite a surprise. One of the nurses had Willow's doctor in a headlock, and had pinned him face-down on the floor. She held a Taser to his neck.

"What's the meaning of this?" Mother asked.

Shiloh, whom I had promoted as part of my main guard, rushed over and pulled the nurse off of the doctor.

The doctor stood and brushed himself off. "It's nothing, Mrs. Layne. This is just a professional misunderstanding."

"The hell it is," the nurse cried.

"Let her go, Shiloh," I ordered.

Shiloh released the nurse, who sucked in heavy breaths. "Mr. Layne, I listened to your and your mother's speeches. And I must say... It's about time."

I shot Mother and Shiloh an uneasy look. "Tell us why you had this doctor in such an impressive headlock."

"Because he's a criminal."

The doctor began to splutter, but Mother cut him off with a gesture. She faced the nurse. "Explain yourself."

"I overheard the doctor speaking with Vice President Rhodes earlier this morning. At first I didn't believe what I was hearing, so I waited for him to take a break, and then I suited up and searched the biohazard container in the decontamination chamber."

Shiloh gasped. "Why would you do that?"

"I was very careful. I'm not new to this disease. I treated my entire family before I entered New Caelum."

I waved my hand. "What were you looking for?"

"I overheard Mr. Rhodes and the doctor saying they'd given Miss Black a faulty hazmat suit before she entered your sister's room. Mr. Rhodes sliced a hole in the back."

I glared at the doctor and my pulse sped up, but I managed to keep myself in check. "Why would they do that? It increases the risk of exposing us all to the virus. Besides, Christina's immune to the disease, so why would Justin go to so much trouble?"

"She's not immune," the nurse blurted out.

"What? Of course she is."

"I was in the lab the day she met with Dr. Hempel. He had her blood samples from years ago, and from very recently. And he showed her how her antibodies were lessening in strength. She used to be immune; now she isn't."

I stumbled backward, placing a hand against a wall to steady myself. "Does Christina know she was exposed?"

The nurse nodded. Her eyes pointed to the ground.

"Shiloh, get a truck ready for me." Cricket knew she was no longer immune, and she knew she had been exposed. Why would she keep this from me?

"West." Mother placed a hand on my arm. "You can't leave now. Your future is running this city. You just gained their support. The city needs you."

I turned to Mother. "My future is Christina Black, Mother. I let her go today because I made her a promise that I would." I never would have let her go otherwise. "But this city I love so much—this city that needs me—it just gave her a death sentence. She sacrificed everything."

chapter forty-three

Cricket

I watched Caine administer the treatment to his three patients. Like Willow, they were all very sick. Unlike Willow, they didn't have seemingly infinite wires and tubes coming from all parts of their bodies. We simply didn't have as many machines, or the power to run them.

Dressed in protective equipment, Nina sat by Dylan's side.

Dax simply stared through the glass at his brother. They were twins, but Dylan looked nothing like Dax now as he lay there in a hospital bed, so much thinner than he had been only a week ago and bleeding from his ears.

The people I loved were here, taking care of each other. I would find comfort in that.

I wanted to hold Dax's hand. To tell him that everything would be all right. But I couldn't.

I couldn't risk the touch.

And I didn't want to lie to him. No matter what, I had never lied to Dax.

I walked into the main lab, where I had stored the vials I'd brought back from the city. I removed the remaining bloodstones from my necklace—leaving only the small tree of life—

and then placed both the beads and my PulsePoint where Caine would find them. Then I grabbed the two vials I needed, needles and syringes, and tucked everything into my pack.

Next, after one last glance toward Dax, I slipped out through the back stairwell. He knew me better than anyone. He would understand that I was just doing what I had to do.

chapter forty-four

West

The evening sky was dark with stone-gray clouds that promised snow and possibly ice. I looked up at the old, run-down hospital and wished I had the power to turn back the clock on these past six years.

I wished a lot of things.

I took the steps of the hospital two at a time. The hallway where I had left my best friend and his girlfriend was quiet. I tracked Cricket's PulsePoint to the lab, but I didn't see her there. I turned and walked toward the hallway leading to the iso units. That's where I locked eyes with someone familiar—Dax. But still no Cricket.

He immediately began looking around frantically. I was sure he was also searching for Cricket.

I walked closer, but he spoke first. "I don't know where she went. I haven't seen her in..." His voice trailed off as he searched his memory. The lack of hostility in his words actually surprised me.

"Did she... say anything to you?" My voice cracked involuntarily.

"Like what?" He cocked his head, narrowing his eyes. He must have seen something in my expression and in the way I was already backing away slowly toward the exit, because suddenly his shoulders slumped, and his expression was one of understanding. "You won't find her. She runs when things get tough."

He didn't mean it as an insult to his friend. He and I both knew from experience.

But I'd find her. I had to.

"Cricket lives by two philosophies," Dax continued. "She would never do anything to expose others to Bad Sam. And she promised herself a long time ago that she would never allow others to watch her suffer through a disease like that again. Not even you."

....

chapter forty-five

Cricket

I somehow found the energy to put together a fire on the balcony of the estate. Sitting on top of a sleeping bag, I brought my knees in to my chest and rocked back and forth while watching a ribbon of smoke drift upward.

For six years, I had lived with the idea that I could face anything. After all, I had already faced the two most painful events I thought I could ever possibly face in my life: losing both parents *and* contracting a disease so awful that I prayed it would take my life. And though I didn't believe a person ever quite got over those kinds of grief, I had learned to live with both. I didn't think anything would ever trump it.

Until now.

"Why did he have to come find me?" I whispered. Unwelcome tears surfaced and spilled down my cheeks. My stomach tightened, and a lump formed in my throat so large that I couldn't get in a breath. I hadn't succumbed to my own tears in so long, I didn't even remember what it felt like to truly cry.

I curled up inside the sleeping bag, wishing that I could get so small that I would disappear. My body shook as I turned my face toward the ground and let myself settle into the heartbreak. "I didn't even get to tell you goodbye," I whimpered into the blanket.

Hugging myself, I sobbed. It was a while before I surrendered to my exhaustion and slipped into another realm.

When I felt my body being lifted, I was sure I was dreaming. And I welcomed the fantasy world—a world that smelled of... West. Arms encircled me as I curled up against something large and warm. I managed to turn my head, but my eyes were heavy. I was so tired.

Fingers traced my hair along my forehead... and down my cheek. It wasn't until I felt the touch reach the scars on my face that I realized I was not in a dream.

My eyes flew open. My body jerked, and I was hugged tighter. "Shhh. It's me. It's West," he whispered close to my ear.

I stared up at hazel green eyes that glistened in the light of the fire. "West? What are you doing here?" I pushed against him, tried to break away from him, but he was strong and wouldn't budge.

"You can't hold me like this, West. We can't—" I cut myself off with a labored breath, left over from the long, hard cry I had allowed myself. "Oh West," I sobbed, turning my face into his chest this time. Even if I was infected with Bad Sam, he was immune. At least I didn't have that to worry about.

I didn't know how long we lay there. He rocked me at first, then he placed me in front of him and covered us with some sort of blankets. They felt like the down comforters we'd used on the roof of New Caelum.

"Sleep now."

And I did. For how long, I didn't know. When at last I awoke, it was to the smell and sounds of a stoked campfire. Warmth and limbs were wrapped around me like vines. It wasn't a dream. West was really there.

I tried to turn over to face him, but the instant I moved, his arms tightened, keeping me in place. I almost laughed at the possessiveness of it.

"Why are you always so eager to flee?" he asked, his morning voice coming out raspy.

I smiled. "I'm not even trying to get up. I'm just trying to face you."

"Oh, in that case." He let me turn over so that our faces were inches apart. "Good morning."

"How did you know..."

"Doesn't matter." He let his hand slide to the nape of my neck and massaged the muscles there. "I'm here now. And I'm not going anywhere."

"I won't let you watch me get sick and die."

"You don't get to make that decision. That's *my* choice."

A tear fell from my eye, and West was quick to swipe it away. "And here I didn't think I had any tears left," I joked.

With pressure to my neck, West leaned in and kissed my cheek where the tear had left a trail that turned cold in the late fall air. "You can cry as much as you need. I'm willing to bet these tears are way overdue."

"Mmmm. Maybe."

"Did Caine give you the treatment?"

I shook my head. Then I sat up and reached for my pack. I pulled out the two vials and the syringe, and laid them between us.

365

"What are these?"

"One is my antibodies and bloodstone. It might help me survive the virus again. The other is Dr. Hempel's creation; it might help to regenerate the antibodies in my blood. It could prevent me from suffering at all." I sucked in a deep breath and let it out slowly. "It could also kill me."

West looked up at me, his eyes wide. "You don't know which one to take."

"I didn't, but I do now." Now that he was here. After I prepared the medication in one of the syringes, I tied a band around my arm above my elbow.

West placed a hand over mine. "Let me." He took the syringe from me and injected the medication directly into my vein.

I replaced the supplies in my pack and lay back down. Then I let my hand rest on West's waist, and I stared into his eyes. "Why did you come?"

West slid his arm around my back, bringing me closer to him. Then he shrugged, leaned his head closer so that his breath feathered against my face, and after a sensual kiss, he whispered, "The timing was right."

Subscribe and Receive a Free *EMERGE* Story

To thank you for being such an awesome reader, I've written a special *Emerge* story — "The Meeting" — just for you, and it's FREE to all newsletter subscribers. You can subscribe and see what else is available from Heather Sunseri at http://heathersunseri.com/novels.

By subscribing, you will receive notifications of all new releases from Heather Sunseri, special offers, and any free stories Heather writes especially for her subscribers.

Also by Heather Sunseri

The *Mindspeak* Series

Mindspeak

Mindsiege

Mindsurge

Tracked

The *Emerge* Series

Emerge

"The Meeting" (An *Emerge* short story)

Acknowledgements

I'm weird, I think, in that I enjoy reading the acknowledgements of a book. It's one thing to write a story. It's a whole other thing altogether to actually publish a book for the whole world to see. And in doing so, a lot of people and a lot of stars must align.

To my most amazing husband. Thank you for encouraging me every single day to keep reaching for my dreams. And for being the first to read that junk we writers like to call a first draft. With *Emerge*, I gave new meaning to the word "rough" in rough draft. Also, thank you for wrapping *Emerge* in the most beautiful cover you've designed so far.

To my beautiful children. I couldn't ask for more supportive children. To my daughter, who is quickly understanding what it means to write and publish a book as her first book is scheduled to come out very soon. And to my son, who provides unlimited hugs and shoulder rubs when Mom's had a long day at the computer.

To my dad, who this book is dedicated to, for inspiring my love for science. I knew I wouldn't follow in his footsteps and be a veterinarian after I watched him perform a C-section on a cow when I was very young, but that didn't stop me from enjoying and respecting all things scientific when I grew up, leading me to clone humans in one book series and destroy America with a deadly virus in another.

To David Gatewood, editor extraordinaire. David was integral to the final version of this story. He brings a certain fierce intelligence and organization to a story, and those things take storytelling to a much higher level.

To Jessica Patch for inspiring me daily and always pushing me to be a better writer and a better me. And for being another one of those early readers. It takes great patience to read my early drafts.

To my ninja typo checkers: Melissa Bybee-Fields, Jamie Deann, and Jenny Kays.

To Lori Kennedy Neville. Thank you for naming the Samael Strain, the virus that killed 99.9% of Americans six years ago. You are a perfect example of why readers are so awesome. Thank you for helping me with this in a Facebook conversation.

To that Kentucky group of writers (you know who you are) who keep me sane in a sometimes irrational world.

ABOUT THE AUTHOR

Heather Sunseri was raised on a tiny farm in one of the smallest towns in thoroughbred horse country near Lexington, Kentucky. After high school, she attended Furman University in Greenville, South Carolina, and later graduated from the University of Kentucky with a degree in accounting. Always torn between a passion for fantasy and a mind for the rational, it only made sense to combine her career in accounting with a novel-writing dream.

Heather now lives in a different small town on the other side of Lexington with her two children and her husband, Mike, the biggest Oregon Duck fan in the universe. She is a recovering CPA, and when she's not writing, she spends her time tormenting her daughter's cat, Olivia, and loving on her son's Golden Retriever, Jenny.

Heather loves to hear from readers. Please sign up for her newsletter—*A Piece of My Mind*—to hear when future novels are released by following this link: http://heathersunseri.com/newsletter. You can also connect with her in several other ways:

Heather Sunseri
P.O. Box 1264
Versailles, KY 40383

Web site: http://heathersunseri.com
Email: heather@heathersunseri.com
Facebook: http://www.facebook.com/heathersunseri.writer
Twitter: @HeatherSunseri

Photo by Candace Sword

Made in the USA
San Bernardino, CA
12 June 2016